Eden's Sagas

Michael P. Andre

This book is a work of fiction. Names, characters, places, and incidents are fictional. Any resemblance to any person living or dead is coincidental.

DEDICATION

I want to dedicate this to my wife and family.

ACKNOWLEDGEMENTS

I want to thank my sister, Joanne, for her editing assistance and Amazon for its cover picture.

OTHER BOOKS BY THE AUTHOR

First Born of the Moon - And Other Stories (2015)

Healer - And More Stories (2017)

Heroes of the Empire - Doom (2018)

Trek (2019)

Beyond the Beyond (2020)

Telepath (2020)

CONTENTS

FORWARD

In October 2011, the people of Libya cast off their dictator and the "Arab Spring" was beginning in the Middle East with much turmoil in many of those countries. For economic reasons mostly, there were riots in southern Europe (Greece, Italy, and Spain were nearing bankruptcy). These crises were the inspiration for a new short story for my second book of stories. I did not begin writing because I was writing another novel. I began writing it in late 2013 and completed it in early 2014.

While completing Eden, I realised I could write two sequels to it; Building Eden and Home to Eden. My enthusiasm for these stories was so great that I completed them in about two months. Now, I had a decision to make. Because the stories were so long, it seemed logical to keep them together in one book and I had almost enough material for a book on its own. I decided to abandon the original idea of putting the stories in with miscellaneous other stories, to create "Eden's Sagas".

I also felt that the trilogy was not complete – it needed one more sequel – and I wrote Battle for Eden in early 2014.

After the third saga was nearly complete, I was inspired in the early morning of April 19, 2014, to write The Day the Lights Went Out. It was meant as a little story within my second collection of stories but it seemed to fit well in the sagas.

So here you are, I hope you enjoy reading these as much as I enjoyed writing them.

THE DAY THE LIGHTS WENT OUT

Hi, I don't know if anyone will read this but I need to do something to pass the time, now. I watched television until it became too disturbing and depressing to see what was going on. It looked as if the whole world was collapsing. It was becoming too much for me but the TV didn't work anymore and the lights went out that day.

It's hard to tell when it all began; it was so subtle. The world always seemed to be a place that slid from one catastrophic event to another – if it wasn't a natural disaster, humans somehow had to invent their traumatic events; a little terrorist activity here, a little insurrection there, or a leader of one country decided they wanted a slice of another country. So, if it was any one of these or all of them, it would be hard to say which event finally broke the back of civilisation.

Some historians study events of the past to predict the future – was it one event that sunk the Roman Empire, or a million little events? Governments thought they learned a lot about economics and politics and tampered with things like interest rates and stimulus packages to try to beat the system, so people and governments spent as if there was no tomorrow. There was no day of reckoning. All we needed to do was tweak an interest rate here, bail out a country there, shore up an economy here; but it's all about people's confidence levels. Civilisation is like a house of cards. It looks impressive but all you need to do is blow a little air on it and the whole thing comes tumbling down. Even some random event like a butterfly landing on a grain of sand in the Sahara Desert might cause a hurricane in the Americas.

So, what happened? Nothing more than what's occurred before. We need only look back to the Roaring Twenties when everyone wanted to make millions on the stock market. Then that decade ended and we got the Great Depression with its lines of people looking for employment. There was terrible unrest in those years and, as a result, many governments fell.

And what about wars in the twentieth century – we had the Great War – the war to end all wars and, sure enough, about twenty years later we had another world war even worse than that one. That one was supposed to be the last but we ended up with the Cold War. Since then, we've had the Korean War, the Vietnamese War, and a never-ending litany of tiny wars everywhere. We've had a long line of pint-sized dictators since Hitler and Stalin, such as Amin, Ghaddafi, etc., on every continent except Australia and Antarctica. In most cases, nobody could do anything about them. The organisation that was supposed to control things like that was as toothless as the failed League of Nations because we gave vetoes to the biggest thugs.

So now, I can talk about what's happened and what I've seen on television. The house of cards was built and nobody could do anything about it. We let countries like Russia take land away from other countries like Georgia and Ukraine. We let pipsqueak countries like North Korea and Iran develop atomic bombs. We could not control the continued growth of terrorism. We had most governments in the world, and even the people in them, with debts so high that a quarter of a per cent increase in the interest rates would cause many people to default.

And that's what's happening, now. People are rioting in the streets blaming everything on the government and even the world's largest countries are bankrupt, with spiralling inflation and disaffected citizens. It's the end of the world as we know it and we're quickly sliding into another Dark Age.

So, a few weeks ago, I bought lots of canned food, filled the bathtub with water, and kept it full until the water stopped running. I know that doesn't make it all go away but I don't have to watch it. It became a participatory sport that I did not want to be part of, or even watch.

How far are we going to sink? I don't know, except to say that it's happening all over the world from Russia, China, India, and Europe to the good old USA. Nobody could stop it and it's getting to the point of every person for themself. The people with the most guns might win in the end – or will they? It won't be long before the stockpiles of guns will no longer work because there's no one to make the bullets. Just think – a world again without rapid transportation, worldwide communications, or electricity. The only ones who'll survive are the people who have horses, wagons, and farms but they won't be able to sell any food, as there's no gas for trucks to get it to the starving cities.

I can't stay in my apartment much longer but I fear for my life. I have no food left in my fridge that doesn't work anymore. The water in my bathtub is almost gone. The canned and dried food that I had stored is almost gone. My toilet filled to the top but I found an unlocked apartment on my floor that I'm using until that's full, too. The mobs are now raiding the apartment buildings for food, so I'll soon have to venture out and see if I can raid a supermarket but from what I've heard, there's nothing there either. I'll have to join the rest of my fellow earthlings and venture out into what's left of the world and hope that I can survive but my chances aren't very good.

I don't know if anyone will read this. In time, no one will know how to read this. No one can help us, now.

EDEN

Samuel Ferguson stopped working on his chores in the fields. He stood erect and bent backwards then from side to side to stretch his aching back. At the far end of the field, he could see his father and younger brother working with the pigs to create the furrows while he followed them sowing the wheat seeds. He had already worked the entire morning, had lunch, and worked half the afternoon.

He thought about how hard the work was. What a difference it was from the rest of the world that he read about in their books. Why was their group so old-fashioned? They had machines in one of the barns that could do most of that work for them but could not bother leaving their farms to buy gasoline or diesel fuel to run them.

Their grandfather said they could not leave their community to get fuel, so they toiled. He would say that working built character but the equipment would not work anyway, as most of them were too rusty and dried out to run.

Sam bent down and continued his task, seed by seed, filling row by row. Near the end of the day, his father and brother walked the pigs to the pen and set out fresh hay and feed for them. They closed the gate behind them and returned to help Sam finish the seeding.

When they finished, the three of them walked over to the house, washed up, and sat at the table. His mother and sister brought out supper and joined them. Soon, their grandfather entered the kitchen and sat down at the head of the table. He led the grace before the meal then there was a minute of silence in respect for the Lord and they ate.

That night they were holding a meeting with the other two families in the canyon as they always did on Friday nights. It was the Merkle's turn to keep watch for the next seven nights. Each family decided for themselves how they were going to take turns watching. They could take an eight- or twelve-hour shift.

In the over sixty years they had to do this, there were eight times they had to kill someone who had spotted their secret canyon. That was their rule – no one who spotted their location could live.

Fifty-one people consisting of three families – the Fergusons, the Merkles, and the Andersons populated their community which had lost eighteen people over their sixty years of living there by a few deaths of the older members, some accidents and illnesses, and others who decided to leave.

Some of the members of the group did not consider their colony aptly named. Eden was supposed to be a place of ease and comfort; a piece of paradise, and this land was not that. The land was rocky and almost barren. The animals had added some fertility to the land but food was sparse and famines were frequent.

They obtained most of their meat outside the canyon by trapping and hunting by slingshots, or bow and arrow, although they did have some chickens, sheep, and pigs. They reserved the use of their guns mostly for interlopers coming too close to their land, or hunting large animals.

When he was a child, Sam had heard stories from his grandfather that they had moved there after his father had purchased this canyon far from towns and cities, to escape from the masses of protesting people and mobs. He named it Eden because it was peaceful and an escape from a collapsing society.

He built a large house for his family about sixty years ago and soon two other wealthy families he knew joined him to sequester themselves in this one small piece of the world. Soon, they built two more homes for the new families and they added a large fuel tank, three wind turbines, and five banks of solar panels. They connected to the world only by radio.

The news from the world grew increasingly troubling, so they stopped listening to it and went about slowly building a stone barrier over the canyon's opening using the rocks they pulled out of the almost-barren soil within their new home. At that time, they began their practice of guarding their home against outsiders and killing anyone who got too close. This had been their private place since then.

The families held the meeting in the grand hall of Sam's house, which was the only room big enough to hold everyone. It rotated among the families until the group grew too large for the other families to handle in their homes.

The men sat in chairs around the dining table with the women behind them. The young women and men looked after the younger children in the kitchen. The only people missing were, of course, the two guards, one at each end of the canyon.

As the senior grandfather, Ferguson led the meeting. "I now call the meeting of the residents of Eden."

The participants responded together, "Aye, Aye."

Grandfather raised the first point of order. "Our first outstanding issue is our water supply."

The Merkles were responsible for addressing that issue. Their senior spoke, "We've dug our main well deeper but there's not much water flow. Our northern well is still running well and our south well is still dry. There's not enough water for our needs. We anticipate this summer we won't be able to irrigate our crops."

There was a murmur in the room.

"Are there any other places we can dig?" Grandfather enquired.

"Our diviner says no unless we get better rainfall this year. We need water for us and the animals."

Grandfather asked them to continue their efforts. He moved to the next topic. "Our next issue is our power supply."

The senior Anderson responded, "We tried to get our number three wind generator going again but I'm afraid it's irreparable. We're left with only our number two generator now but I'm not sure how long that one will last. It's too old. Those things have been running for sixty years and we have no more spare parts. We can cannibalise number three now if we need to." He did not mention the solar panels. They were now good only for a little electricity through the day, as the batteries had long ago failed to store electricity.

Grandfather groaned audibly and began his report. "The provisions report sounds better than yours. We've had to go outside of our compound for periodic trapping of animals but it exposes us to discovery by outsiders, however, it avoids killing our stock. With last year's poor harvest, we don't have much seed to plant. We're keeping more aside in case we have another bad year. We're going to do the same with our vegetables. We may have to forage for food outside our compound but I plan to do that only as a last resort. The bottom line is, that we'll do okay this year but if we have another dry year, we're in bad shape. We'll spend a lot of time this year praying that God will deliver us good rain."

Everyone chimed in, a little disorganised this time, "Amen."

He ended with, "Let's have dessert, everyone."

Sam heard most of what they said at the meeting and did not like it. He knew things were not good for the families. He hoped for good rain but he could not agree with their refusal to go outside for help. He wanted to help them and had suggested to his grandfather to send out a foraging party and see what they could buy from other people. He knew they had lots of money but it was not going to help them sitting in a big old safe.

He remembered hearing about one of the older boys who got despondent and left Eden. He left a year or so before Sam was born and, like all the others over time who had gone off to pick up supplies, never returned. The general thought was that they found things much better out there and were living rich in some city laughing at them.

He had heard about the Amish who lived much as they did, although they had refused electricity and machinery of any kind. In a couple of years, the community would move closer and closer to being like the Amish who had thrived without them. He stood nervously where he was and felt that he needed to do something.

When he fell asleep later in the evening, he had a fitful night and woke up tired. He had breakfast in the morning and went out to do his chores. When his father joined him, he had to get his misgivings off his chest. "Dad, a lot of our equipment is breaking down. Soon, we'll have no electricity, no running water, and no heating and cooling."

"There's not much we can do about that, Sam. We'll survive; we always live through floods and famines."

"I keep wondering about the others who left. None of them came back. They knew we needed stuff and they never returned."

"A lot of things could've happened to them. They could've been killed, found a better place to live, or got lost and couldn't find their way back."

"Maybe I should try. I'm a good archer and know how to fight, if necessary."

"It's not going to be easy. You'll need to live on your own for days."

"I know how to set snares. You know that, Dad."

"Yes, you're one of the best in many things but how can you succeed when so many others have failed? The people who left were not much better or worse than you are."

"At least I should try. If I fail, I'll come back."

"How many times have we heard that before," his father mumbled.

"So, you don't think I should go?"

"That's my preference and I'm sure, if I asked Mom, she'd say the same thing."

Sam put the thought aside.

The year ended well. There were sufficient crops to have a good reserve and it lasted over the winter but equipment was continuing to break down. After they planted crops in the spring, Sam approached his father again, with generally the same response.

"Dad, I'll come back, if I run into problems."

His dad sighed. "You seem to be very eager to go, Sam. I'll talk it over with Mom."

In the evening, his father snuggled into his wife and discussed Sam's request.

The next morning, after Sam had finished his chores, his father called him over to the barn and they sat on a bench inside it for some shade. "I talked things over with Mom. She's apprehensive, as you can expect but we feel we can't hold you back. You're a young man now, and old enough to make your own decisions. You should have all the facts, though.

"You're already educated enough to know what happened sixty years or so ago. The last time we listened to the radio, it sounded as if the whole world was falling apart. We anticipated it. That's why we moved here; to avoid the big crash that was going to occur.

"Whether in democracies or totalitarian states, uprisings occurred because of soaring inflation and shortages of food. Governments collapsed, and rebellions arose. We tried to listen to the radio for a few months after that but heard silence. Now, we don't know what's out there. We've seen people near here from time to time. That means some people are still out there but with what kind of government, if there is any, is unknown.

"There was chaos there, Sam. You might be walking right into that – or maybe there's nothing left."

Sam sat wretchedly. Would it be a mistake to venture out into that unknown? "If there's no one there, then I'll be able to pick up parts and other things that are left," he said cheerfully to cover his growing doubt.

"We're going to give you five hundred dollars. It's what everyone else got when they left. I don't know if that's going to buy you a whole wagonload of stuff, or a loaf of bread. Get whatever you can and get back then we'll know that it's okay out there and can figure how much money we need for another trip. Take your time to think about it but it might be best to go soon, so you'll use the best of the summer. I'd hate to see you get stuck somewhere in winter."

Sam did not know what to do after that talk.

The next day, he worked in the field and finished weeding it. Lizzie, one of the girls from the Merkle family, came by with some water and a sandwich.

"You look hungry," she said and pulled a small pack from her back.

"Sure am, Lizzie. What brings you out here, though?" Sam asked.

"Well, I finished my chores, so I thought I'd do a good deed." She pulled out a sandwich and held it out to him. "I made it myself."

"Sure, usually you're pulling pranks on people." He smiled. "Did you put bugs in the sandwiches or something?" He took the sandwich from her hand, raised the top slice of bread, and looked inside it.

"Come on, Sam, I haven't done anything like that in years," she responded coyly.

"You must have a very short memory then. It wasn't years."

"You're someone who remembers things too long."

"After some of the pranks you've pulled, there are few people who forget them. I must admit some of them were good but most people don't appreciate them; one of them being me, of course."

"Of course," She echoed with a grin on her face. She stared at him while he ate the sandwich. She handed him a jar of water.

"Thanks," he said. "I wonder what's really in this – some arsenic?"

"Oh, come on Sam, now you're being mean."

"Mean – from the champion of meanness," he said with a flourish.

Her eyes began to tear but she resisted the urge to cry. "Okay, I went too far sometimes but that was in the past. Can't you forget?"

"Okay, I guess I'm not being fair. My mom said you were doing it because you liked me."

She blushed then said, embarrassed, "Liked you! Me, liked you? Maybe in your dreams." She suddenly looked sad and pouted.

"Sorry Liz, I know you didn't like me. You never liked me. My mom was just being a mom."

She walked to the barn and sat down on the bench beside it.

He followed her.

She looked at him intently. "I hear you're planning to leave us."

"I think so. I haven't decided for sure."

"It's dangerous out there you know. Nobody who left has ever come back here."

"Maybe I can be the first one who does."

"Maybe you can decide to stay?"

He looked at her. She was about two years his junior and he had not seen her up close for maybe a year or more. He could see that she was filling out as a young woman. She had a band in her hair with a few flowers sticking out the front of it. He leaned forward and took a sniff. "So that's what I'm smelling."

"Oh, the flowers?"

"You've never worn flowers in your hair before."

She looked shyly at the ground. "This is the first time. I didn't know if you'd notice them."

"Maybe if you had a bee in it, I would've noticed earlier," he said with a little laugh, "and you're wearing a dress. I've never seen you outside of jeans." He noticed that her dress highlighted her femininity. She was quite pretty.

She blushed but said nothing.

"I shouldn't tease you, I guess. For some reason, you've prettied yourself up to see me and that was nice. I'm not sure what I'll do but I'm leaning on going. Eden needs some help and I want to do that."

"You'd also help if you stayed," she suggested. "You're a good worker and Eden needs you."

"Eden doesn't need me. They have plenty of able-bodied people. I could do more by leaving and coming back with something more to offer Eden."

For many seconds they sat in silence, as she nervously bit her bottom lip.

Finally, she said very quietly, "I need you."

For long seconds he was in shock.

"Did you say you need me? You don't need anyone. You're a very independent young lady," he said rather caustically. He thought back to what his mother had told him and said, "You're serious, aren't you?"

She nodded.

"So, when did that happen? You've been mean to me a long time."

"Since grade one," she said shyly as if she were confessing a secret to a priest.

"You know, you're a pretty young lady now. I don't know what to say." He paused. "You know we can't make any decisions, don't you? It's the seniors who say who can be together or not. They might decide we can't be together anyway."

"But we can tell them we're in love and we want to be together and sometimes that can sway their decision."

"Hey, wait a minute. How can I say I'm in love with you when I'm not? Maybe in time but right now, I only think of you as a pest."

"You can change."

"I guess I can but it'll take a long time and maybe never."

"I'm the best one for you."

"How can you say that?"

"I'm the right age and work hard, and I already love you, so you don't need to worry about that."

He smiled and said, "Well, I guess you have a lot to offer. You forgot to say you're very pretty, too."

"I can't say that," she said slightly embarrassed.

"Well, I can. Maybe when I get back, you'll be first on my list and we can see about it."

She smiled and said, "Promise?"

"Here, I'll seal it with a kiss."

He leaned over and gave her a gentle kiss on her lips. "Well, I got to go, thanks for bringing lunch," he said.

They stood up and she quickly moved toward him, stuck her lips firmly on his, and kissed him back for several seconds.

After he gently pried her away, he said, a little out of breath, "I'll see you when I get back. If any of the other boys take your fancy, go ahead and take him."

"I'll wait for you," she said softly. She turned and walked back to her chores.

He postponed his decision for a few days but the wandering itch kept gnawing at him to satisfy his curiosity about what he would see when he left.

Finally, five mornings after his talk with his dad, he said at the breakfast table, "I'm going, Dad."

His father turned to him and asked, "You're sure?"

"Yes."

"Okay, I'll meet with the family heads and let them know."

Sam spent the day packing his essentials. He wanted to go as lightly as he could. He took some dried meat in case food was sparse and a water container. He also packed his flint, razor-sharp folding knife, bowl, spoon, larger knife he could use for defence or slicing food, and his bow and quiver with arrows. He added a raincoat, light blanket, spare pair of pants, two shirts, underwear, socks, and backpack.

In the evening, his mother came to him as he was reading a book. "There's a pretty young lady at the door who wants to talk to you."

He closed his book. "Lizzy, right?"

She smiled. "I told you a long time ago that she liked you."

"She sure had a strange way of showing it."

"She's grown up, now."

"Yeah, I saw that. I don't want to see her. I'm going away and don't want her to wait for me, or be upset if I can't come back right away."

"Why don't you tell her that."

"I already have."

"It's not polite to leave without saying goodbye."

He sighed. "Okay." He walked to the door and left.

She was in a dress again. "Let's sit on the bench beside your barn." She took his hand and pulled him there.

They sat down.

"So, you're going," she said.

"Yes, I've thought about it a lot and I want to do it for Eden. We can't live this way anymore."

"I'm going to miss you."

"I don't know what's out there. Nobody who left came back and we don't know why, so please forget about me."

"You'll be back." She leaned into him and kissed him. "I wore this dress for you, so you can remember me while you're away." She picked up his hand and placed it on her breast.

He pulled it away, quickly. "What're you doing?"

"I'm not wearing anything under the dress. If you come back, you can have more."

"Don't get your hopes up. You might have a long time to wait. I'd better get going. I'm leaving early in the morning," he said nervously. He got up and returned to his house.

"So, how did it go?" his mother asked.

"She's a little too much for me," he responded.

His mother smiled. "It won't be long before you'll appreciate her."

He retreated to his room.

The next morning, when he walked out after he finished breakfast, the entire community was standing outside his house. The Andersons handed him the list of things they wanted him to pick up. He read it quickly. He found things listed in three priorities. The group thought it was essential to get some chickens and pigs. All their animals had become inbred and they wanted to get fresh bloodlines. The next priorities were some equipment parts and wood. The last list included things like clothes and shoes.

The Merkles gave him a wrapped bundle that said five hundred dollars on it. They suggested that he go east as there was supposed to be a town only a day or two from their canyon.

There were lots of hugs and farewells from everyone. He stood there for a few seconds. He glanced at Lizzie. She was quietly crying. He realised that this could be the last time he saw these people. They were the only people he had known throughout his life. He was torn between staying with the familiar and venturing into the unknown. He would look foolish changing his mind now, so he took a deep breath, turned to the east, and began to walk.

On that corner of the canyon was their highest point about three hundred metres into the sky. It was not as remarkable as a mountain; nevertheless, it did give a panoramic view of the land in three directions beyond Eden. Sam had spent many nights and days standing on the peak as a sentinel. Now, he was climbing for another purpose – to descend its other side to begin his trek to unknown adventures.

When he reached the top of the mountain, Sam surveyed the land. To the west, he looked over his small community below. He was apprehensive about his decision. Although he intended to return here soon, the odds were not in his favour. He remembered the other community members who had left before and never returned. He was not sure why and maybe he would find out. Then he could get back and defy the odds.

He stared a long time at Eden. It seemed smaller and more fragile from this height. He could change his mind if he wanted. He could descend the mountain the same way he came up and that would be it. They would welcome him with open arms. He was not sure of himself and felt as if he would never see Eden again if he did not return now.

He gathered his courage. He wanted to help them. They could use the materials he was leaving to find and he resolved to succeed.

He tore his eyes away from Eden and looked north. There was nothing but wasteland in that direction, just an endless sea of grass with rocky areas strutting out from it. As he swung around in a circle, he could see no change in view, other than small clusters of shrubs or trees. It was as if Eden was in the middle of nowhere. If they had never seen any other living beings, he would have assumed that there was no other life out there but they had spotted people travelling from time to time and had had to kill a few who came too close to discovering their little community.

When he finished his scan, he took one last look at Eden, turned, and climbed down the peak heading east.

After a few minutes of walking, he looked back. He could see the line of lodged grass from the trail he had made. He suddenly felt afraid. If someone attacked him on his journey, that trail would lead them back to Eden. It would take a few days of wind and rain for the grass to return to normal. Maybe this was one reason none of the people who had left had returned home.

For two days, he travelled and saw nothing but almost barren land. He finally arrived beside a small creek and was able to fill his water container. He also rooted among the plants beside the creek for bulbs and leaves that would re-supply his food bag. He crossed it and camped beside it. He lit no fire and hid himself within some rushes.

In the morning, he got up with the sun and began to pack but froze. He heard a noise that sounded like animals walking, then voices.

He soundlessly slid down on his stomach.

The noise increased in volume and then stopped. Whoever it was, was not far from him and he was afraid they had spotted him. There was no way he could know whether they would be friendly or not. His hand slid over to his bow and quivered.

For fifteen minutes he could hear water slurping and several people talking but nothing he could discern clearly. Finally, he heard one of them say, "Okay, the horses are watered, so let's get going." There was a lot of noise and commotion then he heard the footsteps again but this time they were getting farther away.

He relaxed, waited for about thirty minutes then peeked above the rushes. There was no one around. He finished his packing then got out of hiding and found the trail of horse tracks. It looked as if they had followed the stream for most of their journey and continued their way with no other stops nearby.

He resumed his trek east for the rest of the day and ended up in a hilly country. He found a low spot to give himself a low profile in case any other intruders came nearby and he went to sleep.

A howling wind awakened him. He grabbed his pack of belongings and pulled out a blanket. He placed the pack under his head for support and wrapped himself in the blanket. For a while, he could not sleep but finally, exhaustion overcame him.

He woke up again and pulled his head out of the blanket. The wind was still strong, so he decided to stay where he was, even though it was morning.

Close to noon, the wind abated and he hurried out to relieve his bladder. He went back to the depression, picked up the blanket, and shook the sand from it. He rolled it up and slid it into the pack. He slung it over his shoulder and resumed his walk. He came to a rise in the land and peeked over it, then climbed onto it. He looked around but the desolation continued to the horizon. He sat down and had lunch.

Soon after he left the rise, he could see the outline of what was once a town ahead of him. Only the brick or concrete bases of buildings remained. As he walked through the town, he could see that some of the bases had charred areas – evidence those structures had burned. Occasionally, the base of a sign rose out of the grass and shrubs.

He was walking on the remains of a road where the grass and weeds had almost reclaimed their domination. Some steel beams near the road poked up from the ground. Farther to his right he detected the remnants of a gas station. Eden could use any gas that might remain below the ground but there was no way he could pump it out or even transport it back home.

He walked on and found a few burned-out shells of cars. He walked toward them. Something caught Sam's eye near the closest one. He picked up a stick on the road and walked cautiously toward it. Suddenly, he heard a growl. He approached a little more and spotted a small mangy-looking dog, its tail up in defiance, growling at him. He had never seen a live dog before but had seen pictures of them in books. Their settlement had never had the luxuries of pets. Only, this dog did not look like a pet, it looked quite wild to him.

The dog did not budge and neither did he. He went a little closer.

The dog looked emaciated. He took a step back, slowly pulled his pack off his back and opened it. He pulled out his bowl and water bag and poured some water into the bowl. He placed it on the ground and took several steps back.

At first, the dog stayed where it was. It had stopped growling but seemed reluctant to move. Slowly, the dog took a few furtive steps toward the bowl, likely out of curiosity. It took a couple more, then slipped his head into the bowl and sniffed. The dog continuously stared at the man while doing this, prepared to take off, if the strange man moved.

It seemed to realise it was water. It took a few quick laps with its tongue and backed off again fearing it was a trap. When the human did not move, he returned to the bowl and lapped up all the water in it. It backed off again.

Sam reached into his bag again, pulled out a small piece of dried meat, and tossed it near the dog.

At first, the dog scurried away, fearful that the object might have been a rock meant to harm it. Slowly, it edged over to the object and sniffed it briefly, grabbed it, and ran several metres from the man to gnaw at the meat.

Sam sat down and watched the dog while it ate. When the dog finished, Sam walked over to his bowl, picked it up, put it into his pack, and resumed his walk. Occasionally, he looked back to see that the dog was following him in the distance. He smiled. Even if the dog did not continue to follow him, he did not care. It was hungry and thirsty. He did not particularly want another mouth to feed anyway. This critter was fearful of men.

Sam was becoming uneasy about the world outside Eden. If this animal was afraid of him, it must have encountered some very nasty people. He was beginning to think of turning around and returning to Eden but surely there must be people here to help him. Surely, the world had not deteriorated that far.

He also wondered if he had travelled in the right direction. His seniors told him that the nearest habitation to Eden was to the east. The remains of the town he passed might have been what they were talking about but there was nothing left of it. How much farther did he have to go to get to the next town?

He stopped for supper and left a small amount of water and dried meat for the dog. He was tired of walking, so lay down and stared up at the sky. He could hear the dog approaching and turned his head to see it lapping water from the bowl and later munching on the piece of meat. There were very few people there but the small group who had stopped by the stream indicated that there was someone else besides him in this desolate land.

The dog finished eating and sat not far from him licking its chops.

Sam got up, looked at the dog for a few minutes, and wondered if he should try to befriend it, or let it go. He was not sure how much food he would need for an extra mouth and did not want to jeopardise his survival. Maybe the dog was not interested in him either, only the free food and water. It did not have to tag onto this human.

He stuck out his hand to the dog and, for many seconds. It stared at it as if it were trying to make the same decision Sam was in the process of making. This would be a mutual agreement or none. The dog tentatively moved forward and stopped. It sat there for several more seconds until it quietly approached him and licked his hand. They made the decision; they were friends.

The next morning, he started and, after two hours, reached a river. He pushed his way through the shrubs, small trees, and reeds lining its bank and stared across the wide expanse of water to the other side. He removed his shoes, socks, and pants, stuffed them into his pack, and waded into the muddy bank.

He realised quickly that he would not be able to wade across it and did not know if he could swim to the other side. He had learned the rudiments of swimming when his father had taken him on trips outside their compound as well as in times when water from heavy rains in their canyon had backed up along the rock barrier that they had built to keep people out. He would need to find another way to cross the river. He could walk along its bank until he found a bridge, or he could build a raft. Finding a bridge might take days then he would have to walk back upstream, so he decided on a raft.

He dressed, took out his knife, and spent a few hours cutting down small trees that lined the bank and stringing together a small raft with the reeds as rope. By the time he finished, it was too late in the day to attempt the crossing, so he set up a series of snares along the bank of the river with the hopes of adding to his food supply. During the rest of the day, he fished and hung his catch high in several larger trees to dry. He rested his tired legs.

In the evening, he collected the small animals he had caught in his snares, skinned them, and hung the meat out to dry with his fish. He fed some to his new pet. He also fashioned a strong straight branch into a spear. If he met some unfriendly humans, he would be better prepared. He practised throwing his knife. He undressed, waded into the water, and swam for an hour or so.

As the sun began to set, he settled into his blanket in a small thicket. The dog came close to him to reduce the chill of the evening. Sam petted it to bond with his new friend.

"You know fella, I'll have to think of a name for you."

The dog looked straight into his eyes.

"I wonder if you already have a name, or maybe you've never had a master. You like getting petted, huh?"

The dog rolled over to get a good belly rub.

"Oh, you're a girl. I guess I can't call you a boy's name then."

As the sun sank below the horizon, he drifted off to sleep.

The next morning, he gathered the few animals he caught in the snares. They ate then he collected his partly dried catch and packed it into his sack. He put it and the dog onto the raft.

"I didn't get much chance to swim around Eden but if I lean on the raft and keep my head up, I can use my legs to propel the raft. Does that sound okay, girl? I know you can't talk back and probably can't understand what I'm saying but I'm sure you won't mind my talking. That way it won't be as if I were talking to myself. I don't have my family anymore. Being alone takes some getting used to."

He took off his shoes, socks, and pants then tossed them onto the raft. He slid the raft into the water and pulled himself half onto it. He kicked his feet to get the raft started across the river. The current, although slow, was propelling him farther downstream. It took almost noon to get across to the other side. He looked up at the sky, then to the other side of the stream. He was quite far downstream from where he had started. That meant he was farther south. He tried to estimate the distance. To get home again, he was going to have to factor that into his plans.

He pulled the raft onto the bank, grabbed his pack while the dog hopped off, and pulled the raft into a stand of rushes. Perhaps he could use it again to cross again later. He hid it as best he could. He stayed by the river and set snares to catch more food and rested his tired legs.

They ate and he made camp in the middle of a thicket. He practised his swimming again and later settled into sleep.

At one point during the night, loud noises nearby awakened him. Several people were shouting and there was a lot of scuffling. He froze and held tightly onto the dog, so it would not be frightened away. As quickly as it started, it quieted down. He heard some footprints and horses leaving the area. He drifted back to sleep.

The next day, the sun woke him up. He peeked out from the thicket. There was no one around. He quietly stood up, picked up the dog, and kept his hand wrapped around its mouth to make sure it did not make a sound. He picked up his spear and trudged out of the thicket.

He looked at the footprints in the mud on the bank of the river. He saw something near the bank a little farther from him. On approaching it, he noticed that it was a body and was not moving. He reached down and felt for a pulse but found none. There was a reddish tinge to the water around the body. A little farther along the bank, he could see another body. When he examined it, he found no life there either.

He stood quietly and thought he heard something. He listened carefully. It sounded as if someone was sobbing. He walked farther along the bank and it sounded a little louder. There was a stand of reeds near the bank of the river and the sound seemed to be coming from there.

He stood frozen for several minutes wondering what to do. One option he had was to return quietly to the thicket, pick up his things, and get away quickly. He could, though, find out what was making the noise and see if he could help. He did not know if it was a friend or foe but if it was an enemy, the person would not be sobbing.

He finally called out quietly, "Who's there?"

The noise stopped. There was only silence. He edged toward the reeds but could not see anything. He slowly stuck out his spear, pulled the reeds over to one side and saw a head. The head turned quickly to spot what had moved the reeds and the person dove forward into the water. The person quickly waded a few metres from the bank and stared back at him, looking terrified.

Sam pulled back his spear, walked farther along the bank away from the reeds, and watched the person in the water. The person did not look like an adult. He must have been another adolescent. Sam had scared him.

Two dead bodies and a terrified person in the water – what a world he was seeing! These three must have been part of the group that had been near his thicket. What they did there, and why two of them were dead he did not know but he was getting apprehensive about this world. He looked at the dog he was still holding and said, "It looks as if you have quite a world here girl, where dogs and youth are afraid of other people."

The dog whined as if it agreed.

He returned to the thicket, picked up his things then went to the bank to sit with the dog to eat. When he finished, he picked up a piece of dried meat, held it in the air, and slipped it into the food bag. He decided he would wait for a while and see what the person in the water did. If he came out, fine. If the guy stayed there, he would leave. He did not want to stay there any longer than he had to. He was nervous that the people who attacked them last night would return.

While he sat waiting, he ruffled the dog's fur and petted her. Finally, he stood up, put down the dog, visited his snares, and collected his catch. He packed his water, food bags, and catch into his pack, and tied it closed. He tossed it over his back and walked away from the bank. He was heading east again.

After three hours, he stopped and prepared his catch and fresh meat for lunch. While he was eating, he thought he saw something along the trail he had walked. He watched that direction for a while but saw nothing, so he started walking again.

By supper, he was in a rocky area beside a rise. He walked along its lower edge and found a secluded area that had some growth around it to conceal him. He entered the area and had supper. He set up some snares again along the ridge. The sun was low in the sky, so he settled in for the night. He heard some rustling a few minutes later. He froze. He slowly edged his hand over to his spear and grabbed it. He pulled it back behind his neck.

He was ready to toss but hesitated. He wanted to be sure of his target first as he could only see the person's shadow. He heard the rustling noise again and finally stood up and came face-to-face with the person he had seen in the river. Both froze when they saw each other. Sam was the first one to move. He slowly slid the spear down beside him and put his other hand on the knife on his belt.

When Sam's spear lowered, the other person relaxed and stood quietly.

He finally broke the silence and said, "Hi."

The other person said nothing.

"Well, aren't you going to say anything?"

The other person just shrugged.

The lack of response puzzled him. "Well, come out in the open so I can see you and make sure you're not carrying anything."

The other person hesitated and then stepped out of the bushes two steps.

He was glad to see no weapons visible but in surprise said, "You're a girl!"

She looked down at her nakedness and wondered if that was going to change things. To her, anyone who would pet a dog seemed safe. Maybe if she was female though, this strange young man may not be safe but she was sick and needed help. She had decided to take a chance.

"Don't you have any clothes?"

She shook her head.

"Well, you shouldn't be walking around naked. I didn't carry a lot of clothes with me and certainly not girls' clothes."

He thought a bit then said, "Well, I've got extra underpants, so you can use one of those. I have only one pair of jeans and they're probably too big for you but I have an extra shirt that should cover you quite well. It's certainly no dress but it'll be long on you."

He rummaged through his pack and pulled them out. "Here, put these on. I'll turn around."

She reached for the clothes, grabbed them, and began to dress.

He turned around and waited. "Are you done?" he asked.

With no response, he turned around. She had slipped them on her and seemed much more comfortable.

He lifted the shirt. "I see you figured out that you had to tie up the pants to stay on. Good." He let the shirt fall, bent down, and rolled up her pant legs, so they would stay up.

"You don't say much, do yah."

"She shook her head."

"You must have been with those people by the river bank last night."

She nodded.

"They must have been terrible people. I saw two guys killed there."

She nodded.

"Were the people also trying to kill you?"

She shrugged her shoulders.

"Well, whatever. Sit down and I'll give you something to eat." He glanced at the ground next to him. "Are you hungry?"

She nodded and sat down.

He pulled his water container and food out of his knapsack, handed her a piece of dried meat, and poured her a cup of water. "We'll have to share a cup. I've only got one of them."

She shrugged her shoulders.

He sat down and watched her eat. She seemed to be eating very slowly and cautiously. She looked so pale and her eyes seemed so dull. As he watched, he noticed some red material on one corner of her lips. For a while he continued to watch her then he reached over quickly and pulled open her mouth.

His action startled her but he gagged at what he saw. There was blood in her mouth and – she had no tongue. That was why she had not said anything. It looked as if there were other injuries to her mouth.

He got up rapidly, whirled around, and vomited into the bushes beside his shelter. It took him some time to recover but he whirled around again. "Those bastards! Those bastards cut out your tongue?" he asked loudly.

She nodded and began to whimper.

"Those bastards. How could they do that to you? Why would they want to do that to you?" He stared at her. No wonder she was so pale. She had probably lost a lot of blood. Now, he was wondering if she would survive. He was not even sure what else they might have done to her. He collapsed to the ground, wrapped his arms around her, and wailed out his sorrow.

She also cried.

He finally pulled away and watched her quietly for several seconds to calm his sobs then said slowly, "Nobody will ever do anything like that to you again. They'll have to come through me first. Do you understand? Nobody; that's a promise."

She smiled through her well-watered face.

"Now, we're going to have to stay here for a while."

Her brows furrowed.

"You're in no shape to travel. You'll have to get better first. The trapping around here was pretty good, so I can snare enough animals to feed us for a while."

She still looked a little worried.

"You're right. We can't stay here through the day, or they can find us. Are the group you were with good trackers?"

She nodded her head slowly.

"Do you think they might try to find you?"

She nodded again.

"I didn't cover my tracks on the way here and you followed me, so we'll be easy to find. There wasn't a storm to wipe them out. We still have light, so I'll have to do some quick work. They probably won't track us at night, so once it gets dark, we should be relatively safe. Take my dog and hold her, so she won't follow me."

She picked it up and petted it while she held on.

He left and cut off a leafy branch from a bush. He wiped out their tracks as far as he could from where they were hiding, climbed to the top of a rise, and looked around. He descended and returned to their shelter. He pulled out his blanket and wrapped her in it.

"That should keep you warm." He stared at her snuggled in the blanket and thought about what those thugs had done. He realised that he did not know her name. How could she tell him, if she could not speak? "Do you know how to write?" he asked her.

She shook her head.

"I'll never know your name."

She opened her mouth to try to sound it out but the noise was horrible, so she quickly shut her mouth.

"I don't need to know. May I call you, Beautiful?"

She smiled and shrugged her shoulders.

"Okay, Beautiful it is."

"I know you'll never be able to say it but my name is Sam. Well, I guess it's Samuel but people call me Sam."

She smiled and nodded.

"I haven't thought of a name for the dog yet, I picked her up in my travels just a day or so before I met you."

He left again to set up some snares and returned. She had fallen asleep. He stayed up for a while but there was no sound except for the chirping birds – which was a good sign. Because the gang had been out the previous night, he had to assume they could be active at any time. He was hoping their fears were unfounded and the gang had left her for dead. The sun was just below the horizon and was showing a bright red colour reflecting off the clouds. It reminded him of the blood he had seen inside Beautiful's mouth.

He grew tired and said to his dog, "Okay, girl, rest but stay alert. Get me up if anyone comes by."

It seemed such a stupid thing to tell a dog but he wanted to lessen the uneasiness he felt and hoped that, if it did nothing for the dog, it might comfort him.

He awoke to rain – torrential rain. He cuddled as close to the girl as he could to keep her warm. The dog seemed to be doing the same thing. There was no point in searching for the raincoat, as their skin was already soaked.

Around noon, it stopped.

He pulled out his bag and gave her some fresh meat and water. When she finished, he ate and gave some food to the dog.

"I want to get up on the rise. There are some bushes there and we can stay relatively hidden."

They rose, he slipped the blanket off her and spread it out to dry on the inside portion of their little protected area so no one would see it from the open area.

They climbed up the ridge and looked around. Nobody was in sight. He hid her in the bushes. He climbed back down, collected the animals he had caught, and prepared them to eat. He reset the snares to catch more fresh food. He dug up a few edible roots, brushed over his footprints, and climbed back up the ridge. They nibbled at the roots and he gave her more fresh meat. She seemed to be having trouble swallowing. He got up again and searched around the ridge for something else that might help her. He was back after about thirty minutes.

"Here, put this in your mouth but hold your face down. I don't want you to choke. It's a rock that has iron in it. I hope some of it will dissolve and help replace some of the iron you've lost."

She carefully placed it in her mouth and, with her head bent forward, continued to rest.

In the late afternoon, he checked the snares, collected the small animals, and returned to the rise.

"Are you okay with eating raw meat?" he asked.

She nodded.

It was not a very smart question, as anyone these days had to occasionally eat raw meat or fish – or even insects. He did not want to light a fire and risk any smoke acting as a beacon for miles around.

He gave her some more fresh meat and she ate it heartily but with difficulty. It was easier to chew and slide down her oesophagus than dry meat would have. In the evening, they descended to their previous lair and had a quiet night.

In the morning, they went back up on the rise and he collected the morning's take from his snares. They ate and rested.

Early in the afternoon, the dog appeared to be rather uneasy and was making a whiny sound. Sam grabbed her and handed her to the girl to hold. He grasped his bow and quiver and crouched over to the edge of the rise. He lay on his belly and kept under cover of a shrub while he surveyed the land below.

Suddenly, appearing up their trail from the river, were seven young men. Five of them were on horses leading two other horses while two of them were on foot trying to find any traces of footprints left after the rainfall.

He was impressed with their tracking skills. He signalled to the girl to get a little closer to the edge and peek over. When she did, she shrunk back quickly with a horrid look on her face.

"So, those are the guys?" he whispered.

She nodded.

He motioned her back from the edge.

He watched the young men below as they neared the side of the ridge. They were on the verge of locating their lair when he grabbed an arrow, placed it onto the bowstring, and readied a few arrows beside him. He suddenly knelt and fired one arrow after the other in quick succession. The first one hit the target but before the target had dropped, he hit another person. The third person was on his way down before the other four finally realised what was happening. They began to scamper away and Sam hit another one who fell to the ground. The last arrow missed its target, as they were scampering haphazardly to make them more difficult to hit. They hid behind some rocks.

Sam quickly dropped down, so the rest of the group below would not see him.

The young men behind the rock looked up at the ridge.

One of them said, "The arrows came from up there."

The leader said, "I wonder if it's the guy we're looking for."

The third guy said, "How do you know it's him?"

"A good guess; the footprints are a little too wide for a woman," the leader responded.

"Why don't we go? Who cares about the girl?"

"I do," the leader said emphatically.

"She can't talk. You saw to that."

"Look, I make the decisions. I don't like people shooting arrows at me. If I let him go, someday he's not going to miss."

"So, what're you going to do then?"

"Well, from where he, or a big-footed she, is lying, we're sitting ducks. We'll have to leave and come back later with some more troops. He can't stay here forever. Whistle for the horses and let's go. Try to hide behind the horses for cover."

One of the guys whistled and a few seconds later several of the horses pulled up beside the rock. They made a run for it.

Sam was ready when he heard the whistle. In the melee, he got a good aim at one of them and shot. The guy fell beside one of the horses but the others got away.

"There they go," he said quietly to the girl. "They've collected all the horses, which is too bad for us."

He watched them ride out of sight.

"I want to get my arrows back, so come over here and look out for those guys. If you see anything, throw a rock down, so I can hear it. Don't even try to yell – got it?"

She nodded.

He walked down with the dog at his heels and retrieved his arrows. The bloody ones he wiped against some nearby grass. One of the guys he hit was still alive but seriously injured, so he put the person out of his misery with his knife. One of his arrows was damaged but he kept it for its tip and end then collected five knives from the bodies. Only one of them was an archer. He grabbed the arrows from the corpse's quiver. They were not as good as his but they would do if he ran out of his own.

The girl watched him from the rise and was impressed with his marksmanship. She had seen seven boys in the beginning and could see five lying dead below her.

When he got back to the rise, she smiled at him with pride.

He knew what she was telling him. "Well, I've trained all my life in archery. I don't like wasting good arrows. Unfortunately, one broke, so I have one less. Hopefully, I can find a good piece of wood to make another good one. I did get ten more I could use in an emergency."

Without thinking, she leaned over and kissed him on the cheek.

He blushed a little and said, "I guess that's a thank you. Remember, I made a promise to you." He paused. "By the way, are any of the guys on the ground the leader?"

She shook her head sadly.

"So, one of the ones that got away was the leader?"

She nodded her head.

"Darn, well, if they come back, maybe I can get him. I'm guessing they'll try again. Are there more of them?"

She nodded.

"Lots of them?"

She nodded again.

"Heck, well, let's leave." He sighed. "We're leaving high ground but we've got to get far from here. Are you feeling healthy?"

She nodded.

He slipped his arrows into the quiver.

"I'd like to give you more time to heal but we'd better get going. I'll gather my snares and any animals I caught. Please get my things placed into the pack and I'll be with you soon."

When he arrived back on the crest about twenty minutes later, he showed her his catch and slipped it into the food bag. "I won't be able to get it properly prepared but I can do it sometime during our walk." He put the food bag into the pack. He slipped the pack, bow, and quiver onto his shoulder. He picked up the leafy branch and his spear then they started to walk. As they walked, Sam brushed their tracks.

"This isn't going to be very effective to a good tracker but I'll do it for a while anyway."

"You must know places around here. Can you suggest someplace we could go? Maybe someplace you think is safe – or at least safer than here?"

She shrugged her shoulders.

"I guess you don't find any place safe."

She nodded.

"Well then, is there at least someplace that might be safer than some and farther away from those friends of yours?"

She scowled at him with her hands on her hips then pointed northeast.

So, he would not get ahead of her, he slipped his hand into hers. She gave his hand a tight squeeze and relaxed.

He wasn't sure if she was telling him anything using the hand squeeze but at least for now, they were safe. Once they had picked the direction, the dog led the way. They were soon climbing more ridges and getting into some low-lying mountains. They chose a spot in there to spend the night. Before nightfall, he set up some snares.

When he returned, Beautiful stood up and unbuttoned her shirt. She was beginning to untie her pants when Sam asked, "What're you doing?"

She smiled and let them drop.

He was confused until he realised what she was doing. He walked to her and kissed her gently. He stepped away, looked deeply into her eyes, put each hand on her shoulders, and said softly, "Get your clothes back on."

She hesitated.

"I know what's going on. I helped you. In your way, you're thanking me." He looked at her sweetly. He could see scars on her skin. "Don't take offence. You thanked me with your kiss. You don't have to go any further than that. Right now, let's focus on getting to safety, okay?"

She was confused. Men expected her to do this. Sam was the strangest male she had ever met. She bent down, picked up her clothes, and put them back on.

"Now come here and let's get some sleep," he said as he pulled the blanket from the pack and wrapped her in it. They both slid to the ground and soon were asleep.

In the morning, they quickly ate the food he had caught and continued travelling through the mountains. He brushed the track when he found it useful to do it. They found another good place to bed down for the night. He set snares again. With three mouths to feed they were consuming as much as he could catch. He was trying to preserve the dried meat for when they would need to eat it.

They had travelled farther than he had expected to go and had made numerous changes to their direction. When he was ready to go back home, it was looking increasingly unlikely he would find his way back. He would not fulfil his goal and would have wasted his time. He had promised everyone at home to get what they wanted and get back within a reasonable time.

At the end of that day, they settled down and went to sleep.

The next day was rainy and chilly. They started in the morning and ended up spending the rest of the day in a small cave they had found. Sam could see that, in her current state, Beautiful was having difficulties. They would have to stay there and warm up.

Sam wrapped her in the blanket and was sitting near her when he heard a noise outside.

"Damn, I hope they didn't find us already," he mumbled.

He cautiously went to the opening and looked around. Before he knew it, a bear had raced to him and knocked him down.

The dog began to bark earnestly and attacked the bear.

The bear released Sam to grab at the dog.

Sam quickly reached back into the cave and grasped his spear. He tried poking the bear with the spear to divert its attention from the dog but it was too late.

The bear grabbed the dog, put it into its mouth, and dug into it with its teeth.

Sam quickly took advantage of the situation and rammed the spear deeply into the bear.

The bear turned on him in all its fury.

Sam grabbed his knife from his belt and dug it into the bear several times. Soon, the bear had his left arm in his jaws and was biting deeply into it. The pain was excruciating. Sam continued his attack on the bear and heard a whistling sound then another one.

The bear slumped to the ground and released Sam.

Sam slid to the ground beside the bear's carcass and brushed an arrow shaft as he fell. He glanced toward the cave and saw Beautiful with the bow in her hand. He blacked out.

He woke up but it was dark in the cave. It must have been night. He could still feel pain in his arm. He slid himself closer to the door of the cave and, by starlight, looked at his arm. High on his arm was a tourniquet made with one of his shirts and the wound was bound with underpants. He slid back into the cave and stared at the blackness of the ceiling. He looked a metre from him and could make out the form of Beautiful sleeping softly. He could not see the dog anywhere but it was likely too dark for him to see it. Soon, he drifted off to sleep.

When he awoke, the sun beamed through the entrance to the cave. The blanket was there but Beautiful was not in it. He tried to get up but the pain discouraged it. He thought of the last few days and knew they would have to continue their journey soon, as the gang they had met earlier might have started to look for them. The rain might have impeded their progress but they had to keep their lead and perhaps get to another town soon, so they could better protect themselves.

Beautiful poked her head in and saw that he was awake. She disappeared for a few minutes and soon returned with a bowl of water and food. He pulled himself up and leaned against the wall of the cave for support. He ate the food and drank the water. "Thanks," he said as he finished his last bite. "I guess the tables have turned."

She looked confused.

"I mean, you're now looking after me."

She smiled.

"So, you know how to use a bow and arrow."

She twisted her hand loosely a few times.

"Not that good, huh? Well, it was good enough to kill the bear . . . Where's the dog?"

She looked at him sadly then moved her finger at the corner of her eye as if she were sweeping away a tear.

He stared at her for several seconds. His eyes filled with tears. "I've never had a pet before. She gave her life for me." He fell silent, deep in thought then said, "I liked the pigs and sheep we had where I lived but they're not real pets like her. I hardly got to know her. What a strange dangerous world this is." He paused again then said, "We have to keep going, you know."

She put her hands on her hips and pointed to him, and the ground.

He tried to get up but there was still a lot of pain. He relented. "Okay, we'll stay here for the rest of the day but we must keep moving. If that gang is using horses, they'll be gaining on us even if we move."

They rested for the morning.

Mid-day she removed his underwear dressing and replaced it.

He noticed that she had some plant material on it and supposed it had some medicinal purpose. He felt his arm was not hurting as much.

She loosened the tourniquet a bit and later brought his lunch. She disappeared in between each of these sessions.

Curiosity led him to slip his way closer to the opening of the cave. He noticed she had gutted the dead bear, sliced the meat into thin strips, and strung them up to dry in the heat of the afternoon sun. She also had scraped the skin and hung it to dry. He did not know how she planned to carry all this food with them.

He did not see her again until later in the day when she brought back his washed underwear dressing. She must have found either a stream or spring nearby.

She placed it near his pack then glanced at him and smiled but left and did not reappear until about an hour later carrying some plants. She cut off the tops, cleaned the roots, washed the tops, and twisted them together. For some time, she sat quietly in the sun.

He moved farther into the cave and fell asleep until supper.

When he awoke, they ate some of the bear meat and plant leaves she had collected. He missed the dog. He wanted to talk to Beautiful but somehow it seemed odd to talk about nothing to someone who could understand what you were saying but not respond. He watched her for some time while she cleaned things up after the meal. He had helped her in the past but she insisted it was her turn to let him rest.

They were up early the next morning. She used his shirt as a sling to keep his left arm immobilised. They ate bear meat for breakfast. After she packed all his belongings, she used the bearskin to make a container to hold the extra bear meat. She poked a stick through it so it would be easy to carry on his right shoulder. She carried the knapsack and the bow and quiver. He carried a spear.

They walked all morning through valleys and passes. At one time, they stopped so he could survey the land to determine if anyone was following them but they could see nothing. They stopped for supper and soon found another spot that looked good for them to remain the night. They were both tired and the walking made them forget their ailments.

Before he lay down, he sat while the sky dimmed with the waning sun. He did not want to stare at Beautiful, so she would not feel uncomfortable but he often glanced at her as he thought. The only girls he knew were like sisters to him. With only three families, it did not take long before the marriage prospects declined. The elders decided who he was going to marry; managing it as best they could, in consideration of the genetics involved. Still, everyone was a cousin to somebody. Beautiful was the first girl he had met who was unrelated to him. So far, he was not impressed with the people he had encountered but he saw in her a hope for humanity – someone innately good. He now felt confident that there were others like her.

Her presence had also raised other emotions in him. He was toying with them in his mind and thought it was odd. He loved the people in his community but for her, he had developed a stronger feeling. It was not pity as one would expect but he was falling in love with her and he was not familiar with this new emotion. He found her a very helpful companion and her gentle ways covered a lot of strength in her that she demonstrated when she shot the bear with the arrows. He wondered what she thought about him but was uneasy about asking her because he might ruin the new relationship that he was sensing between them. He might chase her away. He thought that, under the circumstances, they would not be ready for anything more than they had. His main priority was to find somewhere stable and safe to live.

The next morning, they were at it again. Sam was getting anxious and kept looking behind him. He knew they had lost a lot of time and, if those gang members were tracking them, they should be catching up to them soon. He thought they should have seen those guys by now. There was hope that they might not bother to follow them. Why would they want to follow them anyway? They surely had other things to do. She must have said something that enraged that gang leader who also knew that he was not going to give in without a fight, meaning more deaths. Was human life so cheap?

By the end of the day, they were on more level ground, so they were travelling quite quickly. They stopped for supper in a small grove of trees.

"I'm not sure if this is a good spot to stop. It has advantages because we can hide but they can also hide and rush us without our seeing them."

He looked at the trees. "That clump looks like a place we can climb and hide."

He walked over to it and had a closer look. "The branches entwine together, so there's a good spot to sleep and the dense foliage will cover us well." He walked around it. "Good, there's another way down that gets us to those bushes, in case they attack from there or try to burn us out." He pointed to a small cluster of shrubs.

"Okay, let's drop our stuff here and lay a false trail leading out of the grove. I'll brush over our other tracks, so it looks as if we passed by here."

They spent the next half hour setting up the trail and brushing over the other tracks. She climbed into the tree and he brushed the ground beneath it.

It was a tough climb for Sam. He could only use his right arm to help him but he finally got to where they wanted to be. "We can see the ground below us but no one'll be able to see us. The branches around here snap under people's feet, so we'll be able to hear someone coming. Let's get a good night's sleep."

When they had climbed the trees, he found the branches were good support but not very flat, so were not comfortable, especially for a long period. They got a restless sleep but only heard the birds and land critters through the night. The leaves shaded them, so they slept in.

They got up, had breakfast, and climbed down to begin another day's journey. By noon, they stopped by water.

"I can't see the other side, so this is either a very wide river or a lake."

They put down the things they were carrying and stopped to eat. When they finished, Beautiful grabbed his good arm and pulled him to the water.

"Okay, okay, don't pull so hard. It's probably good to clean ourselves. I haven't washed since the river."

She pulled him into the water and splashed him.

He did the best he could to splash her back with one hand. He got some water in his mouth. "Hey, this is salt water! This isn't a lake – it's an ocean. I read about this. It's hundreds of kilometres across to the other side. We won't be able to fill the water container. We can't drink this."

She listened to him and splashed him with water. He splashed her back and soon they were pushing each other into the water. When they were too exhausted to continue their play, they stopped. Sam had not had so much fun in his life.

They waded out of the water and ploughed their feet through the sand. She bent down and picked up some of the shells along the coast. He watched her. She was such a wonderful person. He took a deep breath. They had to keep moving. It was a nice break but they were out in the open here.

He walked to their equipment and picked it up. She came over and motioned for him to put it down. He moved his arm. It was very sore but it moved. He exercised it slowly and carefully. He did not want to crack any of the scabs that had formed. He went closer to the water and washed off the area. She washed the shirt and underwear and wrung them out. She draped them over some boulders to dry.

She walked close to him and looked at him.

He gazed back.

She took two steps toward him, stood on the tips of her toes, and attached her mouth to his. They kissed and hugged for a few minutes. She did not have to say anything. He knew that she loved him.

They pulled apart and picked up their things.

"Okay, where do we go from here?" he asked.

She pointed north.

"Okay, let's speed up, so we can get there quicker."

They began walking quickly along the coast. About an hour later, they could see something that looked like mountains in the distance.

"Is that it?" Sam asked as he walked. He watched her nod her head.

The mountains began to define themselves into what looked like tall buildings. As they grew nearer, they made out a barrier in front of them made of stones at the base and a wooden fence that was about four metres high which extended into the ocean for about fifty metres.

"Should we wade out and get around the barrier that way, or should we follow it along the land and see if there are any gates along it that we can enter?"

She pointed away from the water.

As they turned left to walk along the wall, Sam noticed in the distance along the coast what looked like a mirage but he quickly realised it was something else and it seemed to be approaching them.

"Quick, that might be them. It might not be but let's not take any chances."

They began running along the wall. He feared that it would never end. To the left of him were smaller buildings and structures. He knew he could hide in them and ward them off from there but he preferred to get to the other side of the wall, if he could.

He spotted a break in the wall several metres in front of him to the right. He took a glance back and could see that they were the gang they were expecting. He recognised the leader of the group.

Arrows began whizzing by them.

Soon, they were beside the break and began climbing the rocks that were about a metre and a half high but it was slowing their advance appreciably. They reached the top and climbed to the other side. Sam whirled around and pulled his bow off Beautiful. He grabbed an arrow and, under cover of the rocks, began to fire at his adversaries. Each shot was true and felled each of the gang members he had chosen. Each time he had to stand up to get a good aim. Nine arrows shot and nine men dropped but he had none of his good arrows left and he quickly counted that over twenty attackers remained. Even with the other ten arrows he had, there were not enough to get them all.

He rose to take another shot.

One of the gang members aimed and, when Sam rose, the archer let go.

Beautiful launched herself to block the arrow and crumpled onto the top of the barrier.

Sam had no time to think. His enemies were now too close for arrows and they were climbing over the barrier with their knives and spears in their hands. He picked up his spear to ward them off. He knew they could kill him, now.

One of the men threw a spear at him but it only grazed the right side of his chest.

Sam threw his spear at the attacker and got him in return.

Another man rushed him then a rock hit him on his temple.

Suddenly, twenty or thirty people from behind him were shooting arrows and rocks and soon were swarming the area. Some of them went over the barrier to attack the fleeing gang that had attacked Sam.

He fell to his knees.

There was silence, then some noise, as the people who had crossed the barrier were returning over it to safety.

A female voice roared, "Did you get them?"

A male voice responded, "Every one of them."

"Anyone hurt?" she asked as she looked around.

The male voice answered, "Only a few bangs and bruises."

"Good," she said. "Get back over the barrier and collect their horses, the dead, and wounded."

Sam raised his head to look at his saviour. She was a tall lithe young woman a few years older than he was. He looked around at the others. There were two that looked as if they were in their twenties, the others ranged from twelve to eighteen.

The apparent woman leader looked directly at him and asked, "Who are you?"

"I'm Sam," he replied meekly.

"Is that your woman?" she demanded coldly.

"Well, I've only known her for a few days but we were together."

Sam got up, climbed the barrier, and bent over Beautiful. He felt for her pulse both at her neck and wrist and could feel nothing. In the heat of battle, he could not think clearly about what had happened. He could see that the arrow had struck her just below her heart and there was blood still seeping from the fatal wound. He slid his fingers over her eyes to close them.

That arrow was meant for him. She dove in front of him to save his life. He had promised her that he would prevent her from harm again and here she was, dead in front of him. Her once joyous body and spirit were now cold and lifeless.

He looked at the leader of the group who had come to their aid. He looked over the other side of the rocks with twenty or more dead bodies lying haphazardly on the pavement of a road and the grass beyond. Somehow, he thought there was an unequal balance. Beautiful's life was worth more than all the other dead lying on the other side of the barrier. He broke down. The group that had come to his aid scattered to do their jobs, leaving him to his grief. Only the woman leader remained to guard him, so he would not escape.

It seemed like forever to him before he finally lifted his head from Beautiful's corpse. He saw the woman watching him.

She went over to him and said consolingly, "She must have meant a lot to you."

He dried his eyes and tried to speak coolly but his sobs were giving him away. "It's the only girl I ever loved. She was a very wonderful person."

"From what I saw, she threw herself in the way of that arrow, so you must have meant a lot to her."

He turned from her and cried some more.

She stepped back and remained at her post. She could see he was not going anywhere.

Finally, he composed himself.

She said from behind him, "Just leave her. We'll collect her and prepare her for a nice funeral. Our leader would like to talk to you."

He turned around and looked at her. She seemed so out of place. She had been the first one to join the battle, firing off arrows like an old sergeant leading the charge of a brigade. At first, no one would notice that she was a woman, as her brown hair was very close cut and she dressed as a man would; only her voice and quite pretty stubble-free face gave her away. Her eyes were as blue as the ocean.

"I want to collect my arrows. I need my arrows," he said dumbly.

"We'll pick them up while we pick up ours."

"Okay." He could do nothing else but comply.

"Here, let me look at you," she said. She noticed the blood flowing from the wound in his right chest and the large bruise on his temple. She felt his temple. "That should be okay. There's not much I can do about that." She unbuttoned and pulled open his shirt to expose the wound there. "Just stand still until I get this covered. It's not bleeding enough that you should lie down. The spear grazed your ribs but I don't think anything's broken." She opened a bag she had on her back, pulled out a bottle of water and poured some of the contents over the open wound. She grabbed what looked like a clean rag and pressed it over the wound. With her other hand, she deftly wrapped another longer rag around his back under his shirt and soon had the dressing tied tightly over the wound.

She noticed that he was favouring his left arm. She pulled his shirt off that arm and looked at it. "Mighty bad injury you've got there. What happened?"

"I got mauled by a bear. Beautiful saved me by killing it with a couple of arrows."

"Beautiful?"

"Oh, I gave her the name, as she couldn't talk. Those shitheads you finished off cut out her tongue."

She stared at him with her mouth open in shock. After she recovered, she said, "How horrible but I guess I'm not surprised. I don't get surprised by anything these days. I didn't see the inside of her mouth. It was closed."

She cleaned off the area around the wound. "It looks as if it's healing well. Keep an eye on it and clean it regularly. You don't want an infection." She pulled the shirt back up the arm.

Sam did up his buttons.

"There, that should do it. Just follow me," she said.

She was deep in thought, as she led him up the road. What a strange name to call a woman but she was pretty. It was too bad for her. It was a sad way to die but very daring. She had saved him from a bear attack and those fiends. It confirmed to her that the girl must have cared for him to do what she did.

She led him to the left and walked farther until they arrived at an old stone building.

He looked around him. There were tall buildings all around him but most of the windows in their lower floors had broken and they mostly appeared empty.

He followed her into one of the buildings and up a set of stairs. On the second floor, she opened a set of doors and walked down a hall to a large boardroom. It was stark though, there were only a few chairs of very different designs and they were set up in no configuration. Sitting on one of them was a man who looked in his thirties. He dressed in sheepskin tops and pants like the rest of the people.

The man in the chair eyed him suspiciously and spoke, "So, who do we have here?"

The woman responded, "He's the man who jumped over our south gate. He had a woman with him but she died in the battle. They were attacked by Colton's gang but he was killed with the rest of them."

"Quite a scoundrel!" He looked at Sam and said, "You couldn't have picked an ornerier guy to fight." He scratched his beard and asked, "Where are you from?"

"Not from around here," Sam answered briskly. There was no way he wanted to give him any information that could lead them to Eden.

The man stared intensely at Sam and said to the woman, "Please leave us alone for a few minutes."

She said, "He's clean. He has no weapons on him." She looked at Sam and said, "We'll collect all your stuff and give it to you later."

Sam smiled and nodded.

The gang leader responded, "Good, thanks. I'll yell if I need you for anything. I don't anticipate this guy's going to give us any trouble."

The woman left.

The man continued to stare at Sam. "So, what am I going to do with you?" He paused. "We don't like people crossing over our boundaries without an invitation. It's a wild world out there. We're one of the biggest gangs around here and we didn't get this way without being strong." He paused again and continued. "Where do you come from?"

"Quite far from here."

"I can tell that. If you were from around here, you'd know about us. You also have a peculiar accent. Tell me where you come from."

"Just away from here."

"On the other side of the big river?"

"Yes."

"What's your name?"

He hesitated for a few seconds but thought there would be no harm in telling him that. "Sam."

"Do you have a last name?"

"Do you guys have last names?"

"Some were told by their parents but most have no more links to last names. What about you?"

"Why do you want to know, if you mostly do not need them anymore?"

"Just curious." The man got up and went to look through the window. It still had a pane of glass in it. He continued talking as if he were talking to himself. "Some people still have the old machine-made clothes. There are still some stores around that have clothes in them but over years of picking through them, there's not much left. In some parts of this city, you can still find them and some farmers still have them and there's you . . ."

"I guess you could call me a farmer then."

"Why did you come to the big city?"

"Even a farmer needs supplies."

"In your pack, you had five hundred dollars. By now, all farmers know money is worthless. If anybody finds any, it makes a good fire starter or poor-quality toilet paper but most farmers don't have five hundred in a bundle, if they have any at all. Most banks were looted many years ago, so there's not much around anymore."

Sam said nothing. He was disappointed, for he now knew he could not buy supplies but if money was worthless, machine parts and even wood might also be worthless. If he found anything of use, he could likely just take it. He was curious about why this person was so interested in him.

"There aren't many farmers around anymore either. The only ones who are surviving have formed cooperatives, fenced off their farms, and can defend them." He paused and turned toward Sam. "Your bow is nothing special, as there were many stores you could have looted it from. Knowing where you came from is important to me."

"Why?"

"I really can't tell you unless you want to tell me more."

"Then, I guess we're not going to get anywhere. I'm not prepared to give you the information you want."

The man turned, slowly walked to the door to the hall, opened it, and said to the woman, "Find a room for this young man and keep him guarded."

She entered and motioned for Sam to follow her. She led him to a smaller room.

"Here, pick up your pack and water container, so you can bring them to your room."

Sam looked around and asked, "Where are my weapons?"

"They're stored somewhere else. You don't expect us to return them to you now, do you?"

"I guess not. I'll get them sometime soon?"

"We want to be sure whose side you're on. We're a very suspicious group. That's one way we've survived."

"From what I've seen so far, I guess it's warranted. I'll also watch you guys to see whose side you're on."

She snickered. "I guess that's how you've survived, too."

As they walked out of the building and over to another one, he asked her, "Who's that guy I just met?"

"He's our leader, Josh."

"Pretty suspicious guy."

"Like all of us; he makes the decisions, so if he doesn't like you, we can kill you."

He stopped and looked at her.

She stopped, too.

"You wouldn't kill me, would you?" he asked sheepishly.

She hesitated and said, "If he asked me to, yes. I might hesitate a bit with you, though but I don't question him."

They started walking together again. "So, you'd hesitate?"

He saw her smile slyly as she said, "Just a little bit."

They entered a building and, on the main floor, she opened a door to what must have been an office at one time.

"Where are the washrooms?" he asked.

"Washrooms?" She laughed.

"Well, you can dig outhouses in the city, can't you?"

"For your information, there's a washroom on this floor but we lock it so no one can use it. We have no running water here. There are light fixtures in the halls but they don't work. Nothing works. We have a shed out back where you can do your thing. We empty it regularly into the nearest sewer and when it rains it carries it off to who knows where."

"Oh, I thought since you're in a big city . . ."

She was forcing back another laugh. "What did you think makes everything you dream of in a city work?" She led him out of the building to the back of the building.

"I guess I read too many books."

"You can read?"

"Yes, we were taught to read."

"How?"

"We had some books where I was and our parents taught us when we were young. We had a basic education. I think I read every book we had."

"We have some libraries here. There's one big one and several smaller ones in the area we patrol. Most of the books are still there but people have taken many of them out and used their pages for more practical purposes. One library's roof has leaked a lot and ruined almost all the books inside. In time, that will happen to all of them. There's nobody who can fix anything and nobody cares. Eventually, no one will be able to live in the city in fear of the buildings and bridges collapsing."

"Where will everyone go then?"

"I don't know, or care," she said brusquely. "I probably won't be around to see it. I guess whoever remains will have to start farming. After the riots of the dark times, there was chaos but at the beginning, from what I heard, people could eat food in the stores, when that ran out, they ate dogs, cats, and whatever else they could . . . even each other. When most of the farmers were killed for their food, it was everyone for themselves. The gangs grew out of this. As gangs, they were stronger to steal food from others. Josh took us over about twenty years ago. He was different. He wasn't a cold-hearted killer like the rest of the gang leaders. People got to like him and we constantly get defectors from other gangs who want to have some peace and decency. We're very big, now. There are over a thousand of us and it's very hard to feed us all."

"What's going to happen to you?"

"I don't know. We survive. We've cut up the gang that attacked you for food. We don't have much use for horses. We have some and feed them at some local parks. That keeps us mobile when we must be. In the case of that gang, only one of the horses was healthy enough to keep. The others we cut up for food."

"You eat people?" he asked with surprise.

"We have to eat. People are meat."

"That's cannibalism."

"I don't know what that is but if it means we eat people, well we eat people."

"My God, what's become of your people! Does Josh say it's okay?"

"Why are you so concerned?"

"Well, it's not custom to eat other people."

"The meat's good. It's very tasty. That's the custom, so I don't know why you say it's unusual."

"Well, in civilised societies we expect dignity of the human body. You can bury them, or burn them but you don't eat the meat off them."

"Well, I guess you're calling us not civilised," she said haughtily.

"Sorry . . ." He paused. "Is that what you've done with the girl who was with me?"

"No, tomorrow Josh will lead a ceremony to bury her. We eat other people who attack us but we don't eat each other. Josh makes sure we're buried and our lives honoured."

"I see. I guess necessity breeds its form of decency."

She looked puzzled by what he had said and dropped the subject. They stood at the back of the building.

Sam entered the outhouse and soon was out beside her again.

They continued their walk to another building nearby and climbed to a room on the third floor.

The woman said, "I guess I'd better go; Dave will be here soon. He's your roommate and will guard you. Just get yourself settled in." She left the room.

He saw one corner had clothes and a bedroll by it, so he set up in the opposite corner.

Within a few minutes, a young man of about twenty entered. He was black, with black curly hair and brown eyes. His clothes were much like Josh's. He stopped in the doorway and stared at Sam for a while.

Sam could see that he was carrying a bedroll under his arm.

He finally opened his mouth and said, "I'm Dave. I was a member of the squad that went to help you out."

"Yes, I remember you, thanks."

"Sorry to hear about your woman."

"Thanks."

"Here's a bedroll to sleep on. It's better than sleeping on the floor."

"Thanks," Sam said. He took it and unrolled it beside his knapsack.

"I guess you talked to Josh."

"Yes."

"And Jill."

"Is that the woman who's been leading me around?"

"Yes, she never told you, her name?"

"No."

"She's like that. She's uncomfortable with us. I think she hates men."

"Why do you say that?" Sam asked with surprise.

"Oh, just what she does. She doesn't talk to guys much and if anyone touches her, she'll attack them. She's not normal."

Sam had found her pleasant enough. This seemed so opposed to what he had seen in her so far.

Dave continued. "Did she tell you about your girl's funeral?"

"Yes."

"It's going to be in the morning, so I'll make sure you get up." He paused. "Well, it's time for supper. Are you hungry?"

"Yes, very hungry," Sam responded.

Dave waved to him and headed for the door.

Sam followed.

They walked two blocks and turned right. One more block on their right they entered a door to what must have been a restaurant in the past. They sat down and soon a boy about twelve came to their table and placed a spoon in front of each of them. He scurried out.

Sam looked around briefly and noticed the grungy look about the room. The dirty wallpaper was peeling off the walls. Because of the lack of lighting, it was dark and inhospitable. There were about a dozen dirty mismatched round tables strewn around the room with many incompatible dilapidated chairs around the tables.

"As you know, nothing electrical works around here," Dave said to break Sam's thoughts. "They cook the food in a fire pit out back."

"I don't care. I haven't had cooked food in a couple of weeks. We feared lighting a fire would give our position away."

"The guys here are not necessarily good cooks but it's hot."

Sam looked at the three other groups in various stages of eating remarking how savage they looked. Several other groups arrived and sat down at other tables.

Soon, the boy returned and placed before them large bowls of meat and vegetable stew.

Sam looked at it and said hungrily, "It looks good. What's in it?"

Dave replied, "Well, I see potatoes, carrots, and maybe squash."

"What about the meat?" Sam asked warily.

Dave looked at him and noted Sam's chagrin. "Well, to tell you the truth, it could be anything. I know you had bear meat on you. We took the liberty of adding it to our larder. I hope you don't mind."

"No, I understand. You also use horse meat?"

"Yeah, sometimes even rats, dogs, and cats."

"Anything else?"

Dave looked at him through the corner of his eye. "You talked about this with Jill?"

"Yeah."

"It all gets mixed up together in the pot, so it could be anything, even bugs and those guys we killed yesterday."

"I was afraid of that."

"I'm surprised you think that way. Where do you come from – the moon?"

Sam poked his spoon through the stew examining some of the meat.

"Look, you're not going to notice anything. The meat doesn't have little labels on it. It's just meat, so eat up," Dave said aggressively.

Sam slowly dug his spoon into the bowl and raised it to his mouth. He was famished and Dave was correct – meat was meat. He slid the spoon into his mouth and ate.

They soon finished the stew and poured the remainder of the contents of the bowls into their mouths. They got up and headed back to their building. Before they entered, they used the small hut behind it. They returned to their quarters and sat down in their respective corners.

Dave said, "Our days are tiring. After dark we usually don't stay up, we get a good night's sleep and wake up with the sun. Of course, we also take our turns at guard duty. Our enemies can attack us at any time of the day, or night, so we must be ready for anything. Don't be surprised if someone comes to wake you up to defend our territory."

"Does that happen regularly?"

"Not as much, now. We've become quite a large gang and we're well organised, so we're at peace at least with the other nearby gangs. They know us. It's mainly outsiders – like you were. Just sit down for a bit while I do my rounds. I'm trusting you to remain here. If you're caught out of here alone, I can't vouch that nobody will kill you."

"Okay," Sam replied. He had experienced life outside of Eden enough to believe him.

Dave stood up and left the room.

While Dave was away, Sam spent most of his time looking out the window watching the deepening darkness of the waning day. Often, he saw people scurrying by the building or crossing one of the roads he could see.

About an hour later, Dave returned. He went over to his corner and said, "It sounds nice and quiet out there." He took off his weapons and dropped them on the floor. He paused then asked, "Do you want me to invite a couple of girls to keep us company tonight?"

At first, Sam was confused until he realised what Dave suggested. "They do that?"

"Most of them, why not? We'd better decide quickly or the pickings will get a little thin."

"I think I'll pass. I want to get a good night's sleep. I haven't had one in quite some time."

"Okay, good night," Dave said, disappointed with Sam's answer.

They both lay down and within a few minutes were asleep.

Dave got Sam up the next morning.

Sam slipped a folded knife from his kit into his pocket.

Soon, they were on their way to breakfast.

When the boy served Sam, he noticed it was stew again, this time with a thick slice of something that looked like bread. He looked at Dave and said, "This, I presume, is bread . . ." He held it out to Dave.

"Yeah, with dirt, rodent shit, and whatever else is in it. But we call it bread."

He ate the bread with his stew and found it a little gritty as if it had some sand in it. "This stuff is marginally edible."

"It's food; a little dirt isn't going to kill yah. It's baked well to kill the germs. It keeps you regular," Dave said with food in his mouth.

They ate in silence and went to clean up at a small washstand outside the restaurant.

Sam used the opportunity to hone the sharp knife he had brought with him with a strop and scrape the small beard off his face.

Afterwards, Dave led him a few more blocks away to an old cemetery.

Sam could see much of it contained many mounds of soil and some freshly dug pits.

"We pay no mind to what may have been here before. It's used for burying, so we use it for that. We need to put our dead somewhere and we have lots of people who've died here, as you can see."

There was a large group of people around one of the pits.

Sam recognised many of them from the day before.

Dave led him to the front of them.

On the ground, lying face up was Beautiful. Her face looked almost pure white and appeared a little bloated. Sam looked into the pit and saw a couple of other bodies inside it.

Jill was there and asked him, "Do you want me to remove your shirt and pants from her, or leave her as she is? Usually, we just bury the dead naked, so we can use their clothes for someone else. Maybe you don't want that."

"No, leave her the way she is," he said sadly. "I'd rather go naked myself than take back the clothes I gave her."

Josh stepped out of the group with a thick book in his hand, opened it, and read several passages from it. Sam had read the book and recognised the passages. They were the ones who usually read over the dead back in Eden. There must have been Bibles in the libraries in this city. After Josh finished, he sprinkled her body with water. Josh turned to Sam and asked, "Do you want to say anything?"

Sam did not know what to say and was nervous that he would start crying again but he opened his mouth and said, "Well, I didn't know her that well but what I saw of her was that she was a good person – a very nice person." Then he shut up before the tears could flow.

It was hard being a man. Men were not supposed to cry. He saw before him people who had become hardened by their life. They stood there stone-faced and with cold looks. He also had to look tough.

Two people bent down and slid her into the hole.

Jill stepped toward him as he peered into the pit and tried to hand him something.

Sam looked and saw that it was a bundle of freshly picked flowers.

She said warmly, "I thought you'd like these for her," as she extended her arm farther.

He looked deeply into her eyes trying to find that cold man-hating woman Dave had called her but saw a much warmer, empathetic person. His eyes searched the crowd near him and glanced at Dave, who appeared somewhat dumbfounded.

Sam sadly reached out, took the flowers, kissed them, and let them drop into the grave.

He turned to Jill and said, "Thanks." He turned his head and looked at the flowers resting on Beautiful's corpse. "What do you do now?"

"We leave it open until we have six bodies then we cover it up."

"Are you going to find a couple more bodies in the next few days?" Sam could see the group by the grave start to break up and leave.

"Wait until you've been here for a while. You'll see it doesn't take long. Do you want a tour of our territory?"

"Do you think Josh would like you to tell a potential enemy about this place?"

"I don't know. I hope I'm reading you right. I don't think you're a danger. I'm not easily fooled." She paused. "So, this is one of our gravesites – we re-use old ones. See that patch over there," she said as she pointed to a small area with an assortment of growing wildflowers. "That's where I got those flowers." She continued to lead him to the other end of the graveyard.

"I take it you don't usually toss flowers into graves."

"I think that's the first time," she responded.

"Why did you do it?"

"I don't know. Impulsive decision, I guess. She was special to you."

"You're going to ruin your reputation."

She looked at him quizzically. "My reputation?"

"Well, I've heard you're known as a grumpy old lady."

"I'm not that old. I'm about your age."

"But you're grumpy?"

She glanced at him then looked around, "See over there at the back of one of those restaurants. You can see the fire pit where they cook the food."

"You look about fifteen," Sam said unexpectedly.

She looked at him, shocked. She finally answered, "Nope, eighteen, although I'm not even sure of that. It could be a year or two one way or the other. Nobody keeps track of that. There are no clocks and calendars here. There are old calendars in some of the buildings. That's how I know of them. A person who can read said that's what was written on them."

"Too bad you can't read."

"Some of my friends taught me a bit. I can sound out the words to figure out what's written."

"Well, I'm a year younger," Sam said. "So, I can say you're an old lady."

"Don't be fooled by our size. When you've starved a few times in your life, you don't grow right. Where did you hear that I'm grumpy?"

"Don't get mad at him but Dave. He didn't exactly say grumpy, he said that you're not comfortable with guys. He thinks you hate us."

She chuckled and changed the subject briefly. "That big building that used to be a school is used for exercising and training. We do a lot of that outside but when it rains or in winter we go in there." She pointed to her right.

He looked at it.

"I have a good reason not to like guys. Life now is tough. I was born to a tough young mother. I never got to know her because she died when I was very young. I never knew who my father was but had an older brother and sister. We tried to survive on our own and occasionally obtained help from some adults but I watched both die at the hands of men and their constant warring. I grew up in a tough world where you grow up too fast. Early on, a gang that was even wilder than most captured me but over a couple of years I heard about this place and ran away. I got tired of being the gang's moll. I've been here for about a year. They've protected me since then. That's the story of my life."

"Wow, that's horrible," he said in shock.

"What was your life like?"

"I was lucky to have a nice family to love and care for me."

She looked at him askance. "That doesn't exist . . . and you left that to come here?"

"I didn't know what I'd find. I wanted to pick up some stuff that might make their lives better. Life with Josh doesn't seem to be much different from anywhere else I've seen so far."

"What do you mean?"

"Well, last evening Dave asked me if I wanted him to invite a couple of girls over."

"And did he?"

"No, I wasn't interested."

She smiled and said, "Okay, there are willing girls but here you're not forced to do anything. I've been invited many times but I can say no and get away with it."

"And for that, they say you hate men?"

She pointed ahead of them and said, "We're close to the wall now. You can see that we have protected lookout areas. There are three entrances to our territory. They're made of rocks to impede anyone's advance, like the one you came through. After all, we need to get out sometimes. We do send out hunting parties to find food, wood, and other things we need. You can also see that we use what we have available. The south wall is mostly wood and logs, as we had houses there to get wood from and had trees that we cut down so enemies couldn't hide in them. The other two walls have all kinds of stuff along them, like piles of cars, tires, wood, rocks, and concrete blocks."

They turned to walk along one portion of the wall.

"Now let's see, where were we?" She paused for a few seconds. "Oh, yes, men. I hate men . . . yes; I guess I hate men the way they are now. There must be a better quality of men than what I've seen so far. I got my reputation because I almost killed a few men who tried to get too close to me. I admit that."

Sam moved farther away from her. She noticed it and began to laugh. She stopped walking and held her side. She was having trouble stopping. She eventually collected herself and looked around. "I'll lose my reputation if anyone saw me do that."

"What?" Sam asked as he stood puzzled a few steps away from her.

"Laughing; I don't know if I've ever laughed so hard and long. You're a very funny man."

"Me, funny? I don't get this. I don't get any of it. What's going on?"

"When I said that I almost killed guys who came too close to me, you slunk away in fear."

"Well, if I told you that I almost killed some women, wouldn't you do the same thing?"

"Yeah, but you're a tough macho guy. A guy who can kill a man with one arrow and here, little old me, got you slinking away. Hooray for me!" She raised her fist in a sign of victory.

Sam shook his head, totally confused. "Okay, let's step back and straighten things out. I grew up on I guess what you'd call a farm. It wasn't a large group like you have here but we were a peaceful, well-mannered, and relatively decent people. We treated each other with respect; none of our women were molls. We got married when we were old enough and there was no fooling around – well, almost none . . . at least nothing was forced, so maybe I'm missing something here."

"Well, here it's every person for themself. When you're born you might be lucky enough to live with your mother but she doesn't live long and you may end up in the streets. From an early age, you experience things you can't imagine, whether you're a boy or a girl. You're at the mercy of anyone older than you. You grow up fast and hard until you can fend for yourself. I live for myself. I don't want to be anyone's patsy and I'm old enough and strong enough to enforce that. The guys might say I'm hard and cold but they know where I came from. They all came from the same place. We all survive. Some girls survive by being nice and fending for themselves in their own way but I chose a different way. Nobody messes with me. I could say I'm the woman from Hell if I want to be." She said the last five words much softer than the rest. "What you see is what you get. I don't hide my insides from people."

He stared at her for some time in silence then said, "You're lying. You're hiding yourself from other people. You're hiding even from yourself. You've covered yourself in this indestructible veneer but there's another side of you hidden deep within you; the soft part that's been plastered over but has been crying to get out under the right circumstances."

Her head hung low as if she were hiding from reality.

He stepped toward her and put his hand under her chin. She resisted the force he was applying to her chin but finally relented and her head rose so he could see the tears in her eyes. He pulled out a piece of cloth, dabbed them, and kissed her gently on her lips.

Sam continued. "As you said, you're not alone in the world. This is a strange new world and we all must live in it. You've done it your way and still survive, and there are lots of others like you. They must be the way they are. Tomorrow they might be dead. Everybody seems to be living for the now and not tomorrow. There seems to be a little more hope here in your small group but you all must survive for the now. Do you blame anyone for the way they are?"

"I guess not."

"But you can live your way, so be who you are and be a hard-assed daughter-of-a-bitch woman, and man-hater," he said quickly. He was forcing a serious look on his face but was failing.

She could see it and began laughing again, even harder than she had the first time. When she looked around, she slowly composed herself again. "You know you're a son-of-a-bitch. You're going to spoil the reputation I've had since I came here. My sides ache. It's been a long time since I last used my laugh muscles. I'll have to get rid of you. You're bad for my reputation."

"I'll shoot you before you can get a shot away," he said confidently.

She quieted down and said softly, "You already have."

"What?" he asked confusedly.

"Your arrow struck me when I saw you crying over your dead woman. Nobody cries, especially a man. Nobody tries to establish closeness with anyone because they don't want someone to hurt them. It's as if we're all zombies, walking around as if we're already dead. You can see your best friend die and not shed a tear, yet there you were, crying. People left because they felt uncomfortable. I had to stay there because I was supposed to guard against your escape. But I could see how genuine your feelings were and you had said that you only knew her a short time." She stopped walking and began to sob.

He first looked around to see if there was anyone visible. When he saw they were alone, he wrapped his arms around her and let her cry on his shoulder.

After a few minutes, she pulled away from him and wiped her eyes with the cloth she still had in her hand. She said, "How about we go for a jog, so I can make an excuse for my red eyes."

"They're not so red," he lied.

She led the jog and he followed, they wound through many streets and she stopped a few times to point out some places along the way. There was the armoury where people made mostly bows, arrows, spears, and light shields; a food warehouse where one open area faced south to dry meat for storage; and two parks to grow fruit and vegetables. At several points, there were old buildings where they kept their horses, raised chickens for eggs and meat, and sheltered a few cows for milk.

Finally, near the centre of town, she stopped at a spot she called their most precious asset. She led him into a building that doubled as a hospital, nursery, and school. Here, he saw some older people and children – hundreds of them.

She said, "Most of the children were born from the women here but some were collected outside – either abandoned or from people who couldn't look after them. Josh says this building houses our past in the older people and the future in the children. More than anything else, we protect this building. It's in the centre of our territory. This is where we'd make our last stand if that ever happened. You spotted the rock and piled car barriers around it. We'd die here. There are two rooms in here with weapons which would be handed to all the old adults and older children. They'd be the last ones standing. We hope that'll be enough."

She walked into a room which housed tens of bassinets on tables and benches. Several children about ten to twelve years old tended to the cries of some of the infants within them. She reached into one of the bassinets and pulled out a small baby. "Have you ever held a baby before?"

"Yes."

She handed it to him.

He took it firmly and cradled it in his arms.

She pulled up another one and held it herself. "This is a time when parents can't raise children anymore, so we provide safety in a collective nursery like this. For the ones born here, the mothers and fathers can be ready to work or fight in the outside world, while they know their kids are here. They can see them when they want – or not see them if they wish. Josh wants them safe. Young women don't have to worry about getting pregnant, because they know the resulting children are wanted and will be cared for here."

"What happened before Josh came around?"

"I already told you," she stated matter-of-factly.

"Yeah, bad question."

She carefully returned the baby to its bassinet and he did the same.

"So, that's a short tour of our place. What do you think?"

"I'm impressed. It looks as if you have doctors."

"The two older ones you saw are trained, so they're training others. Hopefully, they'll die from old age but not before they can train enough others."

"How did you find them?"

"Well, all the original doctors are dead but they trained many to take their place and some have survived in some gangs, or by hiding. Having a doctor in a gang is an advantage. We're lucky to have two."

". . . and several other younger ones."

"Yes, some are quite skilled, now. They get frequent opportunities to practice their skills," she said sadly. "Their reward for taking this grisly task is being exempt from fighting. They only need to fix up the maimed, or ill. They're very busy all the time. It's not much of a reward. They see a lot of death."

"I guess but they also have the joy of bringing new life into this world."

"Not so much when you know what'll happen to them in a few years when the former babies will stand in the line of battle and become zombies like the rest of us."

"You're sure negative."

"I've seen too much too early. I guess you haven't lived in this world. Somehow, you seemed to have escaped it. You haven't been a young girl who had to experience a line of boys have a go at her and not just once but for many days, over many years."

He was silent.

"Well, let's not look at the past, shall we?" she said with aplomb.

"Yes, to the future and I think what you're doing here is a good beginning."

"I hope so," she said with much doubt. "It's a fragile beginning. With Josh's help, it's taken about twenty years to get to this stage."

They parted shortly after.

Jill and Dave switched roles again.

"I see you've spent the morning with Jill," Dave said quickly.

"Yes."

"She showed you around?"

"Yeah."

"Okay, then I don't have to do that. I'm not sure if she should've done that this soon."

"I'm not a monster."

"I'm not saying you are."

They had lunch – stew.

Dave took him to the workout area and they practiced fighting together and with other young men. Sam made some impression on the others.

Late in the afternoon, they had supper – stew.

While they walked to their quarters Sam said, "I'm impressed with your training centre."

"Yes, we have very experienced fighters to train us. Tomorrow we can go to another spot and see how you do with other skills like using a spear, bow and arrow, and slingshot."

"Yes, I've practised a lot with all of them."

"From what I saw the other day, it looks as if you're pretty good."

Sam turned to Dave and said, "I guess we'll see tomorrow."

Dave stared at Sam for several seconds then said, "I was surprised to see what Jill did at the funeral."

"Why?"

"She smiled a little. She never did that before. I thought that, if she ever smiled, her face would crack."

"I guess you were wrong, or it might be that her face can take little smiles."

"I was kidding . . . and why did she give you those flowers?"

"Those weren't for me. They were for my woman."

"Well, it's still odd. She didn't do that at any other funeral."

They had a quiet evening and went to bed early.

The next day, they spent at the training centre again. Sam showed them how adept he was. He could stand and shoot an arrow, as well as shoot one on the move. He rarely missed the mark. He was almost as adept with the slingshot, although he was not familiar with the homemade ones from the armoury. What he learned the most was using a spear. While he was good, he picked up a few improvement tips. The other fighters were impressed with how accurately he threw one. Sam's wounded arm was aching by the end of the day.

On their way home, Dave said, "I noticed you held your left arm a lot."

"Yes, that arm was mauled by a bear."

"It must hurt. Do you want to go to the hospital?"

"No, I'll be okay. I should keep exercising it. It's still quite raw but it'll get better with time. Fortunately, it wasn't my right arm, although I have to use two with a bow."

"Okay. We've had a long hard day. I think we'll sleep well tonight."

Not long after their supper of stew, they bedded down and fell asleep.

"Get up. Get up quickly!" Dave yelled as he shook Sam.

"Why, what's going on?" Sam responded dully. He could see that it was still dark in the room.

"We have many practice drills but this isn't one of them. We're being attacked . . . no time for details."

Sam got up quickly and followed Dave into another room. "Over there is your stuff. Grab it and let's go." Dave pulled something out of his pocket and slipped it on his arm. He pulled out another one and handed it to Sam.

Sam looked at it and asked, "What's this?"

Dave showed him what he had done and said, "It's an armband to distinguish ourselves from the attackers. That way we instantly know who's who and act accordingly. The enemy can only slide it off but we're rarely alone to allow anyone to do that. It shows up. We change the colours regularly to avoid the attackers trying to copy what we're doing. Today's colour is bright yellow."

Sam slid on the armband, grabbed his spear, bow, and quiver with arrows, and followed Dave out the door as he slid the quiver over his shoulder.

"They've attacked us at two gates. We don't know who they are but there are lots of them. Some have made deep entry already, so be ready to fight anytime," Dave said breathlessly.

They ran and were soon joined by others scrambling to defend their territory. "We're going to the nearest gate."

Soon, they could see down the street a lot of commotion caused by their defenders struggling to contain a breakout of attackers on their side of the gate. Although there was no moon out, the stars were providing sufficient light to mark out the attackers. A young boy ran up beside him and said, "I've got more arrows for you, sir."

Dave opted to join the close fight with his sword and ran toward the gate.

Sam decided to hang back and focus his attention on the attackers flowing up and over the gate. Within seconds, Sam was firing as quickly as he could pull arrows out of his quiver. Nineteen were all he had so the boy held up the pail and he began to use those arrows. They didn't have the penetrating power of his arrows which made him compensate by pulling harder on the bow. The pail was soon empty but another boy ran up with more of them. The first boy scampered back to the centre of town.

Sam was tiring and his left arm was aching almost excruciatingly. He was a good shot but not used to firing like a machine gun. He was glad to see several other archers joining the fray. Within half an hour the flow of people was slowing and there were now enough defenders to stem the flow.

Dave rushed toward him. "We've got to get to the other gate, they're losing."

Dave, Sam, and several other archers along with the arrow carriers raced down several streets. Within a few minutes, they saw some gang members without armbands running up the street.

"There they are!" Dave yelled as he pulled an arrow from his quiver.

The archers formed a line and began firing. When the road cleared, the archers ran forward until they could see others running wildly toward them. They formed their line again and fired constantly to clear the way. More boys with buckets of arrows pulled up behind them. Within minutes, they were nearing the gate.

Several archers left, so they could attack from another direction to try to stem the tide there.

Sam moved a little closer. He spotted the enemy's archers moving forward to the backside of the pile of rocks to increase their range. He stood his ground and one by one was taking them out.

They spotted him and knew they had to kill him but stepped back.

Sam smiled, stepped forward, and kept shooting as the enemy's shots fell harmlessly at his feet.

Soon, the enemy fell back farther and trained their arrows back at the defenders trying to contain the attackers.

Sam took several more steps forward and started dropping them again. Soon the enemy's archers backed up so far that they were out of the fight. Now, Sam was almost in the middle of the battle so he backed up significantly to train his sights back on the attackers.

It took another hour for the defenders at both gates to be able to feel relieved and the skirmishes deeper within their territory gradually ended.

Dave, exhausted, approached Sam. "This was one of the largest attacks we've ever had. We almost lost it there for a while. They surprised the guards at the gates and hit us so hard, and fast, that some of them got deeply into our territory. It was very fortunate that several guys were able to alert the inner defences, so they could sound the alarm. If that hadn't happened, the enemy would have killed most of us in our sleep. We're done for the day, unless they attack again but I don't think that'll happen. Not too many of them got away. The reserves and younger members will help with the clean-up."

He looked into Sam's eyes and said, "We'll have a lot of fresh meat for the next few weeks. Those guys deserve to end this way. We don't have to fill our few cemeteries with their bodies. Tomorrow, we'll have to bury many of our people. We lost over a hundred of our fighters and hundreds of wounded filled the hospital. We'll likely count more deaths if some of them don't survive."

Sam was getting to understand their morality. He still felt they were wrong but when food was scarce, he could see how society could sink to this level. He did not know if the population numbers included the babies and youth in the hospital and nursery but that night, they had lost at least ten per cent of their population in one battle.

The sun was peeking above the horizon, now. They walked over to the restaurant for breakfast and ate ravenously.

Another fighter walked toward them, leaned over to Dave's ear, whispered something, and left.

When they finished eating, Dave said, "Sounds as if the boss wants to see you." He led Sam back to their headquarters and opened the door to one of the large rooms.

Sam walked in.

Dave stayed outside and closed the door.

Josh was sitting in an old easy chair that had no covering. All that remained of it was loose filling and springs. He eyed Sam pensively and said, "Well, nice to see you again. I guess you can see what we're up against. Many other gangs greatly covet our territory and our strength. Sometimes several of them band together and try to destroy us. We're counter-culture here. I think many of them feel we're getting too strong and need trimming to size.

"Our practice drills worked well last night. If we didn't act as quickly as we did, our losses would have been much larger and we might have been wiped out. We tend to over-prepare but last night showed us that even with all our practices, we were caught off guard. We'll have to tighten up a bit. What do you think? You were out there."

"I was impressed with your organisation. I arrived at the battle site and a small boy had a bucket of arrows ready for me. When he ran out, another boy was ready with another one. That takes some organising."

"Well, they're trained to do that. The fighters fight and the youth provide them with what they need to fight. Despite it, we came very close to losing."

"Your planning saved you."

"I'd say you had a good deal to do about that, too."

"What do you mean?"

"You can't see yourself. I went out to keep things under control and fight too, if necessary. You have quite some arm, young man."

"I practised a lot."

"That's not just practice. You have fire in you. Sure, you have power in your arm but you know what to do and when. You single-handedly pressed those archers at both gates into retreat. You knew their range and yours and used it to your advantage. You saved many lives out there.

"I don't know if you thought of staying here. I'm getting on in age. I know you're thinking that I'm still young. Yes, even though living past thirty these days is a rarity. I need a captain. I need some new blood, someone who can lead and inspire the troops. A lot of the guys out there last night saw you and were impressed. They're still talking about you, from what I hear. You can be that inspiration. When they saw you, I saw them fight harder. It was so apparent. We need you."

"Well, I hadn't planned to stay anywhere."

"I know," Josh said slowly. "I once had five hundred dollars in my pocket. I too had dreams of collecting a few things and heading home with them but I saw that these people needed me here. If I returned home, even if I could find it, I'd only help them a little bit and it'd do nothing for the rest of the world. I'd likely be dead somewhere. Instead, I'm here trying to make a difference to these poor people who so badly need leadership to take them out of this quagmire and back to civilisation. When they succeed here, I could lead my family out of their homes to come here." He paused. "I'm Joshua Anderson and you look a heck of a lot like, and fight like, a highland Ferguson."

Sam stared at him in disbelief. "You're Joshua Anderson from – Eden?"

"Yes, I am, and I don't think you'll find your way back. I want you to work with me to get the world fixed up, at least on this side of the ocean. I don't want to force you to decide right away. It's completely up to you. I know, I made mine. If you want to go back, I'll provide you with an escort that can see you get safely on the river to get you on your way. I can't go farther than that, as I don't want them to get too far away from here. We may need the fighters. I try to be a man of few words, so that's all I'll say. Let me know what you decide. Oh, and get over to a doctor and get that arm fixed up. It's bleeding."

Sam looked at his arm and saw a large stain of blood on it. It hurt him a lot but he was so busy in the morning that he did not notice the blood.

Josh stood up and shook his hand.

Sam slowly turned and walked out. What a surprise. Josh was alive! He did not remember if his family had told him the name of the person who left Eden before he was born. So, now he knew why Josh did not return. Now, Joshua had asked him to replace him in this task. He was torn. He promised his community he would return. If he stayed, he would be reneging on that promise.

He walked into the street and wandered for several minutes. A voice he had only partially heard interrupted his thoughts. He looked up and saw Jill.

"I guess you didn't hear me. I said hi," she uttered.

"Oh, I'm sorry. I was thinking too hard I guess."

I saw you come out of headquarters. Did you see Josh?"

"Yeah, I did."

"He was probably telling you what a wonderful job you did last night."

"Um, yeah."

"I was at the west wall. I understand you went to the north wall."

"Yeah, why are you asking?"

"Well, you went to the west wall and stemmed the break there, then had time to go all the way to the north wall and stem the tide there. The west intrusion though was the major one. I think they wanted to get us busy on two fronts to split up our forces."

"I had other guys with me, you know. I didn't do anything myself."

"I saw you, Sam. You were picking off the enemy archers one by one and they couldn't shoot as far as you could. You outclassed them. You completely moved them out of the picture. I could even hear the creaking of your bow as it strained when you were taking your shots. I thought it was going to break . . . and you did it with a bum arm . . . I hope you know it's bleeding," she uttered as she noticed the blood on his shirt and some was running down his arm.

"I know. I'm going to the hospital."

"You are? Do you know you're going the wrong way?"

He looked up and around. "I am?"

She started into an uncontrollable laugh.

He stopped and stared at her. He waited until it looked as if she were getting control of herself, then asked, "What did I do now?"

"You're so funny. Here's the brave soldier who can kill hundreds of guys in a matter of minutes and can't even . . ." She broke into laughter again.

Sam had walked close to the west wall where many people were cleaning the battleground and a lot of heads were turning toward her laughter.

She noticed and suddenly stopped. "Damn you, you're ruining my reputation. What I wanted to say was you can't even figure out where the hospital is." She was fighting off another bout of laughter but managed to control herself.

She continued. "You know we can use you here. I was so proud of you." Then she stopped and stared down at the road. "You're leaving, aren't you? You said you wanted to get back home. . . You know, I'm not good with guys," she stammered. "Remember, I hate them, and you don't think much of me but, if you want to give me a chance, I'm willing to give you a chance. Um, what I'm saying is . . . um."

Sam closed in on her, put his hand under her chin, raised her head, planted his lips on hers, and left them there a very long time.

When they finally parted, she said nothing but stood there blushing.

"Lead me to the hospital," he said. "I'll think about staying here."

She took a step but stopped again and threw herself at him for one more caress and kiss then pulled away.

Sam saw everyone looking at them. Some wore stone faces but others had bemused smiles. He put his arm around her waist and she began leading him to the hospital. He slid his hand lower onto her buttocks and she jumped away from him.

"Cut that out," she squealed. She looked back to see everyone looking at them. "You're ruining my reputation."

She sidled up to him again and they began to walk. He pulled his arm from her waist and gave the gazers a thumbs-up sign with his hand.

Everyone broke out into laughter.

She banged her hip against him. "Stop that. You're ruining my reputation."

One of the onlookers realised that Sam was saying more than he had won her heart but was giving them another message. The onlooker cheered loudly and said, "I think he's going to stay with us."

The rest of the onlookers soon began to cheer.

BUILDING EDEN

Ten years had passed since Sam had agreed to stay with Josh and his gang of fighters. It seemed to have passed so quickly. Sam had fathered five children – three boys and two girls with Jill, his mate, a feisty person who claimed to have almost killed several men trying to make a move on her. Sam, though, had won her heart and survived. He nicknamed her, Man-Hater.

Their life had not been easy though, as constant battles with other groups around them had seen them bury hundreds of people who were close to them. Despite the deaths, their community continued to grow through the influx of other people, most of them defectors from other groups.

To feed the gang, they had to supplement what they could raise in the former parks within their expanded area of a large former city by bartering with farmers about three hours south by horseback from where they were and by hunting outside of their territory. The farmers did not need very much from the city dwellers and were in constant peril from heavy attacks by marauding groups from other cities.

Josh had called a meeting with the leaders of the city's fighters.

Josh walked into the meeting room and appeared blurry-eyed and tired; an almost broken man. His hair was showing areas of grey. He had spent twenty-eight of his forty-six years of life trying to build a better world. He looked around the room at the faces of his warriors and said, "Hi guys, it's nice to see you together occasionally. There are so many faces I remember who aren't here but it's nice to see new faces replacing them. We're growing despite our battles but it's getting harder to feed our population. If we can't do something about it soon, our budding society may sink into the morass of our surroundings and everything we built will be gone. I had a dream of building a new society – a new world. I guess it's taking a lot longer than I thought."

He took a deep breath.

"I think we need to take a different approach, now. There are over eight thousand people here but much of our population is too young to take to the sword. We cannot live in the cities indefinitely. As you experience each day, these buildings are crumbling around us. Yes, we're making repairs but we're losing the battle. We must think of the future. What I'm proposing is we form an alliance with the farmers – not just deals to trade. I'm hearing that the farmers are slowly losing. The attacks on them have been more numerous and more forceful. If we lose them, we lose everything. They can grow enough food to feed us. We can't grow stronger without a reliable food supply.

"Our enemies don't seem to care. They aren't thinking of a future, they're thinking of eating, now. We must think of a brighter future and that means farmers and city folks supporting each other.

"We've already joined them in battle against some of the attacks against them but we're having a tough time defending ourselves. If it continues, some people might decide that it's no better here than out there. They may start to leave.

"That's why we must keep our hopes alive. We're large now, as long as the other gangs don't unite, none of them can beat us alone but what I've heard, is that some of them want to make a concerted attempt to get rid of us and the farmers."

"Yeah, that's what I've heard," another leader added.

"Never think that we can survive alone. If we stay together, we're strong. You've got to keep that in mind. We've got a good home here. Most of you have been out there and know what it's like. Do you want to see us disappear? Do you want to give up?"

"No," most of them mumbled.

One said loudly, "I'd rather be dead." A few others echoed the same thought.

"Okay, I'll give you an idea I have." He paused and said, "We can't offer much to trade with the farmers. All we can offer them are doctors, teachers, and . . . protection."

"We've already warded off a few attacks on them," one of them said.

Josh responded, "Yes, and sometimes we're almost too late. What I'm thinking is for some of us to go to live with them. We could build a hospital and school. We could give them tips on how to fight; and even more than that, we could improve our bloodlines, especially of our animals. They also have more horses than we have. If one of the gangs defeated them and got the horses, that would make them stronger once they learned to ride. We must avoid that."

"Yes, but aren't we splitting our numbers? That's going to make us weaker here," a person said with concern.

"We don't have to send half of us, just a good-sized contingent that would give them confidence and they can ward off a significant attack."

Sam spoke, "I think that's a good idea. I don't see it as splitting our forces. If the farmers buy into our plan, we'll have them on our side. I understand the four collectives of farmers have formed a mutual aid agreement."

"Yes, but that means only about eight hundred able-bodied fighters. That's the lowest number they've ever had. That's not much of a force," a leader said.

"And it'll get a lot lower if we don't help them," Josh stated.

"What do you propose we send them then, even supposing they'll accept our plan," one of the leaders asked.

Josh suggested, "Two hundred of our best fighters to impress them, with twenty support people, such as two doctors, five nurses, three teachers, and people to help them build and make or repair weapons. The force could be about fifty archers and the rest infantry."

The men looked at each other. One of them spoke, "I guess two hundred aren't too many but it's significant if we send them our best."

"Are you suggesting that we don't have more than two hundred best people in our forces?" Josh eyed him disappointedly.

The person who suggested it said apologetically, "Well, no but it'll hurt our defences."

"Okay, I'll make up the list. You're all dismissed." As they all started to file out Josh said, "Sam and Jill, remain here."

When everyone left, he said, "Sam could you make a list of your best archers, and Jill, the best infantry?"

They both said, "Okay."

"I'm hoping that you both will volunteer to lead the expedition and convince the farmers of how we can help them and form an agreement with them?"

Sam and Jill looked at each other.

Sam said, "I thought you'd need us here."

"I told everyone I wanted our best and you're the best we have."

"What happens if our enemies attack here?"

"Then your work in training and strengthening our fighters will be put to the test."

Sam turned to Jill and asked, "Do you want to go?"

"I'm where you are."

He turned to Josh and asked, "Do we have a choice?"

"Yes, but the group will be leaving here knowing you're the best and you're not going. Do you want to make me a liar? You come from a farm background, don't you? That may help you to work with them."

"What about our kids?"

"You can take them with you but it may be better that you leave them here until you get a new hospital built and get things established."

"Okay, we'll get the lists together and get packed," Sam said. "What about Dave?"

"I suggest that he assume command of the fighters here."

Sam responded, "Yes, that's a great idea. He'll love that."

Sam and Jill went to their quarters and made the necessary list. He sent one of the runners back with the list to Josh. The runner came back a few minutes later with the message that they were going to leave the next morning.

"So soon, that's not a lot of time for us," Jill said.

"Nothing around here is leisurely," Sam responded, as he wrapped his arms around her. "You know it's been heaven being with you."

"I hate you, remember?"

"Yes, I know but you're nice to be around." He kissed her.

She pried her lips from his. "We don't have a lot of time sweetie; we've got to get packed and spend some time with the kids."

"Yes, I know."

They gathered most of their belongings and wrapped them up. They placed them into a pile by the door. They wandered together to the hospital.

As they approached it, Jill asked, "Do you think you can find your way to the hospital alone by now?"

"After ten years, probably," he said with a smile.

"That's a long time ago, isn't it?"

"The best ten years of my life."

"It's amazing we're still alive."

"We've had some pretty close calls."

"Remember you thought we had toilets and lights? How dumb you were," Jill said.

"I was pretty naive then."

Jill looked at him puzzled, as she was not sure what he had said. She finally said, "That's what I said, you were dumb."

They arrived at the hospital and entered. They wandered to the children's wing and spent some time with theirs. In the end, they sat them down and told them what was happening and assured them that everyone would be all right and they would visit them regularly. They kissed them and said their byes.

They walked over to the mess to eat, spent some quiet time together, and bedded down for the night.

In the morning, they were up with the sun and had their last meal in the city, of course – stew. They went back to their quarters, picked up their things, and hauled them over to the south gate.

It was quite busy with over two hundred people, some with their partners helping, loading up four wagons with their possessions on the other side of the wall. Some of the people were hoping that, if they were successful with the farmers, their partners could move over to the new site later.

They said their goodbyes. Josh wished them well and they were soon on their way. The wagons slowed their travel considerably. It would take them the good part of five hours to reach their objective. Most of the people were on foot but they also had ten warriors on horseback forming a small cavalry contingent.

For two hours they travelled. They stopped to let the horses rest while they had lunch. They were about to start when arrows began flying from the west. Some of the fighters were hit before they knew what was happening. Everyone jumped behind the wagons for protection. On their right was a clump of bushes and high grass.

Once everybody got behind the shelter or dragged the wounded behind the shelter, they started to try to locate the source but no one could see anything.

Sam quickly dispatched twenty of his archers to work their way behind the area where the attackers were hiding and twenty to go around the other way. Jill had thirty fighters crawl toward the grass with some firebombs. Before they could get into position, hundreds of rocks were flying toward them, many of them hitting the exposed fighters.

As the fighters were close to the enemy's location, they lit and tossed first one and then another of the bombs into the grass ahead of them. The slight wind began blowing the smoke and flames into the enemy.

Several other infantry and archers worked their way under cover of the smoke around each side of the site to surround them. Through the smoke, some of the archers saw forms without an armband moving in the grass and shot arrows at them.

The attackers hit several infantry fighters with rocks and moved away from them, attempting to retreat.

Sam sent more archers to each side to assist the ones sent earlier to surround the enemy but most of them escaped.

Sam had some support people tend to the fallen near the wagons and waited. Occasionally, he would notice the enemy in the field and shoot at him or her.

After thirty minutes of fighting, Sam's fighters returned to say they were victorious.

Eight people died in the incident with thirty injured. The injured that could walk joined the troop; the others settled onto the wagons as best they could. The fighters piled the dead onto one wagon and quickly extinguished the brush fire. They tied the hands of their five prisoners and had them walk with Eden's fighters.

Two hours later, as they approached the main gate of the farms, they stopped a distance from it. The gate attendant recognised Sam and said, "Sam, it's you. Welcome. What brings you here, especially with so many wagons?" He held out his hand to shake.

Sam shook it and responded, "I'll tell you later. May we enter?"

"Your wagons, too?"

"Yes."

"Is everything okay?"

"Yes, we were attacked on the way here but we're okay. We've brought some supplies and equipment with us."

"We'll have to search everything before we let you in."

"That's fine. We've got bows, arrows, swords, and incendiaries but I'll discuss those with you tomorrow. You may confiscate all the wagons and their cargo if you wish. It's for your use, so technically it's yours anyway."

The leader appeared a little confused but told them their people could enter but they would have to leave their weapons with the entry guard.

"We have some injured but we have two doctors with us to mend them. Is there somewhere they could work?" Sam asked.

"Sure, the guard can direct them."

They opened the gate and Eden's troops entered, turned in their weapons, and brought all the dead and wounded members into the compound.

In the evening, the city's troops looked after their meals but the lead farmer invited Sam and Jill to his house for a good farmer's meal.

They entered and the leader's wife led them to a large dining hall where the heads of all the farmers of the four collectives were already sitting.

"Wow, this is a surprise," Sam said with a big grin.

The leader said, "We knew you wanted us all together tomorrow but everyone wanted to be here tonight to welcome you."

"Well, thank you," Sam said to the group as he took his place at the head of the table. "It's a great honour to be here." He looked at the food laid out before him and was already salivating. "Let's use our time this evening to have a good time and save the work for tomorrow."

"I'll drink to that," the leader said as he raised his glass in a cheer and everyone followed suit.

Sam had been there several times before and enjoyed the change in cuisine. They started with fresh salad then, instead of stew, they had thick barbequed steak and mashed potatoes with peas and carrots on the side. They ended with a mixed berry pie. By the end of the meal, he was stuffed.

They lingered for a while, making small talk. He was quite tired when they finally parted and they returned to his troops camped in a small fallow field near the farmhouse. The farmers had invited him to stay in the farmhouse but he wanted to stay close to his fighters.

The cock crowing woke him up the next morning. He and Jill were treated to a breakfast of pancakes with bacon and sausage. By ten o'clock, everyone assembled again in the dining hall for the meeting.

The farmers' leader stood up and said, "As you know we've been called together at Sam's request, so I guess he has some good news to give us." He looked at Sam.

Sam stood up. "Yes, it's good news. We've helped each other many times in the past few years. We first provided you with supplies of bows, arrows, and things like that then, more recently, ropes and clothes, including military assistance. When needed, you've brought your injured or wounded to our hospital. You've provided us with food, hemp, wool, and cotton." He paused for a few seconds.

"We'd like to go the next step and form a union with you."

There was murmuring in the room.

"What we propose is to give you faster, more complete services. The main beneficiary will be you. We know that if anything happens to you, we won't survive long and we want to make sure you do.

"We're willing to build a couple of hospitals here to care for your sick and wounded, provide care and schooling for the young, and support for the aged. We'll also send you doctors, nurses, and teachers.

"We'll provide you on-site military presence, hence why we have the wagons with weapons onboard and the two hundred people mini-army here, although some of them are dead bodies, now. We'll try to ship some more in to replace them. We'll also provide support if you plan to expand and you can focus more time on what you do best – farming.

"For us, it means increasing our capacity to make all the things we can make with hemp, cotton, and wool; and provide us with a long-term stable source of food." He paused.

"We also know that we, or you, may be attacked by our rivals to the north and we both have to be strong to survive the onslaught. Together we're stronger which will make us not only survive but prosper together.

"That's our proposal. If you agree, we'll stay here with you and begin to build our union. If you don't, then we'll leave but offer these wagon loads of material and supplies as goodwill. If I may, I'd like to answer any questions you have, and then I'll leave to give you the privacy you deserve to make this decision."

There was a lot of murmuring but nobody asked any questions, so Sam left them to their deliberations.

He did not have long to wait. Within thirty minutes, they called him back and he walked to the head of the table.

The leader said, "We've deliberated and genuinely believe that this is a good move that will benefit both of us. We've already worked closely together but a hospital and permanent formal school will be a great asset to us. You're growing in population, so that would give us a steady market for our excess farm products. Having a standing army will also ensure our immediate safety with less of a need for us to send a messenger for help. We'll work together to help your team lay out a plan for where to place the structures you need to house everyone and for the building for the services you'll provide. I was also informed that some of our younger people were noticing the handsome young unmarried young men and women you have."

Sam chuckled heartily. "I'm glad you're interested in our offer. I hope you know how we operate. We keep our children in the hospital for protection and to allow our people to work and not have to worry about children being around. They have around-the-clock care and the school is right there. You might want to do that for yourselves but it's up to you. Also, we don't have formal weddings or anything; in fact, most people have very informal arrangements, if any. If you know you might die tomorrow, firm bonds are rarely made."

"Yes, we know that. Times are tough. I think your arrangement has served you well and some of us may adopt the practice to ensure our kids are safe. We've lost many of our children during raids and battles because they were at the wrong place at the wrong time."

"Well, I'll pass the word to our people to let them know that they have a new home. I guess we'll remain in the tents we've set up for a while. Um, I hope our being here is not going to break up the structure you've established."

"We talked about that. Adam and Eve's children likely didn't have formal wedding arrangements. Knowing that someone will love and care for any children that come of the mingling of our people makes it easier to take. I guess we must raise the farmers and warriors of future generations. We're practical people."

For the next few weeks, they began the construction of a town. It was to the south of the centre of the farm community, as most of the expansion was likely to take place in that direction. It would consist of a central living area and hospital but, for now, housed a temporary tent hospital.

But things were soon to change. A message came from Josh that the gangs from the northern city had united and were on the move. He was not sure where but was not taking any chances and advised them to be alert. He dispatched fifty additional fighters to the farmers to bolster the farm's defences.

Sam and Jill worked closely with the farmers to set up some drills. They taught children too young to fight to be runners to pass messages and provide fighters with supplies of spears and arrows as the battle progressed. That improved battle strength and communications, while leaving those most able to fight to do their jobs. Every fighter practised their arts for a few hours each day to keep them prepared for the worst.

Eight days later after midnight, the enemy attacked. The warning chime's clanging awakened Sam and Jill from sleep. He hurriedly dressed and saw the gathering crowd of his fighters.

Sam looked at the sky. There were some clouds but it was mostly clear. The stars were shining brightly. The half-moon high overhead was providing additional light.

A farm boy was soon at his side and was panting from his race to their tents. He told them where the attacks were occurring.

His fighters were soon ready. He said, "Okay guys, this is our first test to show how useful we can be to the farmers. Let's show them our best. The attack is along the northwest defences, concentrating at the west gate. Let's go."

They were laden with extra spears, swords, and arrows but ran as quickly as they could. After a few minutes, they could hear the battle. As they approached, Sam quickly assessed the situation.

"They breached the west gate, so let's plug the gap with enemy bodies. Archers, form two lines and be prepared to advance. Jill, take the infantry and contain the enemy's advance from the north gate into the compound."

Jill took command and led the infantry to the north gate.

Sam advanced with the archers toward the west gate. When they got within range, Sam ordered a halt and called for the first rank to fire, then the second rank. He continued that way until they could advance. They took a couple of steps forward and shot a couple more volleys into the enemy lines. Soon, the enemy turned toward them in full attack. Sam yelled, "Hold the line! Fire at will!" He pulled out his bow and joined them, firing as fast as he could pull out an arrow from the bucket and load it to the nick.

The attackers were slowing their advance as they tripped over the bodies of their fallen comrades. Some enemy archers were gathering behind their advancing infantry.

Sam left the rest of the archers to do their job while he focused his attack on the enemy archers. He wanted to keep them from forming up and becoming a useful element in the battle in front of them.

He could see out of the corner of his eyes, arrows hitting his archers. He sped up his attack on the enemy's archers to the point most of them had pulled back out of his range but that meant that his archers were out of their range. He continued to neutralise any archer who dared step forward to take a shot. Now, he too could send a few arrows against the infantry in front of them.

The enemy infantry was getting closer, though – almost too close for comfort. The archers were shooting at them at point-blank range. Two young boys were behind them reloading the pails with arrows.

Twenty members of Jill's infantry soon showed up and filled the holes in the lines of archers and firing spears into the enemy lines. When they were out of spears, they picked up bows from the fallen archers and joined the archers' defence.

While Sam was defending the west gate, Jill ran down another path leading north and soon engaged some attackers that had already penetrated deeper into the compound. Some farmers had already engaged but were faltering. The sudden appearance of her forces quickly turned the tide in their favour. The appearance of farmers on horseback soon had the enemy on the run.

Suddenly, through the north gate, a small unit of enemy cavalry was racing toward them.

Jill and her infantry fended them off with spears and swords. The farmers' fighters began a barrage of rocks with their slingshots which were knocking riders off their horses but the cavalry was soon cutting into the infantry with their sabres. The farmers' cavalry soon engaged them and, after twenty minutes of back-and-forth skirmishes, the attackers were in retreat. Jill was not sure how Sam was doing, so sent twenty of her fighters to assist.

While the cavalry cleaned up the area of enemy fighters, Jill headed farther north to engage a large contingent that was fighting a group of farmers. Within thirty minutes, that group of the enemy was retreating out and over the barrier of the north wall.

Back at the west gate, many enemy fighters had finally penetrated the farmer's compound and were torching buildings and fields. Sam caught up with a group of them. The enemy had a mix of archers and infantry who had hidden behind some of the trees and small buildings in the area. Using what was left of the infantry and archers, Sam tried to flush them out. If he spotted any of the enemy, he downed them with an arrow.

Suddenly, to his left, Sam spotted some movement but it was too late. Several archers' response, was shock then they were cut down in a hail of arrows.

Sam's archers fought hard as the enemy pulled back behind cover. When the farmers' cavalry arrived a few minutes later, the battle ended and the few remaining enemy fighters surrendered.

Sam and Jill left their fighters near the three gates to prevent a further attack while the farmers began the process of gathering the wounded and taking them to the hospital tent, then collecting the dead on both sides and laying them out for identification. They locked their prisoners into a small barn.

When Jill had finished securing the north gate, a messenger came to her to give her the news about Sam.

Her first response was shock, then of needing to know more but the runner could only tell her that he had been injured and was in a hospital tent.

She raced to the hospital and saw many dead and injured people strewn about the ground. Most of them were still unattended and waiting their time for the doctors to examine them. She went over to one of the doctors and asked about Sam. He, at first, wanted to use the excuse of being too busy but he relented and told her that two arrows had hit Sam and, to her consternation, gravely wounded him.

"Can't you do anything for him?" she asked.

"We got the arrows out and bandaged him up but there's not much else we can do for him. There may still be some internal bleeding. He's lost quite a bit of blood. In the old days, he could get a transfusion of blood and better surgery but with what we have now, that's all we can do. He'll have to do the rest on his own."

"Can I give him blood?"

"That's a nice gesture but we don't know if your blood would give him life or kill him. Look around you. We have so many others that need help right away and there are only two of us. Please accept the fact that we've done what we can."

She looked at the wounded around her. The doctor was right. He couldn't spend much time on any one patient, even if it was Sam. She was losing the best friend she ever had and had ever loved.

She wandered around the site and found the tent Sam was in. She could see him laboriously breathing but did not go inside. She knelt beside the door but could not see him long like this. She wanted to race to his side and hug him but there were so many other urgent things that needed doing. She wanted to remember him as her friend, tower of strength, and lover, not this helpless being fighting for his life. Tears filled her eyes. She took a deep breath.

A farmer raced up to her and said hurriedly, "Come, follow me."

She got up and ran after him to a point just inside the north gate. The farmer stopped by a tree and pointed to a person sitting on the ground using the tree trunk to support his back.

"This guy made it through the north gate. He's got two arrows in him but he wanted to see you or Sam immediately."

She knelt and looked at the wounded man. She recognised him as a denizen of the city. He looked as if he were in pain. She said, "Hi, this is Jill."

He turned his eyes toward her and recognised her. "Hi, I came here to tell you that the city's under attack." He stopped to take a deep breath. "The enemy has breached the outer perimeter and the city is under siege within the inner barrier." He stopped again briefly. "The city's holding out for now but I can see you won't be able to help. I got caught in the crossfire before I could get through the gate here . . . It looks as if it's all over for us." He took a couple of deep breaths then his head slumped onto his chest.

She knew he was dead.

Jill knelt there for a long time. She felt so helpless. She was losing control. The picture was clear though. The people in the city north of them, who had been their mortal enemies from the beginning, had attacked the farms, probably to knock them out and destroy them quickly. Once they had secured this area, this army would have joined the army that attacked the city and finished the job but they hadn't wiped out the farms and were stuck for now with putting the farmers and the city under siege. The farmers would last a long time under siege but the city would not. The fighters there would run out of water and food. Then the northerners could finish the job in the city and travel here to finish off the farmers.

She stood up. There was no time for mourning. There was no time for crying. There was only time to get revenge on the northerners if she could. It would be for Sam and Josh. She could not let what Josh established die as an unfulfilled dream but it depended on the farmers.

She turned to the farmer beside her and said, "Would you ask your leader to call a meeting of the farm heads as soon as they can? I know everyone's busy but people can work while we talk."

"Yes, Ma'am," he replied, as he hurried off.

She looked at the corpse sitting against the tree and said, "Let's hope your journey here was not wasted."

She motioned to a person carrying a body and pointed to the dead man by the tree.

He nodded and hurried on his way. He would pick it up on another trip.

She sighed and walked toward the leader's house. It looked as if a fire had damaged it and some of the fields around it. Here and there was either a dead body or a person moaning in pain. She helped one onto her feet and walked her to the hospital in the centre of the compound. Jill ignored the fact that she was hungry but did have a drink of water.

She wandered among the people spread on the ground around the hospital tent. It was greener here, as the fire had not reached this far. Her feet were tired from the long walk. She encountered one of her lieutenants and asked him to present her with an assessment as soon as he could put one together. She wanted to know how many people were still in fighting condition.

The leader of the farmers rode toward her on his horse. He got off and came toward her. "I hear you'd like to have a meeting. I think we should, too. I'll set one up for breakfast. We want to assess our damages and will be more prepared for it."

"That'd be fine, thanks. I'll also need a bit more time."

He returned to his horse and rode off.

Before breakfast, Jill had her report. Out of over fifty archers she had, thirty-five were able to continue. Nine were dead and the others were too injured to fight. Of the infantry, she had over a hundred left. That was not going to be enough but that was all she had.

She walked into the dining room a rather sullen person and sat down. The other leaders slowly filed into the room and sat. There was a lot of murmuring as the youths brought in the food. The farmers were discussing their situation with each other. Jill was too burdened by her thoughts to pick up most of their conversations.

They began to serve themselves and eat. At the end, the youths cleared the table and the lead farmer said, "Would you like to say anything, Jill?"

"Yes, I got our status. We have about a hundred and thirty men and women who can still fight. Before a messenger from the city died, he said that the northerners had broken through the outer defences of the city and it was under siege. I know the remaining enemy forces also have us under siege but I'd like to break out and attack the enemy forces in the city because it'll not last long without food and water. I think you'll be able to hold off the siege here with what you have."

The leader responded, "That's a suicide mission."

"I know," she said nervously.

There was silence in the room. The leader looked at each of the farmers along both sides of the table and said, "We've come to rely on the relationship we've had with your city. If you fall, it won't be long before we do. We're stuck with each other. If you hadn't been with us today, we would not have survived the onslaught. We would not be here right now. You've proved to us that you're willing to lay down your lives for us. We can do no less for you.

"Every battle we've had, we've always been on the defence. They expect that of us. They expected to overrun us by now but we're still here. Now, they'll sit out there and expect us to wait until the city falls then bring their forces over here to finish us off but we're not going to sit here anymore.

"We've done our tally. We had eight hundred fighting persons at the start of the day. We've always tried to grow but battle after battle, enemies have worn us down and that's the best we can do after all the years we've been here. Now, we've got only about five hundred who can still fight, which won't be of much use to you but we have over two hundred horses. Most of them are workhorses but most of those are rideable. That gives us almost two hundred heads of cavalry.

"Most of us have been talking during the day, not all together and in bits and pieces but I can speak for all of us. Of our five hundred men and women, we'll field two hundred of them on horses. One hundred are skilful with the bow and can supplement your 35. We also have nine crossbowmen. The rest can fill in your infantry. That's not a big army and it may not be enough but that's all we have. The young boys and girls and the more aged of us can defend the farms while we're away in case anyone else attacks us.

"To be successful, we must eliminate our besiegers. At noon, the enemy will be surprised because, for the first time, we're going on the attack. Our cavalry will strike the south gate first, as they won't expect an assault there. We'll hit so hard and fast the enemy won't know what happened."

We'll sweep north and attack the enemy besieging the west gate. As we do this, our defenders there can join us. When we strike the north gate, we can do the same. If we're successful, all fighters on foot can march north to the city with several preloaded wagons of munitions and food. The cavalry can mop up and catch up with us later."

Jill smiled. "Well, you have a plan and it's very optimistic. Do you have a plan B if something goes wrong with Plan A?"

"Nope, Plan A has to work. I guess Plan B would be to withdraw to the farm and wait for the main force to come and wipe us out in a week or so."

"Then I guess we go for plan A. It's well thought out. We've got to succeed for both of us," Jill said pensively.

"We've got a lot to do to get things sorted out, so this meeting is adjourned. Let's hope this isn't our last meeting. Everyone be ready for noon. We've had a long night, now we'll have an even longer day."

Before noon, everyone gathered at their posts. The cavalry saddled the horses and got their equipment ready. The infantry grabbed their equipment and wandered over to their positions either at the west or north gates. The planning people loaded some carts with provisions and extra arms and pulled them into position near the north gate. The people who would take over the defence of the compound while the fighters were away, got into their positions.

As the sun passed its zenith, the south gate to the farmer's enclave opened and the cavalry stormed over the small enemy detachment that was there.

The enemy did not have time to flee.

Fifty horses broke off and moved east to the ocean to eliminate any enemy troops along their south boundary. Along that border, all they encountered were sentries who patrolled that area to report activity to the enemy forces to the west. They gathered a dozen prisoners and dropped them off at the south gate to add to their prisoners in the barn. The unit then raced to join the larger group.

The larger group raced west along the southern boundary of their enclave cutting down sentries placed along that area then travelled in a wide arc from their barrier to approximately a hundred metres long so no one would escape their sweep along the denser siege area along the western side of the enclave.

When they approached the west gate, they met heavy resistance from the enemy forces there. They slowly pressed the enemy to move north along the enclave's barrier. The farmers' archers at the west gate moved out and supported them in the attack, hitting the enemy with volley after volley of arrows. As the besiegers got too close to the barrier, the archers continued their assault from that side.

The cavalry pressed the enemy into a running retreat north and toward the border. No one was able to escape. It was like a huge broom brushing dust along a floor. The horses were tiring though but the farmers pressed on until they reached the northern border of their territory. The cavalrymen's sabres, sickles, and spears were cutting down the beleaguered enemy.

The farmer's cavalry was now north of the farm and had turned east to form a net to stop the enemy's forces from escaping and informing the besiegers in the city what was going on there. They spread out and kept their eyes open.

Suddenly, at the north entrance, Jill's archers quickly formed up and began a barrage of arrows against the enemy forces outside their gate.

The enemy's archers shot back but in doing so, were giving away their location.

The archers focused on these targets and, within minutes, the enemy's defence petered out.

The archers pulled back and Jill's infantry opened the gate but instead of engaging the enemy, they ran along the wall to the east.

The enemy's leaders were unsure of what to do and were hesitating until the enemy's forces in advance of the cavalry pressing from the west were running through their defences.

The cavalry was stopping the enemy from getting organised into their formations.

Jill's archers advanced and sent another barrage of arrows on the enemy, killing and maiming most of what they hit.

Panic was overtaking the enemy's attempts at reorganising.

Within an hour, the infantry that had left the compound had reached the ocean. They formed a line and began their advance westward.

The cavalry effectively surrounded the enemy forces and advanced from the west and north, while the infantry advanced from the east.

The main body of the enemy was panicking and trying to escape but was deterred as soon as they reached the perimeter which was getting smaller by the minute.

In a desperate attempt to turn the tide, the enemy attacked the northern gate.

The salvo of arrows from there reduced their threat.

As the enemy troops approached the gate, the farmer's infantry poured through it to engage them. Within an hour it was over.

What remained of the enemy forces raised the white flag, even if they risked death, as friends and foes considered people who surrendered as cowards.

As the farmers collected the enemy warriors, they told them to sit along the wall beside the north gate. While the cavalry mopped up and hunted for any stray enemy fighters, Jill had a meeting with the farmers' leaders on the field of battle.

"How do things look?"

The farmer's leader responded, "We lost almost twenty horses and more riders but we'll add other riders. I thought we could continue but I think it would be better to rest the horses and we can start tomorrow. A lot of my people and horses are very tired."

Jill agreed with him. "We lost a few fighters but a rest would help everyone. We don't think any enemy fighters escaped. The cavalry is looking for stragglers now and we'll keep doing it but we were quite thorough."

"Okay, we'll start early tomorrow. What should we do with the captives?"

"Do you have somewhere to store them?" Jill asked.

"We can tie their hands together, lock them in a barn for now with the rest of them," the farmers' leader said.

"We'll be eating soon, how about we give them a good meal," Jill suggested.

They moved the captives into the farmer's barn with the others and kept them under guard.

During supper, Jill talked to the lead farmer. "We didn't suffer huge losses but I don't know if we have enough fighters to attack the city's besiegers. We lost quite a few archers and infantry."

"I know. It was a gruelling day. The farms are so large now it's a long way around them. I could get more people if you want." That means losing more people to defend against any attacks while we're gone. Plus, we have to guard the prisoners."

"Don't take any unnecessary chances."

"Yeah, but we have to break the siege on the city. If we can't do it with what we have, we'll have to find more people."

"Well, give me any you can spare."

After supper, Jill left and walked to where the captives were. She opened the barn door. Her eyes scanned its interior and guessed that there were over eight hundred captives who looked well enough to fight.

"Did you get something to eat?" Jill asked.

Several of them nodded.

"That's good. Your usual treatment of prisoners of war is to kill them but we don't do that unless we have to. We'll be holding you here until the war is over because we don't want you to return to your gang and end up fighting us again.

"If you want to be peaceful, you'll be given a choice – migrate or join us. We provide lots of service to our people that you've never had, like care for children, the wounded, and the old. We have doctors here and carpenters and farmers. Of course, we also spend a lot of time dealing with people like you, so there are times we must defend ourselves.

"We're regrouping to attack your people surrounding our city. If you want to begin your life with us, we'd welcome any help you can provide right now."

One of them said, "We have no real love of our leaders but if we join you to fight against our people and you lose, we'll be killed as traitors."

"By allowing yourselves to be captured you've already been labelled as traitors. They'll kill you anyway. If you join us, fight hard, and if we win, you'll be free. Talk to anyone here to find out what we're like."

"We already know. We wouldn't have surrendered, if we knew you'd kill us anyway," one of the fighters who appeared to be one of the leaders said.

"Well, talk about it amongst yourselves. We need every person we can get."

"And if some of us are afraid to fight?" another fighter asked.

"We'll understand. We could use you though. I'll be back soon with answers."

Jill left the barn.

The leader of the farmers returned from talking with his associates and joined her. He said, "We can get about three hundred more fighters by lowering our age limit. Usually, we keep it around eighteen. There are also a few older people who've volunteered."

"Good, get them together and ready to leave tomorrow at dawn."

Jill returned to the prisoners. Their spokesperson stepped forward and said, "We've got about six hundred people ready to fight for you."

"Good, we're leaving tomorrow."

Jill walked toward Sam's hospital tent. Her head hung low. Whether they won or lost, Jill was going to be lost without him – he was her whole world. When she arrived at the hospital, she found that nothing had changed in his status. He was still fighting for his life.

She stayed with him for about an hour then leaned over and whispered into his ear, "I don't know if you can hear me but I love you. Fight for your life, my love. Never give up. I'll be gone for a while but I'll be back in a few days." She bent her head to his and kissed him. Slowly she got up and left the tent to sleep.

The next morning, everyone gathered at the north gate. Labourers had filled three wagons with provisions for the battle. For three hours they marched north. They stopped well outside the south gate of the city. Jill and the farmers' leader snuck closer to the gate and lay on the rocks to peer inside the compound. There was no one nearby.

"It looks as if they don't know we're coming," Jill said. "They likely have their forces close to the inner enclosure. I hope it doesn't mean that the city has fallen."

"Well, we'll soon find out," the leader remarked.

"Have the cavalry quietly move to the north gate. Since they'll be the last ones to their post, they'll lead the charge. You take your infantry and archers, head to the west gate, and move in from there. I'll stay with our troops here and give you time to get yourself set up. As soon as we hear the charge of the horses, we all move in."

Even with the quickly moving horses it took over three hours before they could hear the horses' hooves pounding on the pavement.

Everyone was on the attack. The three-point attack was forcing the enemy's fighters to move closer to the city's defences allowing the city's forces to fire on the enemy with their archers, at least until the battle became a hand-to-hand melee. Then the city began an attack over its barriers.

The fighting continued for over two hours until the remaining enemy forces laid down their weapons.

The fighting was over but their losses were high – too high.

They spent the rest of the day bringing food and water to the city and carrying the wounded to the hospital.

In the evening, Joshua called a meeting of the military heads. He listened to how the farmers' battle went and how many people had been killed and wounded.

He sighed. "Such a loss of so many young lives. Thank you for helping me free our city from the siege," he said as he looked at the farm heads. "We wouldn't have lasted much longer."

Jill looked at the leader of the defectors and said, "Welcome to our new leader who led his defeated troops to help in the task. I'm glad you decided to join us. You lost a few of your people but at least your wounded will be well cared for."

The leader nodded appreciatively.

Josh said, "I'm tired of all this fighting and am wondering if we can end it once and for all." He looked at the former enemy leader and asked, "Would you provide me with the defensive state of your city if we attacked it."

"Gladly. Right now, there's only a small unit to defend it. You've never attacked us, so we went all out with practically all our forces to eliminate you. I'm glad we failed. I don't want to say much more, except I recommend you include any doctors and nurses you can spare with your attacking troops."

"Hmm, I guess we could do that. So, you think with what we have left, we can defeat your city's forces?"

The leader said, "It won't come without cost but I'm confident we can. I'll talk to your current prisoners and see if I can recruit some of them to join us."

"That'd be appreciated."

"It'd be like liberating our city from the tyranny of our leaders. Most of them are still there. Once we're inside, I'd like to execute them."

"Well, that wouldn't be necessary."

"To us it is. Wait until you get there, you'll see what I mean."

"I'll leave that for your judgment then." Josh drooped his head for several seconds then raised it to look at the farm heads and asked, "Would you be willing to help us in this endeavour? I know you must be anxious to get back to protect your farms."

The senior farm leader responded, "Yes but I can see how important this mission is. What I propose also is to take some of the burden off you by loading some of our wounded onto our wagons and sending them back to the hospital at the farm. When they heal, they'll add a bit of support to our defences."

"That's a good idea," Josh replied. "I'll set up a couple of crews to work overnight to get some wagons ready for them to leave tomorrow. Thanks, everyone. We're going to be busy for the next few days. Everyone, get a good night's sleep."

The group broke up.

Jill wandered down to the ocean and stared at its great expanse. She crumpled to her knees in the sand, weeping.

Dave had seen where she went and followed her. He stared at her slumped on the beach for a while.

She turned to him and told him what had happened to Sam.

He was shocked for several seconds then knelt in the sand, wrapped his arms around her, and hugged her. He could sympathise with her. He was losing, or maybe had lost, a good friend.

He sighed and wondered what he should do. Was it better to leave her alone, or continue to comfort her? He looked up at the great expanse of ocean and sky. Looking at it made him seem so small. He was less than a microscopic bit of dust in the universe. He decided to stay with her until she controlled herself enough to return to the city to prepare for the next day.

In the morning, the troops got up and ate breakfast. Jill received a message that the former enemy leader had over three hundred new prisoners join his ranks. The night crew had done a good job of preparing the wagons to send the injured troops back to the farm and they were already on their way. Within an hour after breakfast, the ragtag army marched north.

For three days they travelled until they could make out the city's profile ahead of them. They made camp, so they would get up the next morning and reach it early in the day, perhaps surprising them.

The next morning, they had breakfast before sunrise and headed out before they could see the sun rise above the horizon. Within minutes, they entered the outskirts of the city. The troops that were familiar with the city led the way.

Forty-five minutes later those troops removed a barricade without incident. They entered while Eden's troops spread themselves out along other roads, walking closely to the sides of the buildings to avoid detection.

When the leading group reached a guarded barricade, they asked to enter. The main guard recognised them and let them in. Three leaders from the group asked to see the gang leader. There was some hesitation as he had just gotten up but one of the leading traitors told them they had important information from their troops in the north.

The guard led them to a large building in the centre of the enclave. The traitors waited a few minutes while the main guard went in to see the boss. After a few minutes, he returned and said, "He's surprised such a small group returned. He expected a large victorious army with many slaves."

"We have news to give him, so can we enter?"

"Sure," he said, as he opened the door wider.

The three traitors walked in and closed the door behind them. Six fighters were in the room.

The traitors continued to the adjoining room where a rather annoyed-looking middle-aged man they knew as their boss confronted them.

"We have news from the front," the leader of the three said.

"Well, what is it? If you're returning now, the news must be good."

"Yes, very good actually. You're being surrounded and we have been asked to tell you to have your troops lay down their weapons to avoid unnecessary killing."

"What?" the boss raised his voice to ask incredulously. "By whom?"

"By a united farmer-city army."

"You're kidding!"

"Have your fighters disarm, now," he said firmly.

"I'll never do that. I'd rather have everyone in the city die before I'd do that." The leader hurried to a window to warn his troops but the three of them ambushed him. Within seconds his body was slumped on the floor – dead.

The noise had raised the interest of the boss' assistants in the next room and three of them burst in to see their leader on the floor. They pulled out their swords but the three traitors had already spread themselves out to move in quickly before the others could get themselves armed. Instantly, they moved in for the kill.

They hurried into the next room, caught others unaware, and killed them. They hurried to the door, opened it, and signalled to their troops. Several of them raced out of the area to get the gates to the city opened for Josh's army to enter.

The lead traitor turned to the person who had waited by the door and said, "I'd advise you to get your fighters to lay down their weapons or face death."

"What the hell are you talking about?" he cried out loudly.

"All your bosses are dead. There's no point in fighting."

He pushed by the three and spotted the bodies through the open door of the next room."

"You killed them?"

"We had to. Lay down your arms now, or in minutes this place will be swarming with fighters and you'll all be killed."

He looked around then yelled out, "Kill these imposters, they're traitors! Kill them all, quickly."

There was some hesitation due to the surprise involved with what was going on. Within a few seconds, the enemy troops began collecting their weapons.

When the traitors could see that they were in trouble, they raced toward their leaders at the door to the boss' building. One of the leaders whirled around at the person who refused to give up and stabbed him in the heart.

The enemy troops raced toward the defectors who crowded into the building for defence. They locked the door behind them.

The enemy troops began to batter the door, while another group raced to the back but the fighters inside the building quickly locked that door. They also shuttered the two windows.

While the sound of banging on the doors boomed through their ears, Josh's troops raced through the open gate and swarmed into the compound.

The banging on the doors stopped when the warning drums sounded and the enemy turned to the defence of the city. The traitorous troops in the building opened the doors. The archers stepped out and began to fire at the enemy. The archers of Josh's army fired at the enemy from the opposite direction. The battle lasted less than thirty minutes after the cavalry entered the scene.

When Josh entered the compound, all was still. Only the sound of women wailing and crying babies broke the silence.

Josh, Jill, and Dave surveyed the city and the sights presented astounded them. Except for its army, the city was a showcase of poverty. Half-starved babies could hardly cry. Children were skin and bones.

Josh turned to the leader of the traitors. "Now I understand why you asked for doctors and nurses and didn't want to say much. This picture says it all."

The leader of the traitors gathered his troops and Josh went over to talk to them.

Josh pointed to the leader and said, "This is your new boss. Do what he says. We'll stay here a few days to help you clean up around here, and then we'll leave you a few troops to help defend your city. We'll also leave you some doctors and nurses to help care for your wounded and sick people. Right now, get over to the wagons and get everybody fed."

The troops broke off, walked quickly to the wagons, and began emptying their contents. Other troops were setting up tents in the streets until the people could clean the buildings.

Josh turned to Jill and Dave. "I think my troops can handle whatever needs to be done here. You guys lead the farm's troops back home. I'm sure you're interested in finding out how Sam's doing."

They nodded and began their preparations to leave.

That evening, all the leaders met over a celebration supper. Josh got his chance to thank everyone for their help and to get to know their city's new team of leaders.

In the morning, the farmers hooked up their wagons, loaded their sick and wounded, and headed south to their farms.

After a week, the newly cleaned city was looking a lot more presentable. The city's management team stood proudly at attention before Josh and his troops. Josh said as he stood by his horse, "The city now looks more like it's ours. I think the people are happy now and have welcomed the change. The hospital is being set up. There's a lot more left to do but you'll have our continued help to do it." He stepped forward and shook their hands. He climbed onto his horse and, as he and his fighters left for their city, the few people left in this city lined the roads and waved their thankful goodbyes.

It was a slow trip for the farmers. As they rode and walked into their farm compound, the farmers welcomed them with cheers. The farmers had heard that their troops had been successful and the northern city was now theirs. Most of the returning farmers broke ranks as soon as they entered their territory. Dave and Jill though, stayed on their horses and quickly rode to the hospital tent.

When they arrived, the doctor came out to greet them. "I guess I know why you're here."

"Yeah," Jill said as she slipped off her horse.

He smiled at her, which relaxed her greatly.

"I guess you've got good news," Jill said impatiently.

"For a long while, we thought we'd lose him. He developed an infection which made it worse and then, he suddenly took a turn for the better and has been improving ever since."

Jill took a deep breath. It was the news she wanted to hear. "Is he awake? Can we see him?"

"Certainly, come along."

They followed the doctor by several tents until they spotted Sam inside one of them. She went straight to him.

Sam had a big grin on his face. "It's about time you guys got back here," he said coolly.

"When we left, you were almost dead."

"Well, I fooled you."

"I'm a little disappointed," Jill responded.

"Oh?"

"I was making arrangements for Dave to replace you, now I'll have to drop him."

Dave suddenly had a shocked look on his face.

Sam spotted it and said, "He might not want you to drop him."

"Oh, you mean I can keep both of you?"

"Well, certainly. You're a healthy old lady. I think you could handle it."

Dave finally said, "Come on you two. You guys are embarrassing. I'm not stealing anyone's woman."

Sam retorted, "Who said anything about stealing? I'm talking about sharing. I'm getting old and I'm not in my prime anymore and need help."

"Oh, for Pete's sake can't you guys talk seriously about anything?" Dave responded curtly.

Sam replied, "I am serious."

Dave looked at them smiling at him and shook his head. "Anyway, I'm glad you're much better. I don't know what Jill's talking about, as I've made no passes at her. Of course, if you had died that might have been another matter . . ." He took the doctor by the arm and led him out. "I think the two love birds want some privacy."

Jill watched them leave, knelt by the cot, and said softly, "I'm so glad you made it."

"I think Beautiful helped me," he said quietly.

"Beautiful?"

"I had a dream about her. I think I was on my way to the other world and she stopped me and told me to go back."

Jill kept silent.

"Anyway, here I am," he said.

Jill crawled into the cot beside him. He wrapped his arms around her and gave her a deep kiss. She snuggled beside him. She had withheld much of her emotions for days of battles and worry, now she broke down and began to cry.

Through her sobs, she said, "Don't get any idea that I love you."

"No, I know. You still hate men. I hate you, too." He hugged her warmly as he stroked her long flowing hair. He brought a handful to his nose and sniffed. He said, "You know, you stink."

She poked him in his ribs. "What am I supposed to smell like after days of travelling and fighting?"

He winced in pain and took his turn to kiss her then responded, "Aren't you supposed to take a bath and soak in perfume for several hours before you see me?"

She pulled away and began to laugh. "You're a funny man, Sam; a very funny man."

HOME TO EDEN

Eight years after the war against their neighbours in the north, there had still been battles. There always seemed to be someone to fight. Being a large group did not prevent other gangs from trying to steal from the city or the farms. Sometimes there were large battles, and other times light skirmishes. Most of the time the battles occurred when there was a convoy of farm goods going to the city, or armaments and other material heading the other way but it never seemed to end. However, inside their compounds, they were relatively at peace.

One day, Sam accompanied a shipment of goods from the farm. He was anxious to meet Josh. When he entered the city, he walked over to headquarters.

Josh welcomed him with open arms at the front of the building. "I'm glad to see you. Let's head over for some food. You must be hungry."

As they walked away from the building over to one of the eating areas, Josh said, "I hear things are going well on the farms."

"Yes, their move farther south and west was successful. They've got some good land under control, inside and outside their boundaries. We haven't completed their defences yet, nor the hospital but they're well on their way."

Josh filled him in on the northern territory. "Our twin city is well fortified now and things are going well. They're interested in establishing some farms between our cities soon, so I'll talk to you about it one of these days. It's a long way to haul farm goods from the south. You might want to alert the southern farmers and see if there are any volunteers for that project. They might be looking for more land themselves."

"I can do that. There's good land to the south too, except as I told you, there's another city south of it. The farmers have continually had their food and animals stolen and their compounds attacked. They're very anxious to get their fortifications improved before summer ends. The fall is the time they get hit the hardest."

"We're already planning to send some more troops down there."

"That'll bring comfort to them. They fear for their lives."

They reached the eating area and sat down. A server soon delivered their meals.

"You should visit us more often. I much prefer the food the farmers cook to this monotonous stew," Sam said.

"So, do I but it's easy to cook for a mass of people. It's nutritious and that's all we need."

"I agree but I didn't come here to talk about food."

"I'm all ears."

"I guess I don't need your permission but I wanted to let you know, as you have some interest in it."

"Yes?" Josh sat up in his chair.

"We're relatively stable, now and I've been thinking about this for some time . . . I made a promise a long time ago to return to Eden. I don't think I have much of anything to bring to them but I wonder if they'd be willing to come here."

"Them, leave Eden to come here . . . I don't know," Josh said pensively while he munched his food. "This is no Eden."

"Depends on how you look at it. Sure, we have battles to fight but we eat well and have places to live. We have hospitals, schools, and lots of protection. Their little Eden can support only a limited number of people. There's no place to expand and with only three families they're having problems with getting healthy babies because of inbreeding. The same thing was happening with the animals.

"This is my Eden, now. We've made a new home. I don't think it'd take much convincing to get them to want to move here. We've created a new world here – a new Eden."

Josh sat quietly for a few seconds. "It's far from being Eden but I guess if Eden is a land of dreams, this is the next best thing to it that we have on Earth; at least what we know of it. From how we're growing, it's a success. Our old Eden is stagnant; a beautiful place with lots of struggles but it's not growing. It's just surviving. Yes, I think you should try to find Eden again and invite them to come here. You should keep true to your promise and that goes double for me. Don't tell them I'm here though. Let it be a surprise. Who knows, maybe I'll be dead before you get back."

"As you wish."

They finished eating and walked back to the headquarters building. Josh asked, "What do you need?"

"I'll need some wagons and maybe I can bring a few things I've been collecting to give them if they decide to stay where they are. I'll need some troops. I'm not sure what we'll encounter during the journey. We should have armaments, food, and water. They'll likely want to bring some stuff back with them if they want to come here."

"Four or five wagons should be enough. Take two hundred people with you and pick who you want."

"We'll try to cross the river at that bridge I heard is south of us."

"That might be risky. That's not our territory. That's close to that ornery bunch of people not far south from our farm."

"We can try a northern bridge but the closest one is in bad shape. People do cross it on foot but horses and wagons are likely to make it collapse. I don't know how much farther north we would have to go to find another one."

"Well, try the southern bridge but don't take many risks. We don't want to lose any of you."

"I think our families might offer us some assistance. If we make it back to Eden, they'd likely want to bring their guns and ammunition to supplement our supplies for the trip back."

"Oh yes, that would be handy but I don't think they have a lot of ammunition left. What's there has deteriorated; a lot of the shells misfire."

"It's old but it's better than arrows when they do fire."

"When are you going?"

"I'll pick fighters from here and head out the day after tomorrow. It'll take time to load the wagons and get ready. As we pass the farms, I'll collect the rest of the fighters from them."

They had reached the headquarters building.

Sam said, "Thanks for your support. We should be back in less than two months, well in time for the harvest."

Sam handpicked his group which included a nurse and a doctor who he knew had regularly practiced fighting with the other men. He was going to be away for a long time and wanted to keep the troop healthy. He ensured that he had a few carpenters to fix anything on the wagons if they broke down. He loaded five wagons with their provisions, arms, some tools, and the parts he thought would be useful to the denizens of Eden if they decided to stay where they were. He selected ten horses to pull the wagons and eighty horses for scouting and use as a small cavalry if he needed one.

On the appointed morning, the five wagons headed southwest. As they passed the farms, they got seventy more people to join them.

Their first four days were uneventful. They reached the river and followed along it for another day. They were now well outside the southern and western boundaries of their territory. Two days later they spotted the bridge. They scouted the area and found the bridge was sound. Sam noticed farther south the towers of a wind farm.

"Look at that, Jill," he said excitedly, as he held out the binoculars to her. She leaned over her horse and took them. She looked to where he was pointing.

"What's so special about a bunch of poles?"

"That's a wind farm. None of the blades are turning, so either they're run down or turned off."

"So?"

"That's power, sweetheart. Remember you showed me around the city and said that the buildings had lights and washrooms but nothing works. If we can fix the towers and hook them up to the city and farm, the turning blades can run generators and make electricity to turn on lights."

"How're we going to do that?"

"Some of the people where we're going would know how. We'd eventually bring civilisation back to the world."

"You know this is in someone else's territory."

"Yes, but hopefully someday we can expand out here."

"I don't think anyone is going to give us this territory and from what we've heard they're not a friendly bunch."

"In time, we can take it from them, or maybe they'll want to merge with us."

"You're a bit of a dreamer, Sam."

"Maybe I am but everything starts with a dream."

She smiled. "My man of dreams; we're constantly at war and you dream of light bulbs. You're a funny man, Sam but keep dreaming."

He smiled back and said, "At least I don't have to dream anymore about the perfect woman."

"Hey, hey," she returned. "Remember, I still hate you."

"Yeah, sure, you have ten kids and you hate all of them."

She grinned, "Only the boys," and rode in the direction of the wagons.

He packed away his binoculars and caught up to her.

They crossed over the bridge and travelled due west for six days then headed north along a smaller road for another six days. They stopped while Sam thought about his next step.

After supper, they sat around the fire. Sam took the opportunity to address the group. "We made fast time on these roads. I've guessed how much ground I covered in my walk and tried to compare it to where we should be. So, I think we'll have to fan out and try to see what we can around us. I've already described what the terrain looks like, so you know what to look for. Break up into seven groups of twelve and take the horses out for two days in each of the other seven directions of the compass. That means we'll see you in four days. The rest of us will hold out here and guard the wagons."

Four days later there was nothing to report. They moved four days farther north and tried again with no luck. They tried the same scheme again. The next direction they went was west for six days until they made another fan-out.

Sam was getting frustrated. He rested one day to do some thinking. He was certain he should go no farther north and likely was close to how far west he needed to be, so they headed four days south. Finally, the report came in that one patrol sighted something encouraging southwest of them.

The rough ground was making it hard to travel but two days later they were in sight of what Sam recognised as home. When they got within three hundred metres of the rocks in front of the canyon, he halted the team.

He looked up to the sky. It was early afternoon.

He shaved and changed into the old clothes he had put aside. "Okay, I'd better go in alone or we'll be pelted by arrows. I'm hoping they'll recognise me. Just stay here until I get back," Sam told Jill.

Jill approached him and asked, "Do you want to eat before you go?"

No, they'll likely offer me something."

"Can I go with you?"

"No, two people might frighten them. They won't know you. I'm not going armed."

"If they see you with a beautiful damsel with you, it might help." She batted her eyelashes.

"Yeah right, although you look a lot more like a woman than when I first met you. You're not a damsel; you're a man-killer, aren't you?"

"But they won't know that."

"It's those evil eyes you have."

"Are they going to recognise you without hair on your face?"

"I left without any, so they should recognise me better, although they usually have younger people as a sentinel, so I might not be recognised at all."

"Aren't you afraid of getting shot?"

"I'm not afraid of anybody these days. Heck, I touch you regularly with the possibility of getting killed."

"Yeah, you've ruined my reputation."

He leaned over and gave her a goodbye kiss. "Hate you."

She responded, "Hate you, too. Don't forget to come back."

"Is that a little tear in your eye?"

"What! You're only gone for a few hours. I won't miss you even a little bit."

"Not even this much?" he asked, as he showed her a one-millimetre gap between his thumb and index finger.

"Well, maybe only that much. I'm more afraid you'll get lost."

"I found this place," he said proudly.

"Yeah, after fifty days of looking and the help of over two hundred people. That's only a few days less than it takes you to find the hospital," she burst out laughing.

"Well, how can I help it with the distraction of your radiant beauty," he said with aplomb.

She burst into laughter again. "You're a funny man. I'm not a kid anymore."

"And you get more radiant every year," he said with feeling.

She laughed again. "You're going to kill me with laughter. Why don't you save those lines for when you get back here?"

"I want you to long for me," he said alluringly.

She looked back at the other people staring at them with big smiles on their faces. She turned back to him. "You'd better get going. You're going to ruin my reputation."

It was the fighters' turn to laugh.

He turned, gave her a quick kiss, and began his walk. He had no idea what had happened in Eden since he left. After eighteen years, would they recognise him? Would his parents be alive? He got halfway up the rock pile when he heard a male voice call out.

"Stop where you are."

He stopped and said, "I'm unarmed. I come in peace." He held up his hands.

"Then why do you have a small army down there? We don't want anyone around here, so go away or we'll kill you. We'll kill you all."

"I'm Sam Ferguson. I left Eden eighteen years ago and have come back to see the elders."

There was a long pause. He finally said, "Just wait where you are. Don't move, or I'll shoot."

Sam stood rock still for over forty-five minutes. His feet were beginning to hurt. Then he heard the young man say, "I've got my gun on you, so don't move a muscle."

A head poked out from behind a rock.

It was a little far away for Sam to see much.

"Come a few steps closer," the voice said.

Sam climbed several steps.

The head popped out again then a body appeared.

Sam stared at the form trying to recognise him. After eighteen years a child's appearance changes somewhat.

"Sam, you old bum, is that you?"

"That's who I said I was. If I'm guessing right, you're Bill."

"Bingo. You passed the test."

"You've changed a bit since you were little. Now, you're all grown up."

"You've aged, too. We never expected to see you again."

"To tell you the truth, I never did either. It's taken a long time to find this place again."

"Yeah, eighteen years! What's with the army down there? You don't expect us to let them in, do you?"

"No, they've made camp, so they can stay there for now."

"I don't suppose they're going to surprise us in the night."

"Bill Ferguson, they're under my command. You don't figure I'd have them attack you."

"Under your command – so, you're ahead of an army?"

"That isn't exactly an army but they do what I say. It's a long story that maybe I can tell you some time but I'm here on business, so are you going to invite me in?"

"Um, well Mom and Dad were quite surprised to hear this. You know, they almost had a heart attack."

"So, they're still alive. That's nice to hear."

"But, grandpa's dead. The Andersons are leading now."

"So, old mister Anderson is still kicking, too! Good for him."

"Well, we'd better go down and see everyone before you call your army on me."

"You must get your humour from me."

"Well, we're brothers, aren't we?"

They walked together up the rocks to the top. There, Sam shook hands with the young man who first noticed him and headed down the other side.

Almost thirty minutes later, they were approaching a large gathering of people in front of Sam's old home. Right in front of everyone was his sister and he supposed her husband, and his mother and father. There were lots of hugs, kisses, and tears of joy. Then he had to go through the ritual of shaking everyone's hand.

The rest of the people broke up because they knew the family would want to be together.

When they entered his old house, his mother said, "I guess things in here haven't changed much since you left."

"No, not at all; it's as if I never left."

"Well, you've been gone eighteen years. You're all grown up. You've changed a bit though. I can see scars on you."

"Oh, that's nothing. Only a mother would notice them."

"So, what have you been doing all these years?"

"So, I don't have to repeat most of it, I'll postpone that discussion. I know it'll kill you to wait."

His mother bit her tongue.

"Don't be upset. I'm still alive and I'm here," he said. "I've had a very busy eighteen years."

"Are you hungry, or did you eat before you left?"

"I'm hungry."

"Good, I'll cook you something. We ate about an hour ago." She busied herself while his sister showed him his ten-year-old nephew.

Sam got to know him and his new brother-in-law. Sam already knew him but not too well; he was two years younger.

His mother called him to the dinner table and he ate heartily. He always loved his mother's cooking. While he ate, he talked to his father.

"I know you don't want to say anything about what you've done since you left, so I won't bother asking that question. All I'll say is I'm glad you're back," his father said smiling.

"I am too. I've got a lot to say about that, Dad. I'd like you to call everyone together. I'd like to inform them about some things and hear what they have to say."

"Okay, I can do that. I guess you'd want to have it tonight. I think they'd love to find out where you've been all these years."

"Tonight, would be great."

He finished his meal. "Is it okay to take a walk around the canyon? It'd be nice to see it again."

Both parents nodded their heads. He left, wandered through the fields he once sowed and weeded, and through the barn to watch the chickens clucking. He got to see the other animals. A lot of them looked rather sickly. He wandered through other fields looking at the hills surrounding him.

Suddenly, he heard a female's voice behind him say, "Hi."

He jumped and said as he turned around, "You startled me. You shouldn't sneak up like that." He was face-to-face with Lizzie. "Oh, it's you. My, you're a full-fledged woman, now."

"So, where have you been?"

"On the outside."

She could see some scars on his face and arms. She reached out and touched a couple of them on his arms. "How'd you get these?"

"It's a long story. It's rather rough out there. At least once I almost died but it's getting better."

"Are you going to stay here, now?"

"I don't know."

"That's what you said last time and you left."

"Well, how've things been here?"

"Okay, we're surviving. This year looks as if it's going to be pretty good but we've had a couple of bad years."

"And the power systems and stuff?"

"Power's gone, as of two years ago. It means hauling water around but it's okay. The water's been okay. I missed you though."

"You never married?"

"No. Nobody wanted to marry a pest. They've got to keep the population down anyway."

"So, you waited all these years. You knew nobody had returned."

"I never got the opportunity. It's a small group here." She paused. "Now that you're back, would you like to get to know me better? Maybe you'd give me a chance?"

"I can't Liz. I'm not available."

"What! Why?"

"You can guess."

She glared at him. "You said you'd consider me. You lied." She slapped him across the face.

"Liz, it's been eighteen years. Things happened in that time. I'd like to be your friend though."

"Friend, I don't need a friend, I need a husband," she said as she began to cry.

He took her into his arms and held her tightly. "Sorry, Liz."

He thought about it. She must have felt very lonely over the years. In this small enclave, if a person did not link up with somebody, the leaders would arrange a marriage, if there was someone. Liz lost her opportunity. It sometimes happened. Technically, he could become a husband of sorts. There were no rules anymore. In the canyon, sometimes a person would marry a close cousin. In the outside world, people didn't marry, at least not formally. Most people lived for the day and linked with a girl for a day. Long-range relationships were rare.

So, if he was in a relationship with another woman, who cared? He knew Jill wouldn't care, especially if he explained the situation to her. She knew there were no rules. She knew she had his heart. There was no lack of confidence there. He had a big enough heart to share.

No, he shouldn't do that, at least not in a rush like this. Liz was more traditional and might not be willing to share his love. He had more important things to do than that. He could deal with that later.

He released her. "Do you feel better now?"

"Only if you could do that forever." She pouted.

"I've got too many things to think about right now. Just let me think, okay?"

She sighed and walked away.

He watched her leave then continued his tour of his home. By the time he finished, it was suppertime and all the men and some women were sitting and ready for the meal. Everyone ate and, at the end, they held up their glasses in a toast to the only person who had returned to Eden.

It was Sam's turn to talk. He gave a summary of his journey and his life over eighteen years, leaving out his things, like the dog, Beautiful, Josh, and Jill. He told them about the city, the farms, the battles, the hardships, and the journey there.

He finally said, "I returned because I made a promise to you. In one of the wagons are some things that might help you repair some of your equipment. I've fulfilled my obligation. If you want, in the future, I can bring another load here of other things."

He paused and looked around the table. "I want to offer you something that might be better. As I said, there are lots of hardships and trials in our world but nothing much different from what you have here. There's greater potential for us to succeed, expand, and grow. You don't have that here. You must keep your numbers stable and, on your list, you asked me to pick up some more animals to reduce the inbreeding you have here. Out there you don't have to do that. We have a wonderful huge farm just south of the city and plans to start a new one north of us. We have hundreds of large animals and thousands of chickens. If you want, there are even great places to hunt, if you keep a lookout for interlopers. And best of all, you have thousands of people on your side. You don't have to worry about who you marry. You can have any sized family you want and we have care facilities, schools, and hospitals to help you."

Sam looked around the room. "We're constantly looking for ways to make things better for us. We don't have electricity yet, but on our trip here, I spotted an abandoned wind farm. That might be our next dream. I invite you to come back with us to our Eden, and you can choose what you want to do. Our farmers are always open to new people, or if you want to live in a city, we've got that, too. So, I can help you live here better by bringing you things from time to time, or you can join us."

There was silence in the room. Everyone looked at each other wondering about the proposal put before them.

"I'll leave you to talk about it. Say the word and I'll start unloading your things and be on my way. I'm trying to get back before the end of harvest."

He got up and left.

Lizzie followed him out.

"Don't you want to be in on the discussion?" Sam asked.

"I prefer to be with you," Liz said.

"I told you your chances were slim with me. You can come back with me even if the others decide to stay here. I doubt the elders would refuse you from leaving if you wanted to go."

"I don't know. It seems a little wild out there."

He told her that, because of it, they had their sense of morality. He told her they ate people and that love was a luxury most didn't have. He told her why.

"I wonder if I'd like living under those circumstances."

"It's a life though. They thrive. You're just surviving here. We've got lots of wonderful children. Maybe you'd like to work in the hospital with them and be a teacher."

"To look after someone else's kids."

"What's wrong with that?"

"It's not part of my dream."

"It's not part of your dream here. There are almost no kids."

She looked at him sadly. "I wanted to have kids of my own – with you."

"But, you wouldn't, if we stayed here. We might have only had one, or two at the most. With us, you can have as many as you want. That's what people do. They have the freedom to leave their mate whenever they want. It's a wild world out there but we look after all the kids. We treat them as our future. The old people are also treasured because of their memories of the past."

"Is that what you do?"

"No, because people also have the right to stay together as long as they want. I chose a woman and she chose me. We're happy, so we stay together. There's also a possibility that you could be with both of us."

"You mean to live together?" She thought about it a few seconds then said, "That sounds too creepy."

"And you have the right to think that way too."

"I'd always be thinking of the day she'd die, so I could have you all to myself." She drifted off toward the house.

He smiled and stared toward the peak he climbed to leave Eden – this false Eden. The real Eden was out there now. They all survived to create a new Eden. Now, if only they could understand that and follow him to it.

Within an hour his father joined him.

"We've decided to leave here."

"They know the risks?"

"We're not leaving much. We have no more electricity. Our emergency rations are gone. A couple of bad years of crops and we have no backup. We know you have a little more than we do. We moved here to escape the chaos and certain death. We had not planned to stay here forever. Maybe this is our signal to join the outside movement for a return to civilisation."

"I'm glad, Dad."

"Everybody's heading home for a good night's sleep. It's going to be a busy day and maybe more, depending on how long it takes to get our things out of here. We'll try to keep it to a minimum but we'll try to take as much as we can. We've got two wagons here we can haul to the other side to help. I doubt anyone's going to come back here."

Sam returned to the house and got a sound sleep in a comfortable bed; the nicest sleep he had had in eighteen years.

He got up before anyone else, left a note saying that he would bring over helpers, and walked back to his camp.

When the farmers got up, there was a flurry of activity. They ate and began to sort things out. A group of young people wheeled the two wagons to the bottom of the rock pile and pulled their wheels off. They returned to do other things.

Sam appeared over the top of the rocks with a lot of his people. They approached the farmers who stopped their work to greet them.

Sam said, "Guys, meet the people in my old community. You'll get to know them over the next few weeks. Especially meet my mother and father, here and there." They stepped forward, so people could see them. "Those three are my sister, her husband and their son." They stepped forward. "And there's my brother. He's single, for any of you girls who may be interested."

His brother blushed.

Sam looked behind him. "These are my people. It's going to take too long to do individual introductions. The main ones are my two lieutenants Jill and Dave." He pointed them out. "I brought a hundred fighters over to help. The other hundred will guard the wagons and help with the packing at that end. So, they'll have something to do right now, they're going to be moving rocks from the top of the barrier to make it easier and easier to get things over."

When they broke up, the extra workers fanned out with each of the farmers. Only Sam and Jill remained with his family.

Sam said, "I guess you guys should meet what I should call, my wife, Jill."

There was shocked silence for several seconds then his mother spoke excitedly, "You're married? Wow, that's wonderful." She came forward and gave Jill a warm hug. "Welcome to our family."

The rest of the family soon did the same.

"Wow, I'm so happy," his mother repeated. She paused for a few seconds. "I hope I'm not being forward to ask if you have children."

Jill looked at Sam then over to his mother and said, "I see you have very small families here. I'm going to sound like I'm a rabbit but we have ten kids – four boys and six girls."

His mother and father looked at each other in shock. His mother said, "Wow, ten kids! That's more kids than we have here right now."

Sam proudly slipped his arm around Jill's waist. "We're a growing community, Mom. I'm just doing my best to help out." He chuckled.

Jill smiled and hit him with her hip. Everyone laughed for several seconds.

Jill said, "My count is wrong, Sam, there's another one on the way."

"Another one! You didn't tell me! You should've stayed home."

"I'm not an invalid and I wasn't pregnant when I left." She looked at his mother and said, "That's what happens when you live with a man in a tent."

They all laughed again.

His mother said, "I think we're all going to get along fine. That's what you can get when you marry a Ferguson."

For the rest of the day, they worked. A group of women prepared lunch then later, supper. They killed a couple of their weaker pigs for the meals and sent some of it out for the others at the wagons. The fighters were happy as they were running low on food. They had brought only enough for a little over two months and it had taken that time to find Eden.

By the end of the day, the clouds looked ominous, so they put tarps on some of the things they didn't want to get wet. Late in the night, it began to pour.

The Fergusons woke up and looked outside.

Father said, "Well, we can do inside jobs today, packing things up."

They watched Sam's fighters picking up and chucking aside the rocks and boulders on the rock wall to make an opening there.

Sam said, "Fighters don't like sitting around doing nothing."

His mother said, "At the rate they're going, they'll have a deep channel cut out of it by the time we need to leave."

They saw some of the younger members of the farmers join them.

"They're making it a one-way trip. The canyon is going to be open again. There's no turning back. That took years to build up."

"Maybe that means a new beginning, Mom," Sam said.

"I guess you're right." She sighed.

By the end of the day, they had packed almost everything they wanted to bring.

Sam looked at the pile. If everybody made as big a pile as they had, there would not be enough room on the wagons for it all.

The next day was sunny again. Most of the ground had dried up. By working through most of the night in shifts, the fighters had removed enough rocks to make a clear path into the canyon. It was only wide enough to get the wagons through but that was all they needed. The fighters drove their wagons into the canyon and began to put the wheels on the two wagons the farmers had placed beside the pile of rocks.

While watching them, the young farm members grumbled about having to take the wagons apart in the first place.

Later in the morning, all the family and military heads met in the dining hall.

Sam opened. "I've been looking at what everybody has and maybe we have to slim down the load a little."

The senior Anderson said, "We'd like to be comfortable where we go. You guys aren't very good at packing things."

"Let's prioritise then. I like the idea of bringing all your guns and ammunition. We can use that. Food is also a good idea, as we'll be using a lot of it as we travel to New Eden. Your animals can walk along with us. They'll slow us down but a few extra days won't hurt us. Some pillows won't hurt but the rest of the stuff, I don't know. Pack the stuff we'll need to use along the way into the food and weapons wagons. We can pack our tents and equipment into one wagon. That'll leave four wagons for you. Look in the wagon we've brought to you and discard what you don't need where we're going."

"We have one other wagon that's kind of rickety we can add," the senior Anderson said. "We have some little carts people can pull, or we can hook them onto a couple of pigs. Around here we used pigs for work. We didn't have the luxury of horses."

"Well, if you can stack it, or carry it, it's your choice. I don't want the wagons overloaded or they're going to break down before we get home and you'll end up with less than your basics."

"We'll chance it. There're a lot of memories in this canyon."

The next day, the farmers packed the remaining things into the wagons and carts, decided what they were going carry, and oiled and greased the axles well. By the end of the day, they were ready. They had a good night's sleep and an early start to the morning.

They had eaten most of the chickens they had but decided to keep the rest alive for fresh meat as they progressed. Many of the fighters volunteered to carry some of the things the farmers wanted to bring along. In the end, they had everything they wanted.

Sam was impressed by how effectively the farmers had stashed, packed, and secured all their goods but was wondering what need there was for a grandfather clock, an upright piano, and other musical instruments. He tried to tell them they may be able to find those in the city, although many of the objects like that had been chopped up and burned as firewood during the winter. Instead of a wagon train, it looked like a carnival. Along with the eight wagons, they had six carts pulled by pigs and three smaller carts pulled by people. The farm families had one last chance to look around their homes of more than eighty years and say their goodbyes.

By midmorning, they were on their way.

They headed out through the opening to the canyon and turned south. When there was a hill or clump of trees blocking them, they turned east then south. By the second day, they found an old small road that led south. For several days they followed it until it ended in a T intersection. They decided to continue south across the country until they reached the large roadway that would lead to the bridge. They turned east again until they could outline the bridge. They stopped.

Sam said, "It's getting late in the day, so let's make camp inside that clump of trees, so nobody can spot us from the road. Dave and I will get onto the hill behind the trees and we'll scout the bridge from there."

While the wagons and carts made their way into the trees, Dave and Sam climbed the hill, pulled out their binoculars, and peered at the other side of the bridge.

"I see something," Dave said.

"Yes, and I don't think it's anybody from the farm. They don't go this far south."

"They're close to the bridge. How did you know to stop here?"

"I saw something glinting in the sun. I may have decided to wait to cross the bridge until tomorrow but that convinced me. It might have been that guy closest to the bridge who's wearing something shiny on his chest."

"Yes, I can see him."

"Who do you think they are?"

"Well, it could be a group that crossed from this side or lives farther south of the farmers. It may be the raiders from the south who've attacked them before. There aren't many there but they might be scouts in front of an army."

"We can't be sure but I'd hate to make the wrong guess. We can't do anything tonight but we should keep an eye on them in case they cross the river. Let's get down to camp."

"Um, can we wait here a minute?" Dave asked.

Sam looked at Dave with a puzzled look in his eye.

"Can I ask you something?"

"Sure," he said with hesitation.

"You know the girl, Lizzie, from your village, right? I think she's around your age."

"Yes, she's around my age and I know her," he said with interest.

"Do you know her well?"

"I've known her since she was a tiny tot. She was quite a precocious young lady. She liked playing tricks on people, even me. I think she had a crush on me."

"Is she over it, or am I getting into personal things here?"

"Why are you asking these questions?"

"Um, well, ah, I helped her family pack and I saw she wasn't attached to a man. She's quite attractive and, ah." He stumbled over his words.

Sam was getting great pleasure at watching him squirm.

Dave continued unsteadily, "I'm not that young anymore, I ah, would like to settle down a bit – something like you. You're settled with Jill and I, ah, like that."

"And you think Lizzie is the one for you?"

"Well, I don't know her well enough yet but I've liked a lot of what I've seen of her in Eden and now on the trail. She likes children."

"What about all the women you've seen over these years?"

"They're not the same. I don't know if they're settling women."

"I see, so why are you telling me this?"

"You have some experience in this area. Heck, you had that first girl who gave her life for you and now you have Jill. What did you do to attract them?"

Sam smiled. "You know, Dave, you just have to be yourself. She's got to get to know you for who you are."

"How do I do that? How do I get to let her know about me? She probably doesn't notice me."

"Just be there."

"Be where?"

"Okay, I'd better say this slowly. You can't throw yourself at a woman like Lizzie. Don't overwhelm her or you'll frighten her off. So, you must use stealth. If she needs a hand with something, give her a hand. Pretend you don't notice her. You're just a helpful person, so you help everyone. Do that from now on. Be yourself and eventually, she'll notice you. When she does, she'll like what she sees. Then, she might be interested in learning more about you. You're not dealing with a city girl here. She's a farm girl, so give up the city girls. If you keep going with them, you may as well give up right now."

Dave looked sombre.

"I'm telling you, Dave, she's a one-man woman, who's going to want a one-woman man. If you're serious about settling down, start now."

Dave said slowly, "Give up other girls."

"Yes. That's what settling down is. Jill and I love each other. Yeah, we tease each other but we know that what we have is genuine and there's nothing like it. That's what you both must figure out. Is it the right thing for both of you? If you find out in the end that she's not interested in you, you let her go. Love can't be forced."

Dave nodded his head.

"Is this what you wanted? Should we get back to camp, now?"

Dave nodded again.

They walked down the hill and back to camp.

Before supper, Sam invited several leaders to a meeting outside his tent. "Dave and I had a look at the bridge and spotted some people on the far side. It may mean nothing but we know this is the time of year the southern city conducts their raids on the farmers. I'm not going to take chances."

He paused. "Dave, have two sentries keep an eye on the bridge and let us know if they try to cross it. Jack, you're a good swimmer, right?"

"Yes, so I'm told but the river is quite wide," Jack responded.

Sam said, "Ride north for about four days, cross the river, and alert the farmers of a possible attack from the south. They'll know what to do. Then ride on to the city and let Josh know about it. I hope we have enough time to alert them. This bridge is about four or so days from the southern part of our new territory. Any other issues?"

No one said anything.

"Okay, let's pack it in for the night. We'll have to decide what else to do tomorrow."

The meeting ended.

Jack picked up a few days' rations of food and water, got on his horse, and left. The others went to their tents to settle in for the night.

The next day, Sam and Dave were back on top of the hill with their binoculars.

"What do you think, Dave?"

"I think their main forces have arrived. They don't seem to be in any big hurry."

"They're probably ensuring the harvest is in before they attack."

"Most of what's there is hidden in the trees and shrubbery on the other side of the river. I can't guess what size of force it is."

"It'll be suicide for us to try to cross, now," Sam commented.

"We could move back up north and find a good bridge to cross somewhere up there."

"It'll take too much time. If we sit here, we might be able to change the tide of the war."

"How?"

"If they move their forces up, we can come in behind them."

"Our group's too small to have much effect," Dave said nervously.

"You might be right but if we can determine how large their forces are, we might take a big risk and try something else."

"What?"

Sam thought for a few seconds, "We can capture their city while they're away, as we did against the northerners. They sent most of their forces to battle us so when we attacked them, there was not much there to defend. That's the risk the farmers took when they helped break the siege of the city. If a gang would have attacked their compound while they were gone, it would have fallen quite easily."

"You've got a point. It might work but they may not leave their city so defenceless."

"True. They seem to have a small force at the bridge. I wonder if it's there to avoid people crossing at that location. They may establish a similar force to the south of their city. That way they can prevent any other force from attacking it."

"Anything can happen."

"Well, we can't do anything, now. We'll have to sit tight and hope Jack makes it through."

For the next two days, it rained quite heavily at times. During it, they kept their vigil. There was little evidence of anything happening.

The clouds cleared the next morning but it was too wet to do much.

The following day, they saw movement on the other side of the bridge. They could spot troops moving farther upstream.

Sam said, "This is it. I hope Jack will soon pass on his message. The farmers won't be able to do too much at this point but hopefully, the defensive works they were working on can hold the enemy troops off until the forces from the city can get there. We'll wait three days, so the enemy's main forces get far away from here. By then, they'll be too committed at the front to think of coming back here to deal with what'll look like a little skirmish."

They remained where they were and prepared to battle. They exercised and practised what they were going to do.

On the morning of the battle, they set up three Eden snipers with high-powered rifles on a knoll on their side of the road and quite close to the bridge. At the base of it, they placed fifty archers hidden in the brush close to the bridge. They were going to make the advanced team look like farmers crossing the bridge. They had harnessed a horse to pull a cart that was carrying the weaponry and provisions they would need for the next few days. Most of Sam's infantry and the other group of archers crept as close to the bridge as they could get on the other side of the road without detection. Most of the people from old Eden remained protected behind the hill to guard the wagons and their contents.

At the appointed time, the horse and cart with a small group of old Eden's farmers rolled onto the road and approached the bridge.

As they neared it, some of the enemy troops stepped onto the other end of it.

The cart slowly rolled forward onto the bridge.

When it got about halfway across it, the leader of the enemy forces called out to warn them that they could go no farther, or they would shoot them. Somebody in the gang said loudly that they should attack, as the cart might contain food. Soon, some of the troops began to rush forward and others followed until most of the detachment was running up the bridge to the cart.

The farmers quickly turned the cart around and moved in the opposite direction.

Other enemy troops on the other side of the bridge joined in the attack. They were gaining on the cart as it finally made it off the bridge. The closest warriors were now only a few metres behind it.

The archers on the knoll stood and started a barrage of arrows into the enemy forces. The snipers on the hill began shooting the farthest fighters on the bridge.

The enemy was surprised and started to organise themselves and fired arrows at the farmers and the visible archers.

The farmers hid behind the cart and fired with pistols at the approaching warriors who were still moving up the bridge guessing this was a small group of farmers that they could take by force. Then the shock came to the farmers.

Some of the enemy fighters pulled out pistols and began firing at them.

The snipers on the hill though targeted them and were now killing any enemy with a gun. When most of the enemy had crossed the bridge, Sam's infantry pulled out of the nearby shrubs and rushed in with their spears. The rest of Sam's forces rushed to the road to take battle. The remaining archers with the infantry stood up and began to shoot at the enemy troops.

Sam watched as an enemy arrow flew toward Lizzie. There was nothing he could do but he saw Dave hurl himself toward her to knock her to the ground. She was about to slug him in the nose when she realised what had happened. He got up quickly, dusted himself off, and lent a hand to help her stand up. She hurried back behind the cart.

Within thirty minutes it was over.

Their losses were minimal but hard to take. A couple of farmers from Eden had lost their lives with a few others injured. A few archers had been injured. Four fighters had been killed and several others injured. The cavalry which had been in reserve was fully intact.

They moved their injured to where the wagons were, then they hurried over the bridge to search for any fighters that had not crossed the bridge. They found none.

Sam called a meeting of his officers and Eden's senior and asked them if they wanted to head toward the enemy's city. There was a lot of discussion but they decided to take a chance. The people guarding the wagons would stay but the others would attack the city.

For the next two days, the attackers headed south until they could see suburban houses. Sam and Dave climbed onto the roof of a house and reconnoitred. They climbed down and continued to walk slowly toward the city's centre.

When the fighters grew closer to the centre, they stopped and pulled off the road placing the cart in a semi-hidden area between two buildings. They loaded up with arrows and spears.

Dave and Sam climbed a few stories up a building and looked toward the downtown core but they were too low to see most of what was ahead. They could see what looked like a barrier across the road. They climbed back down.

Sam called everyone together and said, "Just up the road is a barrier. That must be the edge of the guarded area of town. Let's move quietly. When we get to those taller buildings, your sharpshooters get as high as you can, so you can see into that area and get set up. Archers, find a floor where you get good visibility and get set up. Dave, take about half the infantry, get to the other side of town, and wait for the archers to fire then, either wait for a retreat or rush them as you see fit. Everyone should be as quiet as you can. Jill, you lead the infantry here and I'll join the archers. Use the guns if you need to but save the bullets, if you can. Let's go."

Sam joined his archers on the third floor. He could not see very much, so he pulled the archers onto the roadway and waited for about an hour.

He positioned the archers on the barriers and could see movement ahead. He launched the arrows.

There was more scurrying in the enemy areas but soon there were responding arrows from their side.

Sam heard other activity that sounded as if the infantry on the other side of the enclave had attacked. He urged his infantry to charge and the cavalry urged their horses over the barrier. Soon the whole area was full of activity then they heard shots. There were more shots. Some shots were now coming from the snipers he sent up to the building beside him. Within thirty minutes, it grew silent. Sam climbed the barrier and walked inside it with the farmers. He saw some people lying on the ground, some of them were his men. He joined up with his archers who had moved into the enemy's territory.

Dave came up to him. "We did it; we surprised them. They pulled out their pistols and fired at us. We got them though. I want to show you something." He led him into one of the larger buildings a couple of blocks farther in.

In front of them were women, children, and some men. Most of them were dead.

Dave said, "We didn't shoot in here. It looks as if they committed suicide."

"Damn this world. There was no need to do that," Sam said sadly.

"I guess they'd rather kill themselves than be killed by us."

"We wouldn't have killed them."

"They don't know that. They learn the expected rules, not the unexpected. If anyone else had attacked them, they would have been slaughtered. Maybe not all at once, some might have been tortured first, just for the fun of it."

"Well, gather anyone who's still alive and collect them into one area. We'll have to take care of them. Treat them well. Ensure that they get a hot meal and water. Where's Jill?"

"Last time I saw her she was a couple of blocks north of here."

Sam walked along the road and soon spotted her huddled by a building. He went over to her and said, "What's up?"

She raised her head to him and held up a baby. "Her mother's dead. The baby's hurt but I think she'll be okay." She sobbed.

He watched her looking at the baby and pictured it as one of their own. He shuddered. What a horrible world.

"She's such a beautiful young girl. I think she was shot by one of her people to protect her from us," Jill said.

"I wish someday we can stop all this." Sam looked at the sky. He looked down and held out his hand to Jill. She took it and he guided her up. He looked into her eyes and said, "Josh's dream is to end all this. It's also my dream." He leaned into her and their lips met.

Lizzie had been surveying the damage and was almost regretting leaving Eden. She spotted Sam and Jill by the building. She saw them looking into each other's eyes. Tears began to pour from hers. They had the love she wanted to have with Sam. She now knew how wonderful it was. She realised she could never break the bond that existed between the two of them and she no longer wanted to.

She had the opportunity to marry Sam's brother but he was different. He was not like Sam. Now, she had nothing. She had seen him flirting with one of the women fighters.

Sam and Jill pulled apart. He put his arm around her waist and led her down the street while she cradled the baby.

When he arrived near the centre of town, he told Jill to get the other leaders together. He looked at the group of prisoners they had collected from a search of the buildings in this protected compound. Most of them were children, some were women but there were only a few men. Many of them were injured.

Lizzie came down the street with a little boy and girl in each hand. She had tears in her eyes. She sat down and huddled with them, as she would if they were her own. She looked at Dave on the other side of the street talking softly to three terrified young boys. He was trying to calm them but was failing. They huddled near him watching all the strange people slowly adding to this motley crew of captives.

Lizzie waved over to him. Dave pulled away from the boys to join her but Sam motioned to him to stay where he was.

"Our job is not done. We don't know how the battle is going with our farmers and we don't know if the enemy has any other fighters nearby. We might as well stay here and defend this city. We fought for it, so we should try to hold it. There's no point to all of us going back to the wagons."

He turned to one of the Andersons who had joined them in battle. "If you want to go back to the wagons for added protection, go ahead but I think they should be safe where they are. They're well hidden. I don't think there'll be any enemy troops north of us between here and the bridge but I can't be sure."

The senior Anderson responded that he and his compatriots would stay to defend the city.

He turned toward the leader of the farmers and asked. "Do you want to try to get home to defend your families?"

"We'll never get there alive. We'll keep fighting for you."

"Okay then, we can't be sure where they'll attack us. I want you to organise yourselves so we have sentries on top of some of the taller buildings within the enclave to watch for enemy troops and give us a signal if they spot anything. I think our greatest danger will be from the south. They had a detachment guarding the bridge, so they may have placed another one south of here. They may have heard the shots, or even if they didn't, they may return, in which case, we'll be ready for them. We'll put most of our forces there; keeping a reserve near here so they can support any area under attack. The building beside me will be our headquarters. Let's get our captives under cover. Jill, please oversee things."

The leaders fanned out and began to prepare for battle.

Lizzie led her children toward Dave. When she arrived, she said, "Hi, aren't you being derelict of your duty?"

"Um, well these kids lost their parents, so they've latched onto me."

She smiled. "So, you're a foster father."

"Um, well not really. I just picked them up, or, ah, found them hiding under a bed in one of the buildings. It took a long time to get them out."

"Well, let's see if they'll take to me, so you can do your duty."

Dave knelt to the boys and said, "I've got to go to work right now. This nice lady will look after you for a while, okay."

They hugged him fearfully. "Okay, boys, her name is Lizzie. See, she has two of your neighbours with her. Maybe you can help look after her. This nice lady will get some food for you. Are you hungry?" They nodded their heads and then slowly walked to Lizzie. "I promise I'll be back, okay?"

The boys did not look sure of that.

Dave said goodbye to them and ran down the street to join the groups slowly making their way to their places.

Sam came out of his headquarters area not satisfied with the accommodations. He called to the senior farmer, "It's a damn pigsty in there. I think most of the buildings are like that. If we're moving into that building, we'll have to clean it first. Please set up details to look after that."

The farmer nodded, went over to his people, and gave some instructions.

Lizzie waved Sam over to her and he walked to her.

Sam said, "Looks as if you have a built-in family there."

"They're not family, just strays."

He smiled and mumbled, "At least for now."

"What?" she asked.

"Nothing . . . You called me over?"

"Yes, um, I want to ask you a question."

"Okay, shoot."

"Um, Dave . . . you know Dave, right?"

"He's one of the first people I met here. He's also one of my leaders. So, I probably know him very well. Why?" he asked slyly.

"Um, what's he like?"

He pretended to act surprised. "Why?"

"Oh, just want to know."

"The only reason a woman asks a friend about another guy is when she's interested in him."

She blushed but recovered. "Not necessarily, he had those boys and I wanted to see if he was fit to look after them," she lied.

"I'd trust him to look after the kids. He often goes to the hospital to visit some of the kids there."

"What's he like?"

"He'd make you a nice husband. Not as good as I would mind you but he'd be a good second place."

"I didn't ask that and you're being rather high and mighty about it."

"Come on Lizzie, don't pussy-foot around. You've been watching him for the last few days. I'm not blind," he lied a little.

"Well, you dumped me, so I've got to find someone. Is he single? What's he like with women?" she asked, annoyed she lost her cover.

Sam smiled, put his hand on her shoulder, and said gently, "He knows a lot about women and he's not hitched to anyone."

"So, do you think he'd be interested in me?" she asked.

"He's matured over the years and ready to settle down. I think you'd be just the person he needs."

"Why do you say that?" she inquired.

"You came from a farm where girls tend to be more settled. If you're interested in him, I think he'd be ready to settle down with you. Of course, you must win his heart. I think the two of you would get along very well together."

"Really?"

"If the two of you connect right."

"Like you and Jill?"

"Well, maybe in second place."

She smiled. "So, you're not mad at me for looking for another guy?"

"I only want you to be happy, Liz. With me, you'd always be in second place. With him, you'd be in first place."

She looked at the ground and the five children around her. "So, he likes kids, does he?"

"He loves kids."

She smiled and took the children to a large cauldron of stew and began to fill their bowls.

For two days they cleaned the headquarters building and removed the bodies from the compound.

At midnight of the following day, fighters they guessed were from this city, attacked them from the south. There were only stars lighting the sky. The sentries on top of the buildings saw them on time and dropped rocks onto the road alerting the ground teams who ran to the various buildings and raised the alarm.

By the time the attack came, they were ready, except for the cavalry. Sam's archers repulsed the attack with a barrage of arrows whistling softly through the air. Several times the enemy breached the barrier but the cavalry was able to contain it.

The attackers also fired arrows, supplemented with pistol shots. By morning, the attackers pulled back. Their surprise attack had failed.

With the coming of dawn, Sam hurried around the compound to assess the situation, as the others collected the dead and wounded. He had lost a lot of fighters.

He had an idea. He pulled one person aside to tell her to put the corpses along the wall in such a way that the enemy would think they were still alive. He received a report from the sharpshooters that confirmed Sam's fears that they were greatly outnumbered.

Along the rock barrier, he spotted Lizzie leaning over one of the bodies. He went to her and looked down.

She raised herself and looked up at him.

He saw tears in her eyes. At first, he thought Dave had been hit but when he looked, he could make out the pale form of – Jill. He crumpled to the ground beside Lizzie. He had to be strong. He had to be strong for his people. Jill looked so still, so lifeless, so helpless. He wanted to take her into his arms but Lizzie pushed him away.

"Don't touch her," she said, "She's not dead but badly hurt. She took at least two bullets that I could see. I'll go get a stretcher and look after her. You do what you have to do."

He looked at Lizzie helplessly. "There must be something I can do."

"Yes, you can defend the city. You can muster your troops and do what you must do. Jill would want you to do that. I'll look after her. Trust me. Go do your job."

Slowly, mechanically, he got up. He spotted Dave and told him to get every corpse they had, friend or foe up along the wall, with a spear or gun with it. He had to deter another attack. He had to do it before the enemy thought of climbing the buildings outside the barrier to see what they were doing. He wanted the dead bodies to be along the north and west walls that were currently beyond the sight of the enemy. He was sure the attacking force would quickly surround them. He thought of sending a runner north with a message to Josh but that likely would not succeed with the enemy attackers to the north of them.

So, they were stuck there. They would have to fend for themselves.

He called a fighter over, pointed to Lizzie, and told her to get a stretcher bearer immediately.

She ran to the infirmary and two medics with a stretcher ran out and followed her.

When they arrived, Lizzie backed away and they had a quick look at Jill. They told the fighter and Lizzie what to do and they placed Jill on the stretcher. The aides took each end and walked quickly but gently, toward the hospital.

Lizzie followed.

When the defences were set up as Sam had requested, he had a meeting with his leaders. "I hope we can fool them with the dead. I've no idea how the battle for our farms is going. With any luck, the farmers can hold the line until reinforcements arrive from the city. Meanwhile, we must do our best here. Let's hope our forces win in the north.

"We might as well be aggressive with our foes. I want everyone on alert. If the archers see anyone within range, they should shoot them down. I want the same thing with the guns. We have the high-power rifles on the roofs but I want our other rifles on lower floors. We're going to make them pay, if they get too close.

"I've been informed about our food and water supply. There was some water here when we arrived and we have ours but it'll only last a couple of days. We have supplemented our food supply with the bodies of this city's defenders, so that'll do us for a while. I want everyone who's off duty to spend some time finding anything that can collect rainwater. Even if our forces in the north are victorious, it's going to take several days for them to get here and they may not know we're here. We may be here a long time, so let's use our bullets well. Don't shoot unless you know you can kill them."

He dismissed them and watched them hurry off to notify everyone about the plans.

He hurried to the infirmary and went to their only doctor. He could see him busy with the many patients strewn about the floor.

The doctor knew *w*hy he was there. He went over to him and said, "I want quiet around Jill. I've put her in a quieter room. Two bullets hit her. One grazed her arm and I patched that one up; the other penetrated her chest which I'm set up to operate on. Although no major organs were damaged, she's lost a lot of blood and I must get the bullet out. Don't expect much."

"Can I see her?" Sam said nervously.

"Only for a moment, she's unconscious." He pointed to the next room.

Sam slowly walked there and saw Lizzie sitting on the floor next to Jill.

Liz looked at him sadly.

He looked at the almost naked body next to her. Jill's breathing was very shallow. Her skin was very pale. She was not the vigorous being she used to be. He went down on his knees next to her, bent over and gave her a little kiss. His eyes filled with tears but he quickly wiped them away with his hand.

He whispered to her, "Don't give up. I need you. I love you. Fight this battle for me."

He got up, sighed deeply, and left the room.

Lizzie heard what he had said and cried.

Dave saw Sam and approached him. "Have you seen Lizzie?"

"She's over at the infirmary helping there."

Dave responded, "Oh, I never thought of that, thanks." He headed for the infirmary and looked around for her. He finally found her outside the building playing with the children they had befriended the day of their attack and caring for the baby Jill had found.

"Hi." She turned to him and smiled.

The boys swarmed around him and he tossed them in the air and hugged them. He looked at the younger sleeping baby girl.

"Do you want to go for a walk?" he asked, as he looked at Lizzie.

"Jill's injured and I thought I'd spend some time with the kids to get my mind off her."

"Oh, is she seriously hurt?"

"Looks like it."

"Oh." He lowered his head sadly then raised it. "Well, talking with someone will get your mind off her."

She smiled. "What about the kids?"

"We won't go far."

She sat quietly unmoving for a few seconds then got up. He grabbed her hand firmly and led her away as they told the kids they'd be nearby.

"I've been doing a lot of thinking," he said as they walked a few steps. "We live in hard times and people become hard and cold. Most people are afraid of committing to other people. Life's too short and people get so much pain they don't want any more, so they seal themselves into a protective shell and never form long-term bonds with anyone. You've come from a rather different environment, thank goodness.

"I've often gone to our hospital to get away from things and played with the kids or visited people who were sick and injured. There, I find life. In a hospital are helpless children who don't know anything other than loving and connecting with people. Dying people are fighting for life. They want to live. Outside, people are expecting to die.

"I have to confess that I've known many women in my life. I look inside the hospital sometimes to see if any children are mine. I may have fathered some but I'll never know. Sometimes, I think one looks a little like me but I don't know for sure. Maybe I'm getting old.

"Hah, getting old, when you're in your thirties; that's kind of odd, isn't it? The way it is though, is you rarely have a family of your own. Most of the kids are a collective. They're all together as if they're owned by no one or everyone. No one is responsible. No real closeness. If one of them dies, no one cares really. I guess the people in the hospital care but a mother or father doesn't. They don't want to see or acknowledge any more death.

"I must sound like I'm crazy."

"I'm listening," she said softly.

They were walking through a cemetery where some of the people were burying the recent dead.

Dave continued. "See, those people are free. They have no more pain and suffering. In a way, they're better off. We're the living dead, or people living to die. You can see how young they are, most in their teens who have never really tasted much of life. That's what we see regularly. We though, have a dream. A dream that all this will end and we can live in peace. It'll be hard to get. We'll have to work and die for it but someday children might be able to live until they're old again.

"I want that for me, Liz. I want kids I know are mine. I want to love them and care for them. I want children who can call me father and for it to be real. I want a woman who I can call my own; someone I can love and cherish until my turn comes for the big goodbye.

"I never felt this way until I met you, Liz. I want you to be my one and only woman."

Liz stopped.

Dave noticed, stopped, and turned to her to say, "What's wrong?"

"Nothing's wrong . . . is that a proposal?"

"What's a proposal?"

"It's a strange way to ask it but are you asking me to marry you?"

"I'm not sure what marriage is. I just want to ask you if you wanted to be my woman, like Sam and Jill."

She smiled at him. "You're a strange man, Dave but you're a sign of the times. Of course, I'd like to be your one and only woman, as long as it stays that way."

"I can do that."

"Are you willing to wait until we have a little ceremony?"

"How long is that going to take?"

"Can't wait, huh?"

"We don't have ceremonies here except to bury people. Here, the man just says 'ugh' to the woman, she goes to him, he grabs her hair, pulls her into his tent, and it's done."

"Well, I don't want my hair mussed up. It won't be long. We should tell people and make some plans . . ."

"You don't want to come into my tent?"

She looked into his eyes and sighed deeply. She did want to go with him; after all, one more attack and they could be dead. She had wanted this to happen for such a long time. She wanted it to be the way she always planned. "How about we leave it as a big kiss for now, okay?"

He wrapped her in his arms and kissed her for a long time.

The sound of rifle shots interrupted their embrace as their besiegers began to reconnoitre the barrier.

The besieged archers fired at moving targets.

This activity continued for the rest of the day. The expectation of an all-out battle was high but by nightfall, all became silent again. Sam's troops were on the alert but nothing happened.

Two days later, Sam received some joyful news. Jill was on the mend. He had visited her several times a day and she had still looked pale and lifeless but he had noticed her breathing was becoming more regular. The doctor now felt that she was going to recover.

Two more days passed and Sam's confidence was waning. They were rationing water and anxiously looking at the clouds. For three days it looked as if it would rain. It was as if the clouds were teasing them.

That night the rain came; torrentially. But their tormentors must have guessed the city was low on water and decided to attack before they could get themselves properly rehydrated.

The enemy attempted a pinpoint attack from the south and it took a valiant attempt by Sam's troops to hold fast but it had taken its toll. Although they no longer needed water, they suffered more deaths and many injuries. He had a handful of useable fighters. He still had fifty serviceable people on horseback and less than thirty archers. He also had his three sharpshooters. In an emergency, he could perhaps double those numbers as infantry by using some of the injured.

Sam visited Jill every day and was there when she opened her eyes for the first time since her injury. She smiled and it was a glorious moment for Sam. It meant that he still had her. That dark day when the doctor had told him she might not make it had been his darkest day since he lost Beautiful. He could not go through that again. Even better news was her injuries did not affect the baby she was carrying.

But the respite only lasted two days when, at dawn, the enemy attacked them again. He called up everyone who could stand. If this was going to be their last day, they would go out like warriors and fight until the last person fell.

Then, without warning from the north of town, he heard loud horns blaring. He had never heard that sound before but when he looked down the streets and saw horses and infantry heading toward him, he knew this was the end. They would never survive such an onslaught. He hid in a doorway as they rode rapidly by him. He noticed they rode by the defenders and ferociously fought their besiegers. It was then that he realised this was not an enemy but Josh's fighters racing to their aid. He could see their properly coloured armbands. He collapsed in the doorway.

He recovered his composure after a few minutes, stood up, and walked into the street. The din had moved out of the city's battlements. Their fighters were chasing and eliminating the enemy ahead of them.

Another entourage was coming over the rock defence at the north end of town; the rest of the people remained with the wagons near the bridge and Josh with more fighters. They also had several hundred bound enemy fighters.

Two hours later, everyone had collected in the centre of town. Josh and his fighters were in one group, the farmers another, the families from Eden a third, Sam and the rest of his defenders a fourth, and the captives bunched together by a wall.

Josh got off his horse and walked toward the families. He stood there for a few minutes until Mrs. Anderson stepped forward and approached him. She stared at him for several seconds until she finally said, "Joshua, is that you?"

Josh smiled broadly, walked to his elderly mother and said, "Yes, Mom, it's me. I guess only a mother could tell." They hugged and his father soon joined them.

His mother smiled through her tears and said, "We thought you were dead."

"No, Mom, I was here building a new Eden for you."

She hugged him again. "So, you're the leader of this group?"

"Yes, it took thirty-eight years to get this far. It's ready for you."

Over the next few hours, the remainder of Josh's troops straggled into the enclave and brought in several additional captives. A lot of them had to be taken to the infirmary.

They remained in the city to heal the wounded enough to travel and bury the dead.

Lizzie and Dave had lots of time for themselves. One day, they walked along the beach for a few hours.

"I'm glad the city's troops arrived when they did," Lizzie said.

"They were just in time. Can we go through that ceremony, now?"

"Yes, now we can do it. I was waiting until there was a little peace around here, Jill got well enough to be with us, and I rummaged through the wagons to pick up some things."

"Oh, she's going to be there?"

"I hope so. Thanks for waiting, Dave. I know your 'ugh' ways are all you know."

"I hope you're not disappointed you didn't get Sam."

"Oh, he told you?"

"No, I guessed. I figured you'd only go for the best. He's better than I am in most ways."

"Each person has their characteristics. You're a good man, Dave." She stopped and stared at the ocean. "There must be lots of water in the ocean."

"I bet there is," he responded.

She turned to him and gazed into his eyes. "You're the best person for me, Dave. I love you more than all the water in the ocean."

They kissed passionately.

She pulled away. "Better wait big guy. Sam and Jill are quite a couple, aren't they? I've asked them to play a part in the ceremony."

"Jill can't leave the hospital."

"Yes, she can. The doctor wants her to get up and move as much as she can."

"Oh, then that'd be nice."

"And Sam will be your Best Man."

"Best Man?"

"That's what he's called in the ceremony."

"Oh, this is sounding complicated," he said disappointedly.

"Jill will be my Maid of Honour."

"Maid?"

"That's what she's called."

"I think I like the 'ugh' approach better."

"You'll like it."

"It's too complicated."

"Okay, mister too-complicated, I'll leave the rest for a surprise. Oh, and before we go any further, we're keeping our kids?"

"Our five kids? I wouldn't have it any other way. We might as well have a boost, so we can catch up to Jill."

"Catch up to Jill?" Lizzie looked surprised.

"That's the 'ugh' part."

She shook her head and mumbled, "Men!"

They wandered back to the headquarters building.

The next day, the prisoners stood together before the rest of the people much as Josh had done in the northern city many years before.

Josh offered the citizens the same deal. They could leave town with the victors, or join in rebuilding their city as a civilised community under the protection of Eden.

They were surprised and appreciative. Nobody wanted to leave.

Josh turned to the people of old Eden. "You also have choices. You can move anywhere you want, city, or country. There's a large vacant farming tract to the north of our city that we can cultivate. Some of the southern farmers also want to expand north, or you could join their existing farms not too far from here. Now that this city is ours the existing farms have room to expand safely south, too."

Josh continued. "Some of our people have volunteered to stay here and provide some law and order to get the city well established but most of us want to get back to our town well before winter sets in."

He looked around at everyone and added, "Tomorrow at noon everyone is invited to a special celebration, right here in the centre of town. For now, let's continue cleaning up the city."

The next morning, Lizzie brought Dave a suit and tie. "Here, Sam can you help put this on him? I won't be seeing you until our celebration."

"Why has this got to be so complicated?" Dave whined.

She smiled at him and said to his face, "Ugh," and walked away.

Before noon, the elder Anderson, Dave, and Sam stood on a little platform in the city centre wearing suits and ties. The elder Anderson held a book in his hand.

Soon, a horn blew and Jill appeared with four attendants carrying her up the road on a stretcher. She wore the frilly pink dress Lizzie had worn so long ago in Eden before Sam left there for his journey to Josh's city. Lizzie appeared after her with the young girl she had found as her flower carrier and walked up the road with her father at her side. She was wearing a beautiful white wedding dress with sparkling sequins lit by the blazing sun. Dave gawked at how beautiful she looked. Soon, she was at his side.

Sam helped Jill off the stretcher and supported her.

The elder Anderson led the ceremony and read some quotes from the bible then led them in saying their "I dos".

Jill turned to Sam and said, "Now that we're here, why don't we do this, too?"

Sam replied, "We've been together for eighteen years. I'll be with you for life."

"I know, Sam but it seems nice to say and hear the 'til death do us part'."

Sam looked at the elder Anderson and asked, "Can you, do it?"

"Sure, I can. It's never too late. Elizabeth had this all arranged, you know."

Sam turned to Jill and said, "I should've figured it out."

She grinned back at him.

Dave and Lizzie watched as their best friends made their vows.

Afterwards, they feasted on stew and the old Eden families taught everyone how to do a square dance. A few farmers with their simple instruments started playing music and everyone joined in.

Sam could not dance with Jill but he did with Lizzie and a few other women.

At one point, Josh pulled him aside. "Sam, I'm getting old."

"You've said these lines before. The city talked you into keeping your post, letting me do most of the work and you can keep doing that."

"I know, when I see my parents, I think it's time for me to retire to the hospital to take care of them for the last few years of their lives. I'm asking you to take it all from me."

"You can still be in charge and look after your parents."

"Yeah, but remember what I said when we talked then. My time has come. You're the best person for the job and the people respect you."

"Well, I'll never feel ready but I guess you never felt ready, either."

"Yes, I knew I had to do it. Now it's time to turn it over to another person who doesn't feel ready."

"I'll never be as good as you were, Josh. You're the founder of all this but I'll do the best I can."

"Good, when we get back to town, I'll make the announcements."

Sam returned to the dancing.

Late in the afternoon, Dave looked tired during a lull in the dancing. He looked at Lizzie who was smiling happily. He thought it was enough of all this complicated ceremony. He blurted out, "It's 'ugh' time now" and swept her up in his arms while she screamed, squirmed, and yelled, "Put me down! Put me down! You're spoiling the whole thing! Put me down!" As he carried her off, with a little difficulty, he put his hand behind his back and put up his thumb. Everybody saw it and laughed.

Jill saw it and smiled. She remembered back to her first time with

Sam. She was happy for Lizzie. She would not have changed anything in her life and the choices she made. Sam was a good man and she knew Dave was, too. She looked at the little girl she found on the road and hugged her. She would be a part of her family, now. She looked at everyone, young and old, laughing and dancing together, and realised that there were still many good people on earth – lots of them and, in a few months, number twelve would be born to all this. She put her hands on her stomach and smiled.

BATTLE FOR EDEN

S am sat quietly on his chair beside the ocean. He spent part of every sunny afternoon there in the summer. It was a relatively peaceful place to relax and think. Sometimes sitting there was quiet, with soft waves rippling across the sand on the beach but other times it was noisy with a giant surf that churned and tumbled heavily onto the beach. He watched the birds diving in to catch what they could from the ocean. He thought of Eden.

Almost fifteen years had passed since Josh had turned over management of the three cities and two farms to Sam. There were no questions raised, everyone cheered the decision. Those years had been busy building and growing and relatively peaceful. There was no war. Sometimes outsiders would come and other times they drifted away but most times people liked what they saw and joined them. They had almost thirty-five thousand people now, almost half of whom were under the age of eighteen. There were almost five thousand farmers and most of the rest of the people were in the central city which everyone now called Capital City.

During that time there was a gradual move of the population from the city core to the smaller homes outside of it, as the crumbling large buildings were becoming unsafe. People had dismantled most of the suburban houses over the years to use the wood for fire during winters but there were still many remaining to live in. Because they were small and made of wood, they were easier to maintain and heat in winter. The hospitals were still in the core but in time, they would have to move to smaller schools or local hospitals outside the city centre.

The southern farms had also expanded. It was now less than a two-hour journey south from the capital before people saw sown fields instead of the four hours back then. The farmers still had their compound but they also farmed outside of its boundaries to the north and south. Their territory to the west had expanded to the small river west of them. There was no longer a western gate to guard.

The people from old Eden had settled mostly in the newer farms north of the capital. The farmers were very practical people and had large families themselves and better protected their children using the hospitals.

During that time of relative peace, there was still a loss of life. Josh had retired to look after his parents but they died within five years after they moved there. About five years after that Josh passed away. It was a sad event for everyone. They had lost their founder. The carpenters made a rough statue of him and he had a huge funeral. He was the first person to be buried in his plot in a wooden box. It was like a royal burial. The northern city formally named their city Josh Ville in his honour.

Within six years, Sam had lost his parents. Over the fifteen years he had also lost three of his children; one son to an accident and a son and daughter in an ambush. Those losses were hard to take for him but his biggest loss was Jill, his lifelong partner.

Jill had never healed well from the shots fired at her in the war with the southern city. A few months after the war, she delivered their eleventh child and lived to birth two more but the doctor said she developed complications from a piece of bullet that they had not been able to remove. Without the medical technology of old Earth, she passed away two years ago. He loved their mutual bantering. Without his children, he might have just dug a hole and died but their lust for life was infectious enough to keep him going. Even with their presence though, he felt lonely. He missed his old man-hater.

Part of the reason he sat beside the ocean was because they had spent many hours there. His first love, Beautiful, had also been with him there when they played by the surf minutes before she was killed protecting him. It was the first time he had seen and waded in an ocean. Then, like a flash, she was gone and in a little longer flash later Jill was, too. Now, he could sit beside the water for as long as he liked.

A voice interrupted his thoughts.

"I wish I could read your mind."

He turned his head to see a young woman approaching him. He said, "Every time I turn my head, you seem to pop up."

"I was walking by and saw you. This is also one of my favourite places. I like to go swimming. Do you want to join me?"

"Um, I won't be staying here much longer. Don't you guys swim farther up the beach where there are fewer stones?"

"I don't mind the stones. It's quieter here."

She cast off her clothes and waded into the water.

She was a pretty woman about twenty-five years old with deep blue eyes and long golden tresses flowing almost to her knees. Sometimes he had seen her wear one or two braids. She reminded him of a character in one of his childhood stories called Goldilocks and the Three Bears. He sighed. If he was twenty to twenty-five years younger, she would be a nice catch. He had seen her many times, mostly after Jill had died but he was old, now. People over fifty were considered quite old, although there were many adults in the hospital now who had passed sixty, with fewer in their seventies and only three in their eighties. There was no longer anyone who had memories of what it was like before civilisation collapsed.

While she was still swimming, he grabbed his walking stick, got up and headed to the headquarters building. He spent most of his fifteen years with the northern farmers where his family moved but he was now spending more time in Capital City. He was planning to build several new hospitals that would replace the one near the centre of the city. Attached to one of the hospitals would be a new headquarters wing.

There was not much for him to do, now. It seemed strange that peace would bring a lot of boredom to the cities' administrators. Most of the problems were of policing the little grievances that arose from time to time. Many times, he had to act as arbitrator. He had turned the administrative duties over to his eldest living son, Jim. Two of his daughters were also involved in managing the day-to-day affairs of each of the farms.

He left the building after a few hours and went to sleep at his usual time around nine.

Dave and Lizzie had made the southern farms their home. Most of her family had decided to go with the other families of old Eden to start new farms north of Capital City. Their five initial adopted children had grown by three of their own but it had taken time to get them. Whether it was age or genetics, that was the end of their productive years. They were happy though. Lizzie was a natural farmer. It was what she knew best.

They spent most of the day weeding and were tired after dinner, so went to bed early.

The sound of a triangle's chime woke everyone up. Dave rose quickly. It was nearly midnight. He raced from his house and a yelling boy greeted him, "There's red smoke in the south."

Dave's face blanched. He yelled over to a nearby fighter to get everyone up and get ready to march.

Lizzie raced out behind him and said, "Quick, get back in and get dressed." She returned with him. "I'm going with you."

He knew not to challenge her.

They soon ran back out, grabbed two horses, saddled them, and raced to the southern gate.

Dave conversed with the farmers' leader. "We'd better reconnoitre first. I'll take the city's forces out to see what's going on. It'll be strong enough to support them in a battle but not too large to weaken your defence. Have you lit the beacon?"

"Yes, good luck. If you need more help, send out a messenger."

They were ready in thirty minutes. The cavalry with Dave and Liz headed out quickly to scout the situation while the forces on foot fast-marched north behind them for the four-day journey.

The blaring of horns awakened Sam. He opened his eyes. It was dark, so was in the middle of the night. He dressed quickly and exited his building. He could see a fire in the south end of the city and, at first, thought it might be a building ablaze but, as he walked into the street, he realised it was the south signal beacon they had established after the last war as a quicker way of sending a message for help. He looked toward the north and saw that beacon lit too, so he was not sure at this time where the attack was taking place. He raced to the south of the city and soon a crowd of people enveloped him.

The young woman he met at the beach came up to him and said, "The signal came from the south, so either the farm or city is asking for help."

Sam noted. "The smoke is red, so they're asking for an urgent response."

"Yes, wagons are all ready to go and the cavalry is saddling the horses. It'll take about an hour more to collect everyone together here then we'll be ready to go."

Sam raced back to where he had been and got his equipment ready. He knew they had to react fast. A red fire was the highest level of urgency. It meant total mobilisation. The signal in the north end of town would alert the northern farmers and they, in turn, would light their signal for the northern city, Josh Ville.

Within an hour and a half, seven thousand fully armed city people headed south. Within two hours they rode up to the north gate of the farmers' compound. The sentries told them that the southern city had sent the fire signal and the farmers had mobilised. Following the plan, they marched almost all their fighters to the southern defensive wall of the farmers' compound. They had no further information and were waiting for them to arrive.

It took another two days until the city's forces arrived at the southern fortifications that were mostly built against attack by the city several days away and now part of Eden. It improved since then.

Sam went to see the head farmer. He shook his hand and said, "I understand the signal was sent from our friends in the city."

"Yes, when we got it, we reacted. We've had no communication from them but are ready to defend ourselves with our five thousand warriors, which wouldn't be of much use to break a siege. Dave left here more than two days ago with his forces to investigate."

"You did the right thing. You've got to protect yourselves. We'll spend the remainder of the day to rest and replenish our supplies. Tomorrow we'll travel south to support Dave and leave a thousand people to reinforce your defences until the five thousand warriors arrive from the north."

They left the next morning.

Dave's cavalry pushed their horses and arrived at the city two days after they set out. All that remained of its citizens were dead bodies lying around. The fighters spread out to search the city. Two hours later Dave met with his leaders.

"Okay guys, what did you find?" Dave asked.

Lizzie gave him the summary. "Well, we counted about two thousand dead enemy troops that attacked the city mainly near the south wall and entrance. There were about five hundred dead bodies of the defenders, mostly in the same area, then others scattered around elsewhere. It appears the city put up a good fight but was overwhelmed. It was a night attack based on when they lit their signal fire. We're still searching for any signs of life."

"So, there are over four thousand missing people."

"Right," she responded, "although some of the bodies were found in the hospital. They were the weaker seniors who would've been a burden on the army."

". . . and about fifteen hundred, of those were children and other seniors," he replied. "So, they're somewhere in the city, or the invaders captured the people and took them away with them."

"We're going to search outside the city too, just in case. We're sure they took the people though, because the enemy stripped the city of anything useful."

"Often marauders do that." Dave sighed. "But most often they'll kill the warriors and take the women and children."

"They won't stick our fighters anywhere; they'll keep them as well-guarded slaves, or conscript them forcefully into their army."

"We have a pact with them to protect them. When we're sure of things here, we'll have to come up with a plan to get them back," Dave asserted.

"It's not going to be easy though, as the city was well fortified. The only way that could have happened was for a very large force to attack them. The marauders found this city, so they may soon want to know if there's any human life farther north."

"Yes, so we must keep a large force here to defend our northern territories; however, we found tracks that prove the force was large and they headed south."

"That means we might be safe for now but we must make sure, plus we must track and find our captured citizens."

"While we wait for Sam to get here, let's give our dead a good burial and get a large hole dug to get rid of the enemy bodies. They've been dead too long to be good for anything else and we can have funerals for our people in the morning. Burying the bodies will show the enemy when they return, that people relatively close by were around to do that.

"I want them to know that we're civilised people. They'll find out soon enough anyway. When we're done here, there's no point defending an empty city. The farmer's defensive wall is where we'll draw our line. We know nothing about the enemy and we're going to have to change that, so we'll know what we're up against. Set up camp here for now."

The next morning, Dave had another meeting with his leaders.

His night shift head said, "My team found about two hundred of the city's fighters hiding in the sewer system. They're very distraught. They feel they've been cowards."

"We can talk to them later when they calm down."

"The scouts have found no one else."

"It's a good thing our new enemies didn't continue north and attack the farmers. We would likely have fallen despite their defences. We wouldn't have been there in time to save them," Dave stated.

"Yes, I was thinking of that, too."

The rest of Dave's troops arrived the next afternoon and helped clean the city. Two days later Sam arrived with his army.

Dave briefed him on everything they found and gave him a tour.

After dinner, Dave spent some time with Lizzie and then went to look for Sam. He found him sitting on a large boulder staring out at the expanse of ocean.

"I figured you'd be here," Dave said.

"I like the water."

There was silence for a few seconds then Sam asked, "By the way, do you know anything about the young lady who seems to be around me a lot? You always know what's going on in town."

"Lady?"

"The one with the odd coloured hair – I guess you'd call it . . . golden."

"Oh, I don't know what I'd call it, maybe yellow or orange."

"So, you know her?"

"Yes, she worked with Jim for a while. She's a good fighter. She trains regularly and I've kept my eye on her. As far as I know, she's just a regular girl. She has a couple of kids but no attachments, pretty nondescript until a couple of years ago." He stopped.

Sam turned to him and said, "You stopped."

"Yes."

"Is she 'describing' now, or something?"

Dave had difficulty with how he was going to respond to that question. "Um, she has her eye on you."

"So, you've noticed it, too."

"I think she's been a fan of yours for quite some time but when Jill died, there were quite a few women who considered you a target."

"I didn't know that!"

"Everybody else did. Why not? You're the alpha male but mostly you're a nice guy. I think there are a lot of women who want to settle down with someone and know their partner will also want to. You didn't think you'd be on a lot of women's minds? Of course, you still had your mind on Jill. Maybe it's time you thought of your future and not your past."

"So, there's a line-up of women who're interested, is there?" Sam supposed with interest.

"Not so much now."

"Oh?"

"Anna, that's her name, has let it be known that you're hers."

"So, I don't have a say in the matter?" Sam asked, rather annoyed.

Dave chuckled, "So, when do we have a say!"

"Aren't there older women?"

"Yes, but what's the matter with her?"

"She's too young, damn it."

"She's in her mid-twenties. She's experienced. She knows what she wants. She's a terrific fighter. She's a strong woman. Heck, she's got the other women cowering. And the biggest thing is – she loves you."

"She's told you that?" Sam asked loudly in surprise.

"No, I can see it in her eyes, how she acts around you."

"The way she looks!"

"I saw it in Jill's eyes when she looked at you. I see it in Lizzie's eyes when she looks at me."

"So, she loves me."

"Deeply."

"What about other women?"

"No, it's her. You're the alpha male. She's the alpha female. You'd be perfect together and I'd have to say she's rather good-looking, too."

"Jill would turn in her grave if I'd thought of anyone else."

"No, she'd want you to get off your ass, and stop feeling sorry for yourself and the fact that she's not here anymore," Dave said sternly. "She'd want you to live and be happy. You've been a sullen old grumpy fart the last two years. It's time you stopped mourning and began living again. You're old but you're not dead, at least not yet."

"Not yet." He sighed. "I've been that bad, have I?"

"Everyone understands though. You're a perfect example of what they fear – becoming attached to someone and losing them. You lost Beautiful and came back quickly. It's time you showed people you can love again. Everyone knows she's interested in you but you're not even noticing her. Open your eyes and learn to love again."

"Only a friend could have told me that."

"You're getting old, friend but you don't have to let it take over you. Every older person is a young person encumbered by a deteriorating body. Do you still feel young in your mind?"

Sam thought for a few seconds. "Yes, I guess I do but that comes with an ultimate fear of death."

"Were you afraid of death twenty or thirty years ago?"

"Not much. I didn't think of it. I guess there was the rashness of thinking I'm invincible."

"So, why not now?"

"I guess because it's closer to the big day. I've seen Jill die . . . You see more of the inevitability of it. It's something I can't ultimately fight."

"You've already had a close encounter with it."

"Yes, that's true," he said pensively.

"Was it unpleasant?"

"No, not really but I didn't go through to the end. I love life. I want to keep living."

"Then do it. Do it for Beautiful, if you want, or for Jill. Come back to earth and live. Yes, we're going to die someday but I think everyone has to live."

"Aren't you afraid?"

"Maybe at times but when I snuggle with Liz, I can make it go away. We share our fears and sometimes it reduces the load."

"You're a wise man, Dave."

"I think it grows with time. The devil-may-care attitude turns into wisdom. Maybe it comes with the battle of life."

"Talking of life, we've got to recapture our people."

"Yes, there are ways we can try. We can follow their trail and hunt them down."

"Too dangerous and rash, when we don't know their strength. Unfortunately, we must split our forces. It'd be rash if we gathered all our forces and went after them to leave our territory undefended."

"We've done that before."

Sam thought for a few seconds. "Yes, but we knew the enemy and took a calculated risk. Here, we've got nothing to go on. We've questioned everyone in town but they've given us nothing useful. We don't have enough information to make a good decision."

"Then maybe that's what we should do first."

"I think that's the only thing we can do. Our forces have a good defensive position where they are. We've got a line from the river to the ocean. It's long but defendable but if we're besieged, we wouldn't have enough food and water to hold out for long. At least they can only come from one direction unless they have boats."

"I suggest we pull back to the farmers' border. They've got a strong defendable position and we wouldn't have problems with supplies," Dave said with confidence.

Sam responded, "I agree. Let's send three units of one hundred fighters on horseback to scout the area south of us for maybe fifteen to thirty days, so they return before fall. They should have the authority to take any actions that might be to our advantage but not to sacrifice themselves, if possible. Our main goal is to gather intelligence to tell us what's going on down there. Meanwhile, we can finish cleaning around here and get the rest of our forces behind the farmer's line."

"So, observe but avoid getting too close to the enemy."

"I'd rather save them for the big battle ahead."

"If we have to infiltrate further, one of our best for that is Carl."

"You're son!"

"He won the challenge fights last year."

"But he's one of your sons."

There was a long silence then Dave reiterated, "I know but we can't play favourites. He won because he's sharp and makes good decisions. He's experienced, I know not necessarily in war, as we haven't had one since he was old enough to join the forces. I know he can think his way out of tough spots."

"Yeah, I know how good he is."

"Almost all our children are on the lines."

"Yes, every young able man and woman is in the same position."

"We need someone to get inside if we can. Maybe he can find out what happened to our people."

"Okay, we have a plan. Make your lists and put me on one of them," Sam said.

"What? You're an old fart. You should command the troops here."

"I'm old enough to fight and am able-bodied. I volunteer," Sam said with indignation.

"Everyone will want to volunteer."

"Are you telling me that I'm not one of the best people you have?"

"No, but you're one of the most valuable."

"Balderdash, I've essentially turned over my duties to other people. They won't know I'm gone. They'll think I've gone to the beach. If I can't fight, what're you doing here? I'm better than you."

Dave smiled, "You old coot. Okay, I'll put you on the list but don't get yourself killed."

"Let's go and talk to those people they found."

They went over to the centre of town, entered the headquarters building, and went to the main boardroom. There, huddled together on the floor were almost two hundred people. When they saw Dave and Sam enter, they lowered their eyes in shame.

Sam noticed it and said, "I see you feel ashamed for having hidden yourselves after the enemy breached your walls. Don't be ashamed. The enemy overwhelmed you with a much larger force. They may have killed you or taken you as a prisoner. Your hiding saved you to help us defeat your enemy. We'll be amassing our forces along the farmers' southern defence system. Are you ready to battle alongside us?"

Their eyes rose slightly and most of them nodded.

"We need your help. We want to defeat them and we need everyone to do their part. If you fight valiantly there, you can redeem the shame you feel now."

They all nodded. It was apparent they were afraid to fight them again but they could only further their shame by backing out of fighting, now.

"Please tell us what happened the night of the battle," Sam asked.

One of them responded to the group, "They came after midnight. There were thousands of them. Our archers did their best to hold them back while we woke up the rest of our fighters and we were doing okay at first but there were so many of them. They started to swarm all over us. Some of us fought, others tried to run, and others sat down and put their hands behind their heads. We managed to run and get into the sewer system where they couldn't find us. We stayed there because we didn't know if they were gone. I don't know if we managed to wake up everybody before it was all over."

Sam looked at Dave and said, "It was dark, so they fought quite well considering the circumstances. There were about five thousand city people with about three thousand fighters, so there must have been a minimum of 6000 enemy troops I would guess, likely quite a few more."

"How many horses did you have?" Sam asked the fighters.

"About 200."

"So, they got those too, plus arrows, bows, spears, shields, and swords." Sam looked back at the warriors and said, "Okay, go get some food and have a good night's sleep. You can take tomorrow off to rest and recover then we'll put you on the duty roster. You want to beat them, right?"

"Yes," they mumbled.

"I didn't hear you."

"Yes," they said louder.

"Good, we're going to do our part, so we expect you to do yours. If everyone does their part, we'll defeat this new enemy. We've always beaten our enemies but we've always shed some of our blood to do it. We're glad you're here to help us. At least our forces are more numerous than what you had in your city. It's a shame you got attacked but some of your people are probably still alive and we're putting our lives on the line to find them and bring them back."

The fighters stood up. The spokesperson said, "Thank you, sir. We'll be happy to serve you."

"Don't look at it as if you're serving us. Look at it as if you're serving your neighbours to get their homes back."

The leader bowed and the group left.

"Well, that's two hundred or so more fighters." Sam sighed.

"If we lowered the age to fourteen and got more older people, we could get between four to six thousand more," Dave suggested.

"We may need to do that but not yet. I'd hate an attack by someone else right now. We'll keep them in reserve. Give me your list by the meeting this evening."

Sam wandered back to the ocean. They lost a lot of blood in the brief battle and he knew there was going to be more spilled before this new war was over. One mistake on their part and Josh's dream would become ashes. He was also hoping for some luck.

Soon, he headed for supper. It would only be a few hours for their meeting then the real work would begin.

After supper, Sam received the three lists from Dave. He returned to Dave with a question. "Everything's in order but why is Anna placed in my group?"

"So?"

"I want you to move her somewhere else."

"If I put her anywhere else, she'd refuse."

"Then that would be insubordination. People are punished for not following orders," Sam said curtly.

"One reason she's with you is I tried to give you a strong team. She's one of the best, so I want her there. I also know she'll have extra motivation to look after you – you can sometimes be rash. I want to make sure you come out of this alive. I'm your commander, right? I give the orders. You follow them. So, soldier, do your duty and follow orders or I'll have you punished for insubordination." He said the final words with a smile.

Sam smiled back but felt insulted. Technically, Dave was correct militarily but in other ways, Sam was Dave's boss. Sam decided he would not argue and he would try to ignore Anna's presence on his team. She would just follow his orders and that would be that. He turned away from Dave and went into the meeting room where other leaders were already gathering.

Dave stood up and opened the meeting. "You're all aware of what happened here. It's tragic and we'll have to respond. Sam and I have discussed our options and what we've decided is to move the bulk of our forces behind the farmers' southern defences, as there is no point in defending the city."

He continued to explain what they planned to do. Many hands went up for volunteers for the tracking mission. Dave pointed to Carl. There were no protests about his selection. Dave read the lists of the three groups. They were to leave as soon as each group was ready in the morning. The meeting broke up.

Sam wandered out to the coastline for a few minutes before he headed home and to bed. He heard Anna behind him. He turned to her and said rather gruffly, "Why are you out here this evening? Shouldn't you be getting ready for tomorrow?"

She stepped back and replied, "Um, it'll only take me a few minutes to do that. All I wanted to say was that I'm glad I'm on your team and I'll do my best with whatever needs to be done."

Despite his cold action, Sam noticed the gleam in her eye. Dave was right. He hadn't noticed it before, because he was too concerned with his issues. Was it only his imagination acting in response to what Dave had told him? He did not want to deal with women anymore. These were the times he felt his age.

He smiled, "I know you'll do your best; everyone will. Just go and get a good night's sleep."

"Thank you, sir." She turned and walked away.

He turned back to the ocean and looked sadly over the water. Soon, he got up and headed to headquarters for some sleep.

The next morning, Sam's group was the first one ready, so the first one to leave. There were no wagons this time. They wanted to travel light and fast, so they rode horses and used 8 pack horses for equipment and supplies. They were hoping to gather food as they travelled.

They travelled south along the coast and, at the end of each day, sent out scouts to make sure they were not near any large army. After four days, they noticed that there was a large town only hours ahead of them.

They camped for the night, so they would get into town in the morning.

They got up early in the morning, ate breakfast, and headed toward the town. There did not appear to be very many people in it.

When they approached it and the inhabitants spotted them, eighteen middle-aged women archers all primed and ready to shoot met them. Sam's troops stopped and Sam began to ride ahead. Another rider soon overtook him. She said, "Wait."

Sam turned his head to see Anna and stopped. "What're you doing here?"

"They're women."

"So?"

"Don't you think they might be friendlier to another woman's approach than a man's?"

"Are you challenging me?"

"No sir but they might shoot you and might not shoot me. A woman might not shoot another woman."

Sam glared at her for long seconds then turned around and trotted back to the line.

Anna got off her horse and walked ahead slowly. She tousled her hair to confirm she was a woman. When she got within speaking distance, she stopped and said, "We come as friends."

One of the women who looked older than the others asked, "Who are y'all?"

"My name's Anna. I represent a group of people who live north of here."

"Y'all better get away from here, then. Yah ain't safe here – just git."

"Is it okay if we talk to you?"

"The longer yah stay here the more trouble y'all in. If the Thunderbirds come around, y'all won't last very long."

"Thunderbirds?"

"They're the lords of this land. If they catch y'all, y'all be in trouble. If they catch us talking to yah, then we're in bigger trouble."

"How about if we talk to one of you?"

"And give yah a hostage? Are you all kidding us?"

"We come in peace. We mean you no harm."

"Y'all just a floozy for those men." She nodded toward the group on their horses behind Anna.

"I'm not. You can see we're all not men. We're free to speak our minds. You saw the man start to come here. I went to him and recommended that I come here and he let me. That doesn't look as if I have no say, does it?"

The women had allowed their bows to droop.

Anna continued. "We scouted the area around here and there aren't any Thunderbirds for kilometres. If we wanted to attack you, we'd have done it from the start."

The spokesperson said, "Well, we'll only let two of yah in and y'all can't stay long."

The women lowered their bows.

Anna walked back and informed Sam that the women would talk to him.

He got off his horse and looked at her, annoyed. "You might as well come with me," he said rather crustily.

They walked into the town, while the rest of the fighters got off their horses and left them to graze in the nearby grass.

As they entered the town, the women made way for them. They walked beside a barn and the leader welcomed them with an invitation to tea. They walked over to her house and immediately saw six or seven children gather around them.

The woman said, "Stay away from the strangers, kids, just get into your room and stay quiet."

The children filed into the other room and closed the door.

The woman went to a potbelly stove and poured some boiling water into a pot. She brought it over to a wooden bench, dropped something into it, and closed the lid. She turned around and said, "My, my, sit down and make yourselves comfortable. Don't wait to be told."

Anna and Sam pulled out a chair and sat down at a beat-up wooden table that had seen better days.

"So, why are y'all here?"

Sam explained from where they came and that they were curious about their southern neighbours.

"Well, y'all came to the wrong neighbours, mister. The lords around here won't like the likes of y'all around here. Y'all have two choices, join 'em, or die, and that's if they like yah. If not, yah just die."

"How do things work around here?"

She explained that the Thunderbirds came around every year or more and dropped off some children for the women to look after, get some home-cooked meals, stock up on food and water and, if they had any mature horses, take those from them. They would also collect any children who were old enough to join their army and then leave. All the women had to do was raise the children and farm animals and grow enough food to feed themselves and supply the army.

"How big is this army?"

"Much bigger than the little group y'all have now," she said curtly.

"Can you give me a rough count?"

"What do y'all think I do all day, count the size of armies? Heck, if I were to put a number on it, I'd say a few thousand," she said as she walked to the pot and put it on the table with three cups.

"What's a few?"

"My you're a nosy one. I guess maybe 5000, sometimes more."

Sam paled and tried to hide it. "They don't sound too friendly."

"I wouldn't mess with 'em. I'm suggesting to y'all to get out of here. If y'all live up north, then I'd tell y'all to pack up and move farther north."

"So, they attack their neighbours."

"Darn tooting' they do."

Sam contemplated a few seconds then said, "Well, we can't easily move north. Right now, we're where we are and I'm hoping we can stay there."

"So, you're gonna fight 'em?"

"I haven't decided yet. I hope they won't fight us." He paused. "If you want to live a better life than you have here, you're certainly welcome to walk north and join us. We live on farms and have towns too, although we live together, not like you do here. We don't have roaming armies. Men and women can live their own lives. If some or all of you want to do that, I can have someone lead you there."

"We'd get killed if we moved there with yah. We're settled here."

"Maybe but we're willing to fight for our way of life. We don't attack people like the Thunderbirds but we'll defend ourselves if we're attacked. Would you like to join us to fight back?"

"Yah can't. Yah won't win. We've only seen one army but I've heard that they have at least one other. They have a northern army and a southern army. When they feel everything's under control, they attack farther north or farther south. I reckon in the matter of a few years; they'll be rulers of the whole coast. They pushed into this area maybe five years ago but I think they're moving out faster, now."

Sam's face grew pale. Two armies – if they were of similar size, they could be a formidable enemy. She probably would not know but he wondered if they would defect to a particularly strong opponent.

In the silence, she poured out three cups of tea. She lifted her cup to her lips and took a sip.

Sam and Anna did the same. When the beverage entered his mouth, he gagged but tried to hide it. He looked at Anna and saw her similar reaction.

The woman saw them and said, "Takes some getting used to, doesn't it? It ain't real tea. My grandma says she ran outta real tea, so she came up with this concoction. T'was her habit to have a mid-mornin' and mid-afternoon tea, so she had to invent somethin'. To me, it tastes like poison but I'm still livin'."

They only had a few other light sips to be hospitable.

She enquired, "So, what are y'all doin' tonight?"

"I thought you could talk to other people in town about what I asked then get on our way."

"By the time I do all that, there won't be much left to the day. I'll talk to the others and give 'em time to think. Then they can make up their minds."

She got up, pulled out a pitcher of water from a cupboard and brought it to them. "When y'all are done with your tea you can empty the rest of it into the pail over there." She pointed to a pail by the door. "Then y'all can help yourselves to the water in the jug."

"Thanks," Sam said.

She put her empty cup on the counter and left.

Anna got up, picked up the two cups, and dumped the contents into the pail. She returned to the table and filled them with water. She kept one in her hand and put the other one in front of Sam.

"Thanks, I think that's probably the worst thing I've ever tasted in my life," Sam said after he sipped the water to clean out his mouth.

Anna sat down and looked around the house. She could see that it was built before the end of civilisation. It had light fixtures on the ceilings and a washbasin with a tap. The house looked quite beaten up as if it had had many tenants.

The woman returned within twenty-five minutes.

She said, "I talked with everyone and a lotta 'em is afraid to leave here."

"Just tell them their kids would be well cared for and we'll provide them an escort."

"I sorta said that but I'll tell 'em again. One thin' I did get some agreein' on was to invite y'all to stay with us tonight to give 'em time to give y'all their decision. There're a lotta lonely women here and they're prepared to entertain your troops."

Sam smiled. "It's rather early in the day, so that'll be delaying our journey."

"Well, it'll be well worth their while," she said cheerfully.

"I'm sure as well," Sam said with a smile. "Maybe we can use the rest of the day for reconnoitring then head out first thing in the morning."

Sam and Anna returned to their fighters. After he dispatched the scouting parties, the rest of the troops walked their horses into the farm town. Later in the day, the women treated them to supper. After supper, Sam left the town to find a quiet place to think about their plight. The town was not close to the ocean but he saw a slight rise just outside the town. He climbed to the top of it and watched the sun slowly sinking on the horizon.

A voice startled him. He turned to see Anna behind him.

"Don't come up on me like that," Sam said, irritated.

"I didn't want to make much noise, or you'd likely run away from me."

"Well, just announce yourself earlier. Why are you here?" he asked gruffly.

"Like you, I'm getting away from all the commotion."

"You didn't join in the fun?"

"I stopped having fun, as you put it, a couple of years ago."

"Why, getting too old?" he questioned with a scowl.

"You should talk – you also walked away."

"I've found it's nice to get away from people for a while."

"I hope you're not upset I'm here. I'll go back if you wish, or more likely, I'll find another quiet spot of my own."

"You're here now."

They stood quietly looking at the sun.

"Nice sunset, isn't it?" she remarked.

"I love dawn and dusk – the coming and going of a new day."

There was silence for several minutes.

"Why are you being so harsh with me lately?" she suddenly asked.

"I haven't been."

"You don't notice yourself."

"I treat everyone fairly. I didn't like your butting into my business when I decided to be the spokesperson for the troops earlier today."

"You've been mean longer than that. You didn't want me here with you, did you?"

"That's right."

"You don't think I'm good enough?"

"No, you're one of the best female fighters we have. You have an impressive record. Your scars attest to your eagerness to fight. I found out something about you that bothered me and I didn't want any issues to arise."

"What issues?" she asked, puzzled.

"You seem to be infatuated with someone in the unit."

"Who told you that?"

"So, you're not denying it?"

"No, but that won't affect my willingness to fight."

"I didn't say it would."

"So, who's the lucky fellow?" she asked flightily.

He took his eyes off the sky and looked at her. "Don't play dumb with me."

"Well, nobody should've told you," she said angrily.

"Well, they have. It appears that everyone else knew. Just think, thirty-five thousand others knew but me."

She smiled, "You're counting the babies and they wouldn't know what you're talking about."

He was going to laugh but quickly put a frown back on his face. "I didn't want you here."

"I'm not distracting you, am I?"

He looked back at the sun.

She continued. "I've noticed you for a long time, not only because you're a remarkable man – you know you're a hero to almost everyone but also because of your relationship with Jill."

"My relationship with Jill is a private matter," he said gruffly.

"No, it wasn't. You showed it every day. You were very public about it. Everyone loved listening to the two of you talk. She was your man-hater and you were madly in love with her. I loved hearing and watching the two of you. I wanted to have what she had. I looked around at what was available and all the guys I knew weren't interested in a one-on-one relationship. I was left with no one. When Jill died something died in me too but I could see how lonely you were and how lost you were without her. I wanted you even more but you couldn't let her go. I wanted a man who could love me that much."

"Well, with all the men we have, there must be someone else."

"Yes, there's Dave and a few other couples, particularly on the farm but there's not much of a selection. I asked myself, why not me? You had Beautiful and then Jill. Your heart is large enough to love me."

"I'm an old man now, young lady," he said angrily.

"Old – you're only as old as you think you are," she bellowed. "You're not dead. You're a man. You've got to let Jill go, Sam . . ."

He cut her off. "Sir, to you," he said authoritatively.

She ignored him. "Sam, you've got to let her go. If Jill could see you now, she'd be upset."

"You can't say what Jill would think. I loved her. No one can replace her."

"You're right," she said with directness, "just like no one could replace Beautiful. I'm not trying to replace her. I'm me. You'd have to love me for me. I'm not her but I'm a woman . . . and . . . I love you, so that's a start," she said a little wistfully. "Jill wouldn't be happy to see you as miserable as you are now. You were so happy and carefree. Now, you're just an old grump."

"Yeah, old."

"You don't have to be old either. You need to love someone again. Here I am, offering myself to you," she said with a sense of urgency.

He turned to look at her again. He could see that familiar sparkle in her eye. He wanted to grab her and kiss her and just let go but he could not. He would need more time to think and make his peace with Jill.

Anna was right. Jill was gone now but he also had to contend with the heavy weight of dealing with his ultimate demise. If his life were threatened, he could pull out his bow or a sword and protect himself and he had done a good job of that through the years but his foe now was not something corporeal. It was an invisible enemy from which no sword or arrow could protect him. He was afraid. For the first time in his life, he was very afraid. He turned back to the setting sun.

After he turned away, Anna could see that he was not ready. She had done everything she could. Her cards were all on the table. It was up to him, now. She turned and walked down the rise toward the town.

He turned and watched her go.

When she was halfway to town, she glanced back and saw him. She wondered if she should turn around and return to him but she thought that, if he wanted her, he would have called out. She turned her head back to the town and went to her bedroll to cry.

The party continued well into the night.

Sam had thought his fighters would be ready to go shortly after sunrise but some had to be pulled out of bed much later than that. He had his opportunity to talk to the leader of the women and forty of the seventy-five wanted to escape with their children. Sam got them on their way with one fighter as an escort. He also sent out a small scout group ahead on an old road heading south. Everyone else said their goodbyes and his fighters were back on the road before noon.

In the evening, he sent out several small scout groups and set up camp. The scouts returned about an hour later to say there were no hazards ahead or to the west of them.

In the morning, they headed out to a boring day. They passed by many abandoned farmhouses and several villages over the next few days until they came to another populated town. Again, they were challenged but convinced the people that they were friendly and ended up staying the night.

About a week later, the river closed in on him as it met the ocean. Sam's fighters were now deep in enemy territory. So far, they had not spotted any danger. He had to veer northwest to find a bridge. In two hours, they reached one. He looked it over and found it looked safe but he dared not use it because of the chance of getting caught on the other side of it. An enemy force could easily block him there. He pulled out a wrinkled map he had with him and found where he was. There were two more towns a little northwest of him. He could visit them quickly then turn east to connect back up to the coast road and ride north to home.

The messenger wheezed as he fought to the front of the dais where the king of the Thunderbirds sat and gestured to him.

The king royally waved his officials and fawning concubines aside.

The messenger breathlessly whispered into his ear, "Sir, I've heard from our spies that invaders from beyond our northern border have been talking to our citizens and convinced many of them to join them. The defectors are moving there by foot as I speak. Some of them have northern guides leading them."

The king's eyes widened with rage. "How dare they!" He roared back, "Are you sure of this?"

"Yes."

"How many troops do they have?"

"The spies say very few, perhaps a hundred in a group."

"That's very audacious of them. Let's teach them a lesson, shall we? Send messages to our other armies to begin moving north. Our expansion to the south is complete for now. Let's deal with these interlopers and crush them under our feet. It's about time to expand a little more to the north before the season's over. We've never had anyone do this before. We'll invade them and kill all our deserters. We'll turn the invaders' leaders into our slaves and their people into members of our army."

"It'll take us six weeks or so to get there."

"So, what's the hurry? Once we're there, it'll be little more than a day to finish them off."

"Do you need all your armies to crush a few hundred people?"

"I want them to piss their pants in fear when they see us."

The messenger smiled.

The king said, "Tell my generals to march north but stop short of attacking until everyone's there. I want the northerners to see us in our glory and have it done with quickly."

The second scouting team headed southwest of the trail of the enemy army and followed a road for several days avoiding towns and villages while constantly scouting ahead of them, trying to determine what was around them. They talked with the few people they encountered to gather what they could and continued for another eighteen days until they surveyed the site of an enemy army. They determined that it contained over five thousand troops. Before they could find out more, a group of their attackers discovered them, so they raced away from the scene heading northeast for home.

When the scouts neared Eden, they encountered hundreds of Thunderbird citizens heading north and protected them for the rest of their journey.

Carl rose before the sun. It was his turn to leave Eden and follow the trail of the enemy who had attacked Eden's southern city. He slipped out of his bedroll. He had had a restless night but it was not because of feeling afraid or nervous about his task, it was because he was so eager to start the first major task of his life.

He had trained all his youth for this day. Now, at eighteen, he had to prove himself. What was the use of shooting arrows at targets, learning the martial arts, or participating in simulated battles, if all he did was practice and play in the various championship games that Eden held each year? He had proven himself to be the best over the past two years. The only weapon he had not mastered was the crossbow.

This was going to be the real thing now. He was not sure what he was going to encounter or what he was going to do. He would take one day at a time and use his honed wits to get by. His mission was to track the enemy and learn as much as he could about them, including infiltrating their army if he could.

The previous evening, he had looked at the various maps that he had collected from the various libraries to give him some notion as to the layout of the land south of their location. It had been a thriving area in the old days with many farms, villages, and small cities. There were two or three larger cities farther south.

He cleaned up, dressed, and ate breakfast. It was unusually busy that morning, as many others woke early to do the many tasks necessary to saddle the horses and get the three hundred and one fighters ready to head out on their various missions.

He returned to his quarters and packed his things. He could only pack what he could carry on the horse. He also wore and packed old machine-made clothes to play his role of a wanderer from the West who was exploring the area and not an inhabitant of it.

As the sun raised its leading edge over the ocean, he said his goodbyes, got on his horse and rode away to the southern end of town to find the enemy's trail.

He did not take long to find it. It had rained lightly a few days before but the trail was still prominent on the ground. He rode while it was light and found a good place to camp. He brought no tent, just rolled a couple of blankets on the ground.

Sam had taken his children out several times to show them how to live off the land and had invited several of Dave's children, including Carl who learned a lot about snaring small animals and hunting larger ones, then preparing and preserving the meat. He developed a taste for raw meat. It would be instrumental in his exploits now, as he did not want to light a fire to attract attention to him.

He laid out some snares, then lay back and watched the sun dip below the horizon as the day slowly turned to night. He looked up and spotted some of the star formations Sam had shown them on those nights outside. His favourite that he could relate to, was Sagittarius, the archer. He could see his belt prominently in the sky. He also loved Sagitta the arrow and Scutum the shield. Then there were the horses, Equuleus and Pegasus, and other animals; a fox, eagle, goat, swan, dolphin, and lizard. Although he was not shown them, he also learned that different cultures had their own configurations and names. People, to see images in stars, likely spent many hours a night staring at them, then linking them to stories written about ancient gods. The stars were like stained-glass images in God's skies.

He slowly drifted off to sleep.

In the morning, he gathered the small animals he had caught in the snares and used his knife to obtain the meat. He had breakfast with most of them. There would be enough to feed him for the day.

After a couple of days, his job became monotonous. He came there not to experience camping and living in the wild but to fight. He was already impatient; even though it would be many days before he would catch up to the army he was tracking. This was the longest time he had ever been away from other people.

Two days later he woke up to pouring rain. He was wet, so he got up and packed his things. He tied them to the saddle and, even though the sun had not risen, started on his way. There was not much chance he would fall asleep and there was not much difference between lying down on the ground wet or being on the horse wet. At least he was moving. He did not even stop for lunch, except to occasionally get off the horse to confirm that he was still on the army's trail.

Late in the afternoon, he spotted a large grouping of buildings ahead of him, likely a town.

He stopped and saw evidence that the army camped near here several days ago. He turned to his right and slowly circled the town. When he had gotten about halfway around it, he picked up the trail of the army again. So, they had likely stopped here for a day or two then continued their way. He resumed his encirclement of the town until he arrived at the spot where he had first seen the enemy's camp.

He was wet and cold and, with the evening approaching, was getting colder, so decided to take the chance. He needed to warm himself up before he endangered his life by staying outside and facing his physical enemies – the forces of nature.

He walked his horse into town and found that one of the small buildings had a light on, so he stopped there. He got off the horse and lightly tapped on the door. Nothing happened, so he tapped a little harder. There was still no response. He said with a strong but not loud voice. "I'm a friend and need a place to stay through this storm."

He could see the drab grey curtains in the small window rustle slightly.

He heard a female voice ask, "Who are you?"

He replied, "A visitor from the west who needs to get warm and dry."

There was rustling behind the door then it opened slowly until he was facing a middle-aged woman with an arrow in a stretched bow.

He did not move. He knew one wrong move on his part and she would release it.

A young boy scurried out and looked around then entered the house again. He said, "He seems to be alone. He's got a horse."

For long seconds Carl stood there staring at the point of the arrow. Then, very slowly, she released the tension and he relaxed. He made no other moves.

"Come in and take off your weapons."

He followed her orders and closed the door behind him.

She said, "Sit in that chair and don't move." She nodded to a chair next to a table in the centre of the room.

He moved to the chair and sat down.

She remained standing with the bow and arrow in her hand. After a few more seconds of delay, she asked, "Why are you here?"

He hesitated for a few seconds then said, "I'm from the west and wanted to scout out new lands to farm."

"Hold out your hands."

He raised them.

She moved closer to him and looked at them. Even through the wrinkles caused by the rain, she could see the calluses of a labourer on his hands. "What's your name?"

He answered, "Carl."

She looked at the boy and said, "Go get his things off the horse and bring them in here then lead the horse to the barn and get the saddle off, so everything can dry."

The boy said, "Yeah, Maw," and left.

The woman called out, "Mary, get out here and get this man some food."

A lanky young woman wearing an old ragged dress entered from a rear room, went over to the counter, and filled a bowl with what looked like stew. She walked over to him and put the bowl and a spoon on the table in front of him.

He began to eat.

She said, "It's not very hot, as we ate a little while ago."

He smiled at her and said, "Thanks, it's delicious the way it is."

She smiled back.

Carl looked toward the door from which the girl had come and noticed a head peering out from it. It looked like another girl younger than the one who had served him. "I'm sorry I bothered you, Ma'am, I wouldn't have stopped, if it wasn't so cold and wet. I'd be much obliged if I could stay the night in the barn to keep dry then I'll be on my way."

"Well, I guess you can spend the night but it makes no sense staying in the barn. It'll be warmer here." She paused and then said. "So, you're a farmer?"

"Yes, Ma'am, we have a collective farm quite a way north and west of here on the other side of the big river," he partly said the truth.

"Is this the first place you found?"

"No, actually I crossed over a bridge a few days north of here and met some other farmers close by there but this is the second place this far south."

"Farmers north of here?"

"Yes, Ma'am."

"Not aware of any. What are they like?"

"Normal farmers, Ma'am; a collective I believe."

"Ah, you can cut with the 'Ma'am', name's Jessie. You might as well sit down and get comfortable. So, are they under the Thunderbirds?"

He sat down and furrowed his brow. "Thunderbirds?"

"You don't know the Thunderbirds?" she asked in amazement. She thought a bit more and said, "I guess maybe you wouldn't. It was only maybe five years ago so we didn't know of them either. We're just small-time farmers around here. Not close to any cities, so we've managed to survive. Things changed a lot since they came."

"Oh?"

"Yeah, they came here and took all our older kids and men and some of the younger women, and dragged them off to fight in their army, so we stay here and farm as we always have. About once or twice a year they come by, take anyone of age, take a lot of our crops, sometimes drop off a woman with a child, take care of the women, and disappear. So, those farmers never met the Thunderbirds?"

"I don't think so. They had women, men, and kids of all ages."

"I guess the Thunderbirds will get up there in time."

"You live this way?"

"Not much choice. It's a life; better than being dead."

"You're left out here on your own."

"They protect us. There are other houses here with other women and kids, so I'm not alone. Nobody messes with the Thunderbirds. Maybe you should leave before they find you. They don't tolerate fighting men in their territory. They won't let you farm around here, they'll grab you for their army so if you don't want that, I'd advise you to go back to your farmers in the west or north, or better yet, go very far from here, because someday, probably soon, they'll attack those farmers. They won't stand a chance."

Carl sat quietly and thought. These marauders had set up an interesting symbiosis – a wandering army that used older women as farmers to provide food and nurseries for their and other women's children. Slowly, they expanded their territory, so they could grow even larger. "When was the last time you saw these Thunderbirds around here?" Carl asked.

"A few weeks ago."

"What did they do here?"

"Their usual, and they left us about twenty children, which was an unusually high number but I think we'll be able to feed them."

"Children?"

"Yes, they do that from time to time. Three of the children were infants. They tried to give us more women and children but we couldn't support them in our small town, especially with all the kids they left us."

Carl instantly knew what the Thunderbirds had done. They had attacked the city and captured the people. Now they were distributing the children to the small communities in their territory to have them grow up there until maturity, so they could draft them into their army.

He said thoughtfully, "You know you guys can always join the farmers north of here. There's an abandoned city between here and them but they'd certainly welcome you. They're a friendly group of people. If you started now, you'd be there in a few weeks or so. It's unlikely the Thunderbirds would miss you for quite some time as they're going in the opposite direction. When I was with the farmers, they said that these Thunderbirds had attacked a small neighbouring city and took everyone who survived. I suspect the children they gave you came from that group. I imagine the older ones will be incorporated into the army but the farmers would love to get the kids back."

"I don't think so."

"Why not?"

"Because when they return, they'll know we're gone and they'll hunt us down. When they encounter those farmers, you're talking about, they'll just blow them away. Where will we be then?"

He did not want to give away too much information but he countered, "What you have here is existence, not life. Would you like to stay like this, or try something better? Is this much better than death? Do you want your children to fight in an army their whole lives? Do you want your daughters to be fighters and baby factories for the army?"

She sat quietly. After a few minutes, she said, "I can talk to the other families but I don't think there's much chance everyone would want to leave. There may be a few brave ones who would, I don't know.

Maybe knowing there was someplace else to go may help encourage them."

"It's really up to you. Just look at the kids you have now. In a few years, they'll take them from you. It'll keep happening unless you do something about it. Even if one person avoided all this, it'd be worth it. Please talk to your neighbours."

"I'll think about it."

"That girl, Mary, looks old enough to join the army."

"She's a little small for her age. She's older than she looks. I wondered too but I suspect with all the extra women and children they have right now, they didn't bother. Her time will come, likely in spring when they return."

There was silence for many minutes but their conversation changed to small talk before he and his clothes got warm and dry and the children went to bed. She gave him a little room off the bedroom at the back of the house. When the children were asleep, she entered the room and crawled into bed beside him . . .

He had breakfast with the family the next morning and, soon after, packed his things then headed to the barn to saddle the horse and load his pack. When he finished, he left the barn where Jessie waited for him.

"Good luck in your journey. Take heed of what I said and high tail it out of here and never come back."

"Well, I've got a job to do before that. Thanks for all your help and have a great evening. Consider what I said about moving north."

"Yeah, it's a dangerous decision." Jessie looked into his eyes, smiled, and gave him a brief kiss. She handed him a packet of food.

They said their goodbyes and he headed out of town the way he came.

Jessie looked sadly at Carl as he disappeared down the trail. She turned and looked at Mary. "Now that's a real man, not the animals the Thunderbirds are."

Jessie stood for a while longer thinking. It was a dreadful thought that the Thunderbirds would pluck her children from her within a few years but that's the way it was. She returned to the house to get the children settled for the day.

Later in the morning, she visited each house in their village and invited them to a meeting. By noon, everyone had collected in one of their larger barns. She told them about the visit by the strange man from the west and his finding a free group of people north of them. She suggested that they pack up and move there.

There was silence for several seconds then an argument ensued, discussing the risks and the fact that the gang could kill them. Some, however, wanted to take the risk and by the next morning, they left with their children and adopted children. The population of the village of over two hundred people dropped to less than a hundred.

Carl circled the town and followed the Thunderbird army's trail. He found that the rain had washed out most of the tracks but a large unit like that leaves many tell-tale signs of where they travelled.

The third group of fighters sent out returned after six weeks to Eden with the message that one of the Thunderbirds' armies was on its way north again and was only about two to three weeks behind them. They provided an escort to almost eight hundred women and children migrating north. One person in the migrants said they were aware of at least two Thunderbird armies.

Sam continued his journey, visited two other towns, and got more people to join them. So, they could move faster, he encouraged the deserters to leave with their horses.

He was very deep in enemy territory, now and decided to return to Eden. At the last town, he led the emigrants to the northeast with his group to get to the ocean road.

Their first stop by the road was near the coast. He had not seen it for several days, so he took the opportunity to seat himself on a large rock next to it. It was not long before he had Anna as company.

"At least you didn't creep up on me this time," Sam said gruffly.

"I've never done that. You weren't paying attention to my noise."

"Whatever; you're persistent, are you?"

"Still being grumpy, are you?" she said in return.

"I'm not grumpy. I don't like being bothered while I'm thinking."

"It's going to take a month for us to get back to our lines."

"I'm surprised we could go as far as we did. I don't want to press our luck. We've got to hurry these people along, now. I don't know if the Thunderbirds rest for the winter. We might be lucky and they do. We'd better get back though. If they don't attack us, we can get the harvest in."

"They're still the kids and older people who could help with that."

"Yes, but it'd be nice to get back to the safety of home. I'm getting tired of fighting. I guess it's people's nature to fight. It's been like that since the beginning of time."

". . . and it's also in their nature to love."

He looked at her. "That too. Yes, they seem like incompatible natures. People live in a dichotomy. I guess that's why we have virtues and sins."

"Sins?" she asked, puzzled.

Sam smiled, "Those are hard to explain, especially these days. If you don't understand them or know about them there aren't any."

"Huh?"

"They're for priests and philosophers."

"Why don't you speak plain English?"

"In these times, there's not much time for thinking, just doing," he mused.

"Maybe you think too much."

"That comes with age."

"You keep talking about that. Why don't you stop thinking and just feel? Have you lost your emotions?"

"Emotions can get you into trouble. They can also start wars."

"Well then, I guess I like trouble. I know I love you and that's all I need to know."

"You don't have any deep thoughts or fears?"

"Not right now."

He looked deeply into her eyes and was drawn into them. Their heads closed the distance between them then he pulled away and looked aside.

"Now what?" she asked in frustration.

"I have daughters your age."

She frowned. "You think too much. You want an old bitch?"

"That's cruel, just because a woman's older . . ."

"That's not what I mean and I'm not one of your daughters." She turned away angrily. She felt like hitting him.

"Do you remember that first day on the beach?" he asked.

"What day was that? I've been by the ocean several times with you," she replied exasperatedly.

"The day you took off your clothes and ran into the ocean."

"Yes, why?"

"Why did you do that?"

"You never seemed to notice me, so I was hoping that'd help."

Sam laughed for a few seconds. "You thought I'd notice you?"

"I was hoping so."

"You were that desperate?"

"Look, a woman has to do what she needs to do." She stared at him with her hands on her hips. "Nothing else was working and, by your response, it didn't work."

"Yeah, I guess it didn't work. I did notice that you're a very pretty woman. I could also see some of your scars."

"So, you did notice," she said with some interest.

"Just the scars . . ." he lied. "I wish peace would come someday, so people wouldn't have to ruin their bodies with injuries. When you're a baby you're so pure and unblemished. Then the reality of life hits you and you develop physical and emotional scars. Life is tough but people seem to make it tougher." He looked back at her eyes again. "Don't mind me. I sometimes prattle on."

"Does that mean you think too much?"

"Maybe more like talk too much, or maybe read too much, so I have too many words in my vocabulary."

She gazed back and moved toward him. "I don't know what you said but what're you thinking now?"

"I'm thinking that you're not one of my daughters."

Their lips joined and they kissed . . .

Early the next morning, they were on the road again. For several days they continued and avoided the towns, keeping them at a distance. On the third week of their travels, they came across a group of townspeople walking north. Sam remembered them. Even though he knew that they would slow them down, he joined with them. He placed the smallest children and anyone who walked slowly behind the fighters on their horses.

A couple of days later, he caught up to another group and did the same thing. At the next town they encountered, Sam asked the townspeople for their horses. They reluctantly gave all they had. He had to collect more horses at the next town. They met up with another group on the road that had some of their horses. To make up some time, Sam began travelling into the night.

Sam knew they were days away from safety. He was beginning to relax until one evening the scouts came back to say they had noticed one of the Thunderbirds' armies a few kilometres to the west of them.

They didn't make camp that night and turned off the road to get farther east of the enemy army but it slowed them down too much, so after a few kilometres, he got back on the road. They travelled all night and the next day. They soon saw the outline of the city they had abandoned and stopped there for the night. He could press the people no further.

The next morning, they were up early and marched out of the city. The scouts reported that the enemy was several kilometres behind them, so Sam was beginning to relax a bit more.

The next day, they were travelling early again. They were near the ocean at their next camp, so Sam went out to sit beside it. Anna soon joined him.

"You like the ocean, don't you?" she said.

"Yes."

"Or are you getting away from the usual evening commotion?"

"Well, the kids are in bed, so it happens. They all realise that there may be no tomorrow. People live like that now."

"Like us?"

He glanced at her. "You have a one-track mind, Goldilocks."

"Goldilocks? Where do you get some of your words?"

"That's the name of a girl who had golden hair in a children's book that my mother read to me. It had pictures in it. We had many books in our library but not too many with pictures in them. My favourite story was 'The Little Engine That Could'."

"Could what?"

"Get over the hill."

"I thought you were already over the hill," she said slyly.

He smiled and poked her. "Ha, ha, Goldilocks."

"Well, I'll call you . . . 'my steed'."

"You're what?" he said with indignation.

"Steed."

"Look, you don't call me Steed and I won't call you Goldilocks."

"But I like Goldilocks."

"Let's be a little more mature."

She looked around her and said, "I can see that the water is interesting. No two days are alike and you can sometimes tell when a storm is coming."

"Almost as if the ocean were speaking to us," Sam added.

"What do you think it's saying today?"

"Maybe we're almost home."

"It looks as if we're going to make it."

"I hope so."

"Are you happy?"

He turned his head to her and said, "Yes."

"Good, because I'm happy, too and soon we'll be home."

"There's an army behind us, so it looks as though home is not going to be safe. If there're other armies behind us, we're going to have a war and many lives will be lost."

"You think too much."

"You think so but somebody has to think of that."

"I think of now; and right now, I'm going to lie down on that patch of grass over there and you're going to join me."

"You're going to order me around, are you?" he said wistfully.

"A woman's got to do what she must."

"Yeah, sure. I learned long ago that men don't have much say in what happens to us. A lot of stuff just happens and you might not have time to make a choice, you just act."

"So, what're you waiting for?"

Sam looked at her and shrugged his shoulders, "You'll be the death of me, woman."

"You're not dead yet old man, you're my steed. If you die now at least you'll die happy."

"You think I'm going to have a heart attack?"

"If you keep whining, you'll never find out."

He smiled, "You're getting to be too much for me. I'm too old for all this."

"Just get over here." She grabbed his hand and led him to the patch of grass. "Pretend you're eighteen again."

He rolled his eyes . . .

The next morning, they were ready to go early again when a scout rushed in and said, "I noticed a couple of people with binoculars on the hill just west of us. I think they've spotted us."

Sam raced out of his tent and yelled, "Shit, let's get rolling, people, we're not far from home and we've been spotted, so we'll have to make a dash to it."

Everyone got on their horses. They put as many other people on the horses as they could and began a quick pace up the road.

A few minutes later, they could hear horses' hooves on the road behind them.

Anna shouted to him. "It doesn't look good, does it?"

"We've got to keep positive, especially for the others."

"See what I meant about living one day at a time and taking your opportunities when they arise."

He looked at her. "Whatever happens, I'll never forget you," he said solemnly.

"Nor I; I'll love you forever," she said sincerely.

"I haven't known you for a long time but I'm happy I got to meet you. You gave my life purpose again. You know, I never thought I could love again."

She shouted, "Does that mean you love me?"

"That's our secret for now. We must keep up our appearances."

"Appearances? I don't care about appearances. Do you love me?" she demanded.

"If I say so, you're going to want to kiss me or something worse. You have no sense of propriety."

"Propriety? Can't you speak English? What the hell is propriety? I asked you a simple question," she said a little louder.

"I love you, Goldilocks," He shouted and saw her smile with joy.

One of his leaders shouted, "With the loads on our horses, they'll catch up to us."

Sam countered. "We've got to save these people. We asked them to leave and we must protect them, so they can reach safety."

They travelled as quickly as they dared. If they pressed the horses too much then nobody would make it.

Sam let himself fall to the back of the group, so he could follow the progress of the cavalry behind them.

In the front, Anna noticed another group of people ahead of them and rode up to them to inform them to run. When a rider encountered a slower member, he or she grabbed them and got them on a horse.

They were almost at the clearing of the forest where the farmers' fields were.

The Thunderbirds' cavalry began to shoot their arrows and were just short of them.

Sam had to act quickly. He told the defectors who were fast runners and those on their horses to continue toward the gate. He ordered his fighters to get off their horses and get the remaining defectors on them.

They slapped a few of the horses on their haunches to get them running. The horses and people raced to the farmer's gate while Sam's fighters turned, stood their ground, and fired back at the cavalry with their arrows. They were taking the Thunderbirds down as quickly as they could but they were grossly outnumbered.

Anna saw an arrow hit Sam. She yelled out in rage, "You bastards, you killed my man," and redoubled her efforts.

The cavalry was on them now and they were all cut down with the cavalry's sabres.

The cavalry turned toward the racing horses and people but could see they were almost at the gate of the farmers' compound. They turned back up the road to join their army.

Sam felt the arrow penetrating his chest. There was a pang of pain then he felt nothing, no pain at all. He dropped to his knees as if he were in slow motion then slowly fell on his face. Everything turned black.

For two more days, Carl continued to follow the Thunderbirds' trail. The next day, he found a good shelter under a huge rock by a stream and snuggled into his blankets.

He awoke to the sound of splashing in the water. The sun was up. It was still cool outside but the sun was providing some warmth. He froze. He reached for his bow and slowly pulled out an arrow. He slipped the arrow into the bowstring, pulled it back, and stood up.

The target immediately saw him and froze.

He lowered his bow slightly, so he could see his target better. On the bank of the stream, he spotted a bundle of clothes with a small bag and a bow and quiver beside it. In front of him was a beautiful naked young woman maybe a couple of years younger than he was. She had her black hair cropped short.

She continued to remain rigid but finally asked nervously, "You're not going to shoot me, are you?"

"Well, just stay where you are," he lowered his bow and asked, "What are you doing out here in the middle of nowhere?"

"Who are you?" she asked in return.

"I ask the questions," he said authoritatively.

"Are you a member of the Thunderbirds?" she inquired furtively.

"Are you?"

She smiled and began to laugh, maybe out of nervousness or thinking about the ludicrousness of their situation.

"What are you laughing about?" he asked, puzzled.

"Well, we're asking questions and nobody's answering. You've got an arrow pointed at me and I'm standing here with no clothes on."

He smiled nervously, "Oh, I guess you're right. I wanted to make sure you weren't a Thunderbird."

"And so was I. I used to live not far from here but who are you; another deserter?"

"No, I'm a visitor – a farmer from out west looking for new places to settle."

"You managed to avoid the Thunderbirds?"

"So far."

"They passed by here a few days ago. I thought maybe you were one of them. They have spies everywhere."

"Well, I'm not," he said more relaxed.

"So, are you going to let me get dressed, or did you have something else in mind?"

He took a good look at her and thought he should end her misery. "Um, oh, yeah . . ." he said with embarrassment. He lowered his bow and turned around. "Get dressed."

She waded out of the water and dressed. "I'm done."

He turned to face her. "Sorry about that."

She picked up her leather bag, bow, and quiver. "What you did was risky. I could have killed you; you know."

". . . but I trusted you."

"Never do that again. Don't trust anyone," she said seriously.

". . . but you were dressing."

She chuckled. "You saw me naked, so it was a little late for being chivalrous. It makes sense if I was undressing and you trusted me."

He stood embarrassed. She was right.

"Have you eaten yet?"

"No, I set up some snares last night, so I can check to see if I caught anything. Maybe I caught enough for the two of us."

He visited his snares and brought what he collected to her.

She cut up the small animals and pulled out the meat while he hung his blanket on a tree and collected his belongings from under a rock.

He asked, "If you live around here, why aren't you in the army?"

"I ran away."

"From the army?"

"No, from home; I was getting large enough and old enough for

162

them to drag me into the army but I left home before they could do that. Once you join the army, I don't think you can ever get away. You change when you're in there. I knew a boy from our village who was quite nice and polite – rather timid. The Thunderbirds picked him up and when I saw him the next year his eyes were hard and cold. He didn't even say hello."

"You must have left quite a while ago."

"I'd say three, maybe four years. The Thunderbirds go by size and age. If you're a big ten-year-old, they'll take you but usually the age is around thirteen to fourteen. Fortunately, I was quite small when I was younger but as you saw, I've grown up."

"Um, yeah."

She smiled. "I haven't talked to anyone since I've been out here. I fear going back to my village, as a recruiter might capture me for the army. Usually, I stay away from people. If I had seen you first, I wouldn't have come near you. Now, I'm talking to someone. It feels strange. I'm used to talking to myself." She looked at him. "Maybe I'm talking too much."

"Um, no, go ahead."

"I finished cutting and cleaning the animals. Here, I'll divide what I have in two. It looks like a good breakfast." She held out her hand with a blob of meat on it.

He took it and they ate quietly. When they finished, they walked to the stream and washed up.

"Where are you going, now?" she asked.

"I'm not sure."

"I suggest you get away from here before the Thunderbirds catch you. If you have a home, I suggest you go back."

"I have a home but I have to finish my job . . . You know, I met some farmers north of here who are free from the Thunderbirds, maybe you should head up that way."

"Free from the Thunderbirds?"

"Yes."

"The Thunderbirds own the world."

"They don't own you."

"Eventually they will," she said sadly.

"They won't if you walk north and join the farmers. They're maybe two or three weeks north of here."

"What's north?"

He looked at the sky in the direction of the sun, pointed away from it, and said, "That way. Keep the high sun at your back."

She stood in thought for a while then said, "The Thunderbirds will attack them. If I go there, I'm no better off than here."

"If the Thunderbirds attack them, the farmers might win and you'll be better off."

"The Thunderbirds have two huge armies. The farmers will lose."

"They have two armies?"

"Yes, two huge armies. They travel to our land to protect people – that's why people accept them. People must do what they say."

"They do that because they're afraid of them and everyone who might be able to fight them is gobbled up into the army. There can never be resistance."

"That's what I mean. Nobody can win against the Thunderbirds."

"Then why didn't you stay and join them?"

"I don't know. I guess I wanted to be me for a while."

"And you think you might eventually join them?"

"I don't know, not right away. I don't mind the summers but I find it very cold in winter. I also don't like being alone all the time." She raised her eyes and looked at him.

He gazed back. It was as if he were looking into her soul. He pried his eyes away and then looked down at the ground. "Look, I suggest you head north. There, you can be free and make your own choices."

"No, my land is here. Even though I haven't seen my family since I left, this is where my family is."

"Well, then there's not much I can do for you. I have to go."

"Are you going back home?"

"No, not exactly. Eventually, yes but I have something to do first." He looked at her but only for a moment then had to look away again.

They stood quietly for several seconds.

"Can I go with you?" she finally enquired.

"I thought you wanted to stay here."

She hesitated then said, "You're someone to talk to. I can always come back here after."

He had to be honest with her. "Look my mission here is to see and maybe join the Thunderbirds, so I can learn about them." He looked at her and noticed her confusion. "I don't want to join them. I want to learn about them, so I can help destroy them."

"Destroy them? You can't destroy them."

"Not by myself but I want to see how big they are and what they're like, so when they do attack the farmers in the north, I can protect them."

"They'll crush the farmers."

"That's what I want to stop. I want to stop them from crushing the farmers. They attacked and captured some people in our city south of them and I want to save them from the army and bring them back home. We want to stop the Thunderbirds. We have to beat them," he said in earnest.

"You won't."

"But I have to try."

There was a long pause.

"I want to go with you," she said.

"You can't. You might be killed."

"I want to go with you and beat the Thunderbirds."

He grabbed her shoulders and said loudly, "You can't." He looked deeply into her eyes then, before he could stop himself, he pressed his lips to hers and kissed her.

When he pulled away, she said softly, "I'm going with you."

He replied almost inaudibly, "You might be killed."

"Then we die together."

He pulled her to him again and kissed her with more passion.

When he pushed away, he leaned his forehead on hers to cool himself down.

He finally said, "We'd best be on our way. I'm following the army's trail. Are you sure you want to come with me?"

She pulled her head back to break contact, looked at him, and said, "Yes."

"What's your name?"

"Susan."

"Mine's Carl." He released her shoulders and began preparing the horse to go. When he finished, he added her equipment to his and helped her get onto the back of the horse then he slipped into the saddle.

"Are you good back there?" he asked before he nudged the horse to start.

She wrapped her arms around his chest, hugged him, and said, "Yes."

For two days they followed the trail. They came across a village where one of the inhabitants obliged them with a meal. He suggested that she migrate north.

They were soon on the trail again.

Several days later, they caught up to the army which had stopped for several days inside a rather large town.

He pulled out his binoculars and surveyed it.

He turned to her and asked, "Have you ever been there?"

"No."

"This might be our chance to find out more about their army. We won't know when they'll hit the trail again. First, though. you'd better ditch your clothes. You should look as if you came from the same place I did. I only have one extra pair of jeans but I do have several shirts. You can wear mine, although they'll be a little big on you."

They dismounted then he rummaged through his pouch and pulled them out. He turned and saw that she had already removed her clothes. He turned his head away from her but held out the clothes. "Here, put these on."

"Why do you look away? You saw me by the brook. It's as if you didn't like looking at me or something. Am I ugly?"

"No, I think you're pretty, so let's leave it at that."

"You know, you're the first boy, or umm . . . young man, who didn't want to, umm . . ."

He knew where she was heading, so he interrupted her. "Our people don't take advantage of other people."

"You don't like me?"

He took a deep breath. "I like you very much, just get my clothes on."

She smiled but looked disappointed. She slipped the clothes on and spun around. "Hey, I do look like you."

He looked at her. "They're a little big, maybe roll up your sleeves and ankles."

She did it while he pulled off his belt, slipped it onto her jeans, and tightened it.

He said, "They still look too big but I hope that's not going to cause a problem."

"They'll think we're twins," she said rather gleefully.

"I don't think so. When we get into town say nothing, okay?"

"Sure."

"I may have to pretend you're my girl, okay?"

"Pretend?" she asked, puzzled.

"Ah, okay I'll tell them you're my girl."

"That's better. I like that. I'm your girl," she said as she spun around again.

He shook his head and grabbed the reins of his horse. They walked into the town. He found a small inn and tied up his horse. They entered it and sat down.

A middle-aged woman walked over to them, looked at them, and asked, "Are you with the Thunderbirds?"

"Ah, yes," Carl responded.

"You don't look as if you are." She went over to a counter, pulled out a bottle of liquor, and put it on the table. She walked into a back room and returned with two bowls of soup. "Here you are."

Susan pulled the bottle over to her and took a sip. "Yuck, this is terrible water."

Carl took it from her, pulled it over to him, and took a sip. "Oh, this isn't water, it's alcohol. I've tasted it before but we don't have much of this where I come from."

"You mean you can drink it?"

"Yes." She pulled the bottle back to her and took a long deep drink.

Carl reached over quickly and pulled the bottle from her. "You don't drink it like that. It's not like water."

She grabbed the bottle back and took some more. "I'm thirsty," she said with a hiccup.

"That isn't going to quench your thirst."

She took more of it.

Carl motioned to the server and asked for a glass of water.

The server returned with one and put it on the table.

"Here, drink this," he said as he pointed to the glass in front of Susan.

She released the bottle.

He pulled it to him and noticed that the bottle was more than half empty.

He shook his head and looked at her.

Her eyes were closing.

He took the water, leaned forward, and held the glass to her mouth. She drank some of it.

"Now eat your soup," he said.

She started eating but seemed to have more trouble as time passed.

He pulled his chair close to hers and helped feed her. When the bowl was empty, he slid back his chair and ate his soup. He took a few sips of water from the glass then some alcohol.

He didn't want to take too much of it, because he wanted to keep his wits. He would likely need them soon – and he was right. Just minutes later, six men walked in and headed toward a large table close to a wall of the inn.

One of the men turned his head and looked at Carl's table. They sat down and the server brought them soup and bottles of alcohol. The man who spotted Carl leaned over to the man to the right of him and nodded toward Carl.

The man turned his head and looked at Carl then pulled a knife out of his belt and put it on the table.

The first man picked up his bowl, brought it over to Carl's table and sat down.

"I haven't seen you around. Who are you?"

Carl told them about his being a farmer from the west.

"Why're you here?"

He told him why.

"Well, I guess you came to the wrong place. We have no room for farmers to expand. We already have our farmers."

"Well, maybe I should be heading back then," Carl replied.

"You're on our territory and we have no able-bodied men on any farms. You'll have to join our army."

"What if I don't want to join?"

"That's what the knife on the other table is for."

"So, I have no choice?"

The man began to laugh. He called to the other men, "Hey, this guy thinks he has choices here."

The man beside the knife slipped it into his hand and turned sideways. He slid his fingers lightly across the sharp edge of it while he glared at Carl.

The man seated next to Carl looked at the woman next to him and asked, "And who's this?"

"That's my woman," Carl said assertively.

"We don't own women here. They're shared," the man said menacingly. "Pretty woman, isn't she?"

Carl turned white. He looked at Susan. She was almost asleep and had slumped slightly in her chair.

He wanted to lash out. He wanted to escape. He didn't mind being here himself but now Susan was involved and he was sorry he had allowed her to join him. He felt, though, that she would not have stayed. She wanted to go with him. He hoped she would accept the price they both would have to pay. He knew any resistance would result in physical violence to him and possibly Susan. The odds were against him.

"Well, neither of us owns the other. We choose to be together," Carl finally responded.

"Like you now choose to be together with us," the Thunderbird said with a grin that looked part humour and part growl.

The man with the knife got up, stuck the point of it in Carl's back, and led him out of the restaurant and then down the street to a large building. He turned him over to a gruff-looking middle-aged man who shoved him into a room with some other mostly young men and boys. There was no other opening to the room. He crawled over to the wall and sat against it for support. He had now joined the Thunderbirds.

Carl did not fret though; he knew what he was getting into. He worried about Susan. Did she know what might happen to her? He had hoped they could stay together but sitting among all these men made him realise that he might never see her again. He tried hard to put those thoughts out of his mind. He did not want distractions. He had to focus on the job he had to do. He did not want to get emotionally involved with anyone on his mission and he had broken his pledge. He loved her.

The next morning, they had him take off his farm clothes and don the sheepskin clothes of the group. They led him out of the building, gave him food, and moved him and his equipment to a large tent with some brutish men. He could see that he had little chance of escaping from such an environment.

For two days, they put him through extensive testing. He wowed the trainers with his abilities. After the end of the third day, they stopped testing him and placed him with the elite squad of archers then moved him from where he was into another tent with another set of brutish men. He could keep his horse.

That evening, he learned another one of the army's routines. A couple of hours after supper, some women entered the tent and soon the men were picking one to spend the night. There seemed to be a pecking order among the men. When they finished, there was one woman left. Carl had not participated in the process and was willing to let her leave the tent. Instead, she sat down near the entrance. He got up, walked to where she was, sat beside her, and asked, "Don't you go back to your tent?"

She looked at him out of the corner of her eye, dumbfounded.

He asked, "Why are you sitting here?"

"Nobody picked me."

"I'm new here, um, can't you go back to your tent?"

"No. We don't have a tent. If nobody wants me, I must stay here. They send one woman for every man in the tent."

"Sorry, I didn't know you'd be left here if I didn't pick you."

"Am I that bad, you don't want me?" Her eyes were watering. "Something like this rarely happens but sometimes a man will take a second woman, so I might still get lucky."

"Lucky! Come with me then. It's not very comfortable sleeping on the ground."

"I don't want you to take me because you feel sorry for me."

"Come on, get up."

He helped her up and led her to his bedroll where the light was better. He looked at her, trying to find out why the other men had not picked her. He thought this was a terrible way to do something like that. A woman could have her self-esteem destroyed if she was always the last person chosen. He could see she wasn't beautiful but she was far from being ugly and she had an inner beauty he liked.

She started to remove her clothes.

He quickly said, "Wait, what's the rush? Why don't we talk for a while and get to know each other?"

She looked at him and said, "You want to talk!"

The antics of the largest of the brutes in the tent were distracting Carl. He had been the first one to choose his woman for the night, so Carl guessed that the other occupants must have considered him mister big in this group of Thunderbirds. He motioned for his young woman to sit down.

Carl could hear the brute slapping and, in some cases, hitting the woman with his fist and she was trying to keep quiet despite her pain. Carl was going to sit down but could stand it no longer. He quickly worked his way across the tent and kicked the brute in the side.

The brute sat up and gave him one of the most horrid looks he had ever seen on anyone's face. He reared up and swung his fist.

Carl quickly dodged it and stepped back.

The brute stood up and swung again.

Carl avoided that blow, too. He knew he could not win against this brute with force. He was going to have to use what he had to his advantage; his wits, and speed.

The brute lunged at him again to try to grab him but missed. He raced toward Carl but Carl stepped nimbly out of the way. The brute twisted to the attack again and Carl saw his opportunity. He reached out with his left leg, grabbed the brute by his garb, twisted around, and used the brute's momentum to whirl him over his shoulder hard onto the ground in pain.

Carl said loudly as the brute hit the ground, "Never beat a woman, or for that matter, anyone. Heck, she's one of your troops. Save your aggression for the battleground, not your bed."

He looked toward the woman sitting on the brute's bedroll. She had bruises on her face and was crying.

Carl asked her, "Can you go somewhere else, or do you have to stay here."

She shook her head almost in panic and pointed toward the bedroll.

"Well, I hope he calms down and gives you a quieter night."

Carl turned away from her and returned to his woman. As he approached, he could see she had removed her clothes. "Um, I thought I said to wait," he whispered.

"You'd better not; I don't think you'll live through the night," she muttered in return.

He sat down beside her. "I can sleep very lightly if I need to. I hope he takes it as a lesson."

"He's the top man here. He won't stand for someone embarrassing him like that. It's the way it works here. You challenged him for the top spot. You should've killed him. Now he'll kill you," she said. "I may have been picked last but now I'm with the top man for as long as it lasts. I'm proud to be your woman tonight. I hope I can be good company for you."

"I don't know your name."

"Who cares; I don't need to know yours. It's better this way."

"You don't want to talk for a while?"

"Life's too short for talking. It's a waste of time and I don't want to start liking you."

Carl threw up his arms in frustration. He slipped his sword out of

its sheath and laid it beside his bedroll. He leaned over and kissed her.
. .

Carl was fast asleep. There was a soft rustling a step or two away from him. He woke up but kept his eyes closed while his hand slid slowly to his sword. He could feel the warmth of the woman's body next to him. He opened his eyes slightly but it was dark in the tent from the dim light of the moon. He saw a shadow closing in on him. At the right moment, his reflexes whipped the point of the sword up from his side into the looming shadow and thrust it upward with all his force. He could feel the resistance to its momentum. The suddenness of his action woke up the woman who stifled a scream. The brute's body fell on top of them.

Carl forced the body off them and then closed his eyes but the woman closed in on him and her lips met his . . .

In the morning, he woke up, sat up, and looked around the inside of the tent. To the side of him was the brute who had walked to Carl's bedside with a knife in his hand. Carl's sword was deep in his chest. Things like this were not rare in the world of the Thunderbirds.

The killing had changed the rank status in the tent but he did not take advantage of it so, in effect, the rank structure continued as it was but he obtained newfound respect that went beyond the confines of his tent as the word got around.

It had another strange effect on the routine of that tent. From then on, most of the women who knew they would be visiting that tent tried to make themselves look as plain as they could, so they'd vie to see who got to be with Carl at the end. Some did not bother, as they had no interest in making small talk and making an evening out of what was, up until then, a simple and uncomplicated activity.

The next few days the archers spent training as a team.

As the days passed, the Thunderbirds' leaders trusted Carl enough to allow him more freedom of movement but the time was too short to visit other units, as the army was preparing to move from this town to another one. With his increased mobility, he was constantly on the lookout for someone he knew but there were too many people for him to identify anyone, even Susan.

They left the town and headed south. At the end of the day, Carl tried to mingle with other fighters but he had to be careful. He found out quite quickly that the troops were well-controlled. To manage it well, the generals had spies everywhere; even the spies had spies. Any suspicious activities were likely reported up the chain of command but he had seen no need for discipline since he had joined them. Everyone robotically followed the long list of established rules.

The next evening, Carl spotted Susan hauling some water from the stream near where they had stopped. He hid in some rushes near the bank and, when she returned for more water, he called softly to her.

She glanced over to him but did not stop her fluid motion of dipping the pail into the water. She replied quietly, "What are you doing here?"

"I wanted to see you and find out how you were doing?" he whispered back.

She tipped the bucket upright. "You can get killed for breaking rules."

"Yes, I know. How are you?"

"I'm surviving, as long as I do what they say."

"Have they hurt you?"

"Not physically but this brings back memories of when they first came to our town. I don't like being here."

"You expected this, did you?"

"Yes." She stood, righted the bucket, and turned.

"Then why did you follow me? I told you it'd be dangerous."

She glanced briefly at him again, then turned her head quickly away and said, "I want to help you destroy them."

He could not hear her last words well, as she had begun walking back to her camp.

After she was far enough away, he slid from where he was hiding and wandered back to where he was supposed to be. Along the way, he could see how roughly people, particularly the women, were treated. He felt bad for Susan.

The next day, the leaders kept him busy practising his archery on horseback. He could see the horses grazing in a large open field and estimated that the Thunderbirds had two to three thousand horses. That was quite a cavalry. He was getting worried. If this force turned north and attacked the farmers, it was likely they could break through the lines. What he could see there were over eight thousand warriors, potentially with a three thousand horse cavalry, about one thousand archers and the rest infantry. They had a very powerful mobile force and, somewhere else, they had another force at least as big as this one. Eden would fall.

He got a chance to rest before supper and spent his time thinking of his options. If he tried to leave here to get back to Eden, he would not likely get very far. His only option was to try to undermine them from within but how? So far, he had encountered none of the hundreds of warriors the Thunderbirds had captured from their southern city. If he could somehow organise them, he could at least weaken the Thunderbirds when the time came. That was all he could do. He would not be able to find help in this mass of people, as he had limited opportunities to wander through the camp. He would have to meet some of them though and they would have to pass on the plans to the others. This would have to work.

Later in the evening, he thought he recognised one of the leaders of the southern city's forces. He was watching the horses forage for food. Carl ambled near him and, while watching the horses, said, "Hello, you're Ian if my memory serves me right."

The man continued to stare at the horses but soon slowly turned his head to glance at him then turned it back toward the horses. He replied in a low voice, "You're one of Dave's kids are you, I think Carl?"

"Yes," he responded without turning his head from the horses.

Someone passed by them, so they remained silent.

When the person had passed, Ian said, "What're you doing here? You weren't in the city when we were attacked."

"That's a long story. Right now, I want to know if you're with me, or have you joined them?"

"We had no choice, it was joining them, or die."

Their conversation stopped while several persons joined them to look at the horses. They stayed about five minutes then left.

Carl reopened the conversation. "I know you have no choice but I expect they may attack Eden eventually. Would you be on my side when they do?"

"I'm here but I hate these guys. What do you want me to do?"

"I want you to set up an information chain with your old troops."

"I'm in contact with a few but everything is very controlled here. Someone to the left of you near that fence is eyeing us suspiciously, so we'd better break up. I'll leave first, as I was here first then you be on your way."

Within seconds, Ian left and Carl left a few minutes later.

The next day he noticed that the Thunderbirds were moving north.

For the next few days, the troops held mock battles after their days' journey. That kept Carl busy until one evening he met another former leader of their city's army.

Carl pulled up to him but kept his distance. The leader glanced over and turned away.

The leader said in a low tone that he had met briefly with Ian and would be willing to pass on any information he would receive from Carl.

"Are you guys setting up a messaging system?"

"Yes, but it's difficult and very sporadic. We can't stay here long as we're constantly under surveillance. We're newly captured fighters and they don't trust us much. I've heard that a spy from the north has informed the Thunderbirds that farmers farther north visited some of their northern towns and many of their people are fleeing there. They're pissed off and I'd expect that's why we're heading north. The message will likely be passed on to their other armies."

"Good, we may as well fight them now rather than later but the farmers can't fight them all at once. If anyone is questioned about what's up north you've got to tell them there's not much there and urge them to attack before the rest of their forces arrive."

"Okay, but we'll have to part." He quickly moved away from Carl and rejoined his group. Carl turned and returned to his.

The next morning, they marched north again. At the end of the day when they had settled into their tent for the night, the women filed into his group's tent. He was not paying much attention to their presence until he noticed Susan among them. He got up quickly but one of the men had already selected her. He went up to the man and said, "I'd like that one."

He responded, "I picked her first."

"You're right but this time, I want this one. I'm always letting you guys have what you want. Now, I'd like this one."

The man eyed him coarsely but handed her to him and selected another one.

Carl took her hand and led her to his bedroll. She was smiling brightly. When they sat down, she said, "I'm glad I'm with you."

"I'm doing this to get you away from those animals, although they're a lot tamer than they used to be in this tent."

She smiled gratefully. "I heard about your fight with one of the men in your tent. I was glad to hear I was coming here and was hoping you'd pick me."

"I didn't think you were going to be among the other fighters."

"I was with the leaders for a couple of weeks. They get the new girls first. Now, I'm with everyone else."

"At least we have some time to talk."

"I hear you're a great person to talk to."

"Not everyone likes to talk though. A lot are very business-like."

"Yes."

"But I guess you're not."

"You know I like to talk but not too many guys are interested. I spent a long time on my own with no one to talk to; now I'm with lots of people and still don't get to talk to anyone. I'm as lonely here as I was when I was alone."

"Odd how it can be like that."

There was silence for about a minute.

She broke the quiet. "So, how are you doing?"

"Good, it was tough for the first few days but it's better, now. Although I don't talk to anyone much, I feel I get lots of respect from this group at least. How are you doing?"

"I'm being trained to fight," she said unenthusiastically. "So far, they're trying to find what I'm good at. I wonder what happens if they can't find anything for me."

"I can't see anything to do with killing you'd want to be skilled at."

"I guess not."

"Usually when that happens you end up in the infantry and you find a way to fight or you're killed." He paused. "Well, I guess we may as well get some sleep. It was a long day today."

"Sleep? I didn't come here to sleep. I have to be your woman for the night."

"You don't have to do anything; you can rest from that."

"My chance to be with you and you want to sleep? Regularly, I'm with strangers, now I'm with a friend and you want to drop me?"

"Are you serious?"

"Of course, I'm serious."

"I think you're special."

"I think you're special, too." She placed her lips on his and kissed him . . .

For three weeks the general's troops travelled. They crossed a bridge over a large river and were now finding some towns and cities half empty. The leaders of the Thunderbirds questioned the remaining people and confirmed that the strangers were from somewhere to the north.

At the end of another two weeks, the general of the Thunderbirds' army called for a meeting with the leader of Eden's northern city they had overrun. The general looked at the captured leader out of the corner of his eye and said, "You know we're moving north again. I won't tell you why but tell me what's north of your now deserted city."

"I'm guessing that we're about three days from our old city. About a week's ride north there is a farm community. We've been attacking each other for years. We stole food from them and sometimes they'd steal it back."

"So, you weren't friends of theirs?"

"More like enemies; we couldn't wipe them out and they couldn't do the same to us. We were equally matched. They're getting smarter though. They've built some earthworks to slow us down. I'd imagine that you'll mow them down as you did to us. It's getting late in the year and is almost harvest time, so they'd have lots of food for you guys. It's a good time to attack. They'll be in their fields getting ready."

The general dismissed him and the city's leader left, hoping his misinformation would make the general overconfident.

Dave's fighters kept continuous watch from behind the farmers' barriers. Dave considered his options and did not want to take any chances, so he had a new signal sent out in red fire to the other communities. This second fire would signal for more help. Jim would see to it now that all people in the communities between the ages of thirteen to eighteen and 50 to 60 would begin marching south. This would provide Dave with over five thousand more fighting men and women but it would take more than two weeks for everyone to arrive.

He was also having catapults built using automobile springs to help in the defence of the line. They could send rocks or fireballs made from compressed hay quite a distance into the enemy lines. Instead of relying on the denseness of the forested areas to discourage the enemy from attacking them, he had the openings boarded over. It was a long boundary to defend as about two kilometres of it was open space that was a long trench with rocks piled in front of it. To cut down on some of the exposed length Dave had crews build a three-metre-high solid wood fence from the edges almost to the centre of the boundary. From the ocean to within five hundred metres from the gate, the ocean water flooded the trench. From the river to within five hundred metres from the gate, river water flooded the trench. Even after more than a month of building they still had more than one kilometre with only the rock barrier. It was also keeping the fighters busy during the long wait for the arrival of the Thunderbirds.

The rock wall had only one area open for travel through it but a heavy wooden gate blocked access. The farmed fields to the south of the defences provided visibility for hundreds of metres. Around the more open area near the gate, they built tall towers several metres back from the front and parallel to it every thirty metres to use for observers, crossbowmen, or archers.

They continued to welcome fleeing Thunderbirds' citizens. Soon one scouting group and then another arrived with more of them. Only Sam's group and Carl remained in enemy territory. They escorted the fleeing people to the farms or cities and integrated them into the populace, so they would be difficult to recognise should Eden's defence fail.

Dave called a meeting of his leaders and explained the situation. The information received so far indicated that they would be facing possibly four armies for a total of at least 20,000 fighters. Dave had eighteen thousand with about five thousand youth and seniors on their way. They had 2000 horses he wanted to use for cavalry in the background when there was a breach in the defensive wall. As their fighters were versatile, he wanted to have 6000 archers available backed up by 600 crossbowmen when the enemy attacked. One thousand archers would be on horseback. With that large an area to cover, they would likely be needed.

Dave was hoping that the first Thunderbird army arriving in a few days would engage them. In that case, they had to destroy them quickly, so they could clean up and be ready to fight the next armies that arrived. He would use the youth and senior brigades only as reserve forces if required.

He set up the duty roster on an eight-hour cycle so that two-thirds of the forces would be immediately ready to fight when attacked. He also told them that, if things got rough, he had authorised the use of guns, although the ammunition for them was unreliable and limited. He instructed his leaders to be very positive and instil confidence in their fighters. He dismissed them.

Dave's fighters continued to build the fence and practice regularly. They had to be ready anytime for the arrival of the Thunderbirds.

Several more days passed when, between the fields and bush, there appeared to be hundreds of people and horses coming up the south road. They stopped briefly, about a hundred fighters dismounted and began shooting arrows at the mounted fighters behind them.

The civilians mounted the empty horses and joined the group racing to the gate.

Within minutes, the enemy fighters on horses approached the dismounted fighters and cut them down with their swords.

By then, the fleeing people were near the open gate and entered.

Dave peered out at the sight, turned to one of his captains, and said in shock, "That was Sam's group. They slowed the progress of the Thunderbirds enough, so the women and children could make it safely here. They sacrificed their lives for them."

He hung his head for a few seconds, then looked up and could see the bulk of the Thunderbird army appearing outside their range of fire.

"I don't think that'll be all of them. It's too soon. Let's hope overconfidence causes them to attack us before the other armies get here."

Carl looked across the fields of ripening wheat and could see the farmer's defensive wall in the distance. He felt a surge of adrenalin. He was unhappy they had arrived here, as it meant many people would die but he was also happy that they would get the war between them over with – one way or the other. It would be better now than next year or later.

The general stared at the wall ahead of him and told his aide to fetch Eden's city leader they had talked to earlier. He pulled out his binoculars to survey the site. He could not see much beyond the barrier but he noticed the towers, some of them staffed with people with binoculars. It appeared that the farmers were doing their assessment.

A few minutes later, the person he requested arrived. The general looked him in the eyes and asked, "Is this the place you were mentioning?"

"Yes, sir. This is the barrier they built to keep us out. You can see that's why we were at a stalemate."

"How many fighters are there?" the general asked.

"About the size we were, maybe a few more – 3000, maybe four. They're farmers though. Fighting is not their line of work. They use things like pitchforks, axes, and scythes as weapons but they have archers of their own."

"Any of those can be dangerous in the hands of capable people."

"They're capable but not too organised."

"They've got watchtowers, so they don't look disorganised."

"Not so good that you couldn't destroy them. You took us out in minutes."

"We surprised you at night. We're not surprising them." He thought for about a minute. "So, you'd recommend a night attack, as we did to you?"

"Most of them would be asleep then. You wouldn't have the element of surprise but it doesn't matter, day or night, you can take them. Shit, your cavalry might be able to take them by itself."

"What about other entrances?"

"The ocean covers the east side, a small river on the west and they have a barrier on the north similar to this but you'd have to cross the river and there isn't a bridge nearby."

"When we passed through your city, all the dead had been collected and buried. Why would they bother to do that?"

The leader delayed his response to collect his thoughts. "It might not have been them but if they did, they likely launched an attack on us and found us gone. They're farmers and have respect for the bodies. They don't want diseases to spread to them and their animals. It was quite plain that you overran us. They're likely glad we're gone. Now we can take our vengeance on them."

"We must wait until our other armies get here."

"Why?"

"Because we were told to."

"Isn't it going to be embarrassing for you, if the full army marches through with little resistance? If you won the battle before they arrived, you'd likely get a medal. You'd be able to welcome them to your new territory."

"I don't think so. I follow orders," the general said menacingly.

"Well, it's up to you," the leader said, sounding discouraged. "Maybe give me back my people and we can attack them and take the place ourselves. I have confidence in my warriors. Don't you have any confidence in yours?"

The general gave him a sneer and waved him away.

The city's leader returned to his group.

Before midnight of that evening, the Thunderbirds woke up and began to muster into position with their weapons.

Carl was trying to keep a straight face but was ecstatic. He looked outside his tent and saw that the sky was mostly clear with the stars shining brightly. There was no moon out though, so visibility would be marginal. He had managed to talk a few times to several of their old city's leaders and they had a plan in play. Now, if it would only work.

He knew the Thunderbirds wanted to surprise the farmers, so were going to be moving fast.

The general gave his signal and everyone raced forward in a wave. Two thousand cavalry raced ahead, closed the distance to the gate, and stumbled over the rocks. The rest of the army marched close to the wall and the order was given to send in a barrage of arrows for a few minutes, as the infantry moved close to the barrier.

When the general gave the signal to shoot their arrows, Carl and all the other former city archers stepped back, turned around, and began shooting at the general and his entourage.

The archer beside Carl noticed what he was doing and Carl thought he would get a knife in the ribs; instead, the other person turned around and joined them. By the time other archers knew what was going on, the general and his aides were lying on the ground either badly wounded or dead. In the infantry, former city fighters headed toward their commanders to eliminate them; most were successful.

The city's archers now began knifing the elite Thunderbird archers beside them but soon became targets themselves. Other archers not with the city also began to join the battle against the elites.

Meanwhile, Carl was knifing the archers near him but several loyal archers soon fatally wounded him with their arrows. For thirty minutes, there was chaos in the ranks of Thunderbirds until the remaining officers got control of the situation, so the troops could kill the traitors and turn back to what they were supposed to be doing. Finally, the attack on the farmer's compound began in earnest.

Carl lay on the ground as other fighters stepped on him, each time he winced in pain but it was short. One of the arrows in his ribs had grazed his heart and he bled out on the battlefield. He smiled that he was able to at least stall the Thunderbird's attack. They had achieved their goal. His eyes glazed over. He died in the anarchy of battle.

Susan was nearby with the advancing infantry when she saw Carl fall. She worked her way over to him and bent down. Her troop leader saw her do this and thrust his spear into her as he passed by her. She fell on top of Carl. Several of the fighters behind her compounded her misery by stepping on her.

She ignored the pain. She felt for a pulse in Carl's neck but found none. She hugged him and began to cry.

Dave was on the midnight shift when he noticed movement in the Thunderbirds' camp and quietly informed an aide. They did not want to sound the alarm; everything had to be done quietly, so everyone began doing their duty to get those asleep out of bed.

They already had two thousand horses and riders ready to go as well as a full complement of archers. Only the infantry remained understaffed until they could get everyone else awake to fill in the ranks.

Soon, he could see the enemy's cavalry galloping toward the barrier. The archers and crossbowmen fired a barrage of arrows at them.

The enemy cavalry was soon by the gate where the riders had smeared it with tar and ignited it.

When Dave saw the cavalry's destination, he told the fighters with crossbows to get on the wall to fire on them.

The enemy focused their archers on the crossbowmen, so they retreated from their positions. The enemy cavalry was soon beside the rocks by the gate and clambering over them.

Eden's fighters greeted the enemy cavalry with a barrage of arrows.

When the Thunderbirds realised their attack was fruitless, they turned to run but Dave's cavalry moved in behind them.

Within thirty minutes, Dave's fighters were collecting the horses and leading the surrendered troops to a temporary holding area. The younger fighters cleared the grounds of both sides' bodies and were injured.

Dave could see that the Thunderbirds' archers and infantry had moved close to the wall and there was something wrong. He spotted the general fall off his horse and surmised that their city's troops within the Thunderbirds were behind the temporary chaos behind their lines. He ordered his archers near the wall to fire at Thunderbirds who were not involved in the chaotic actions within the enemy's forces.

When they had neutralised the enemy's cavalry within their compound, Dave ordered his troops back to the barrier and soon the archers were firing into the now more organised assault by the Thunderbirds. After a few minutes, he ordered the farm's gate opened and Dave's cavalry rode out but instead of attacking they rode along the wall for a couple of hundred metres then headed south to encircle the Thunderbirds. Meanwhile, the infantry worked to extinguish the fire on the door.

When the Thunderbirds' cavalry outside their compound moved in to attack and got into range of Eden's archers, their numbers diminished rapidly. The two cavalries engaged in a close-fought battle. When some of the enemy's cavalry tried to escape inevitable defeat, Eden's cavalry surrounded and massacred them.

The Thunderbirds' archers fired into the compound hitting many of the warriors there but it did not last long.

With a heavy concentration of fire from Dave's archers, the enemy's firepower was diminishing.

The Thunderbirds' infantry finally got to the rock barrier and began climbing over.

Soon, there was heavy hand-to-hand combat.

As discipline in the enemy's troops faltered, Eden's cavalry prevented any fighters from escaping.

Within thirty minutes, some of the Thunderbirds began to lay down their arms and surrender. By the end of another thirty minutes, they were surrendering in mass.

Dave walked onto the battlefield while his fighters were collecting the prisoners. Within the farmers' compound, he saw many people he remembered well; some of their finest fighters. He talked to some of the wounded and then wandered outside. He could recognise a few of the faces from the southern city. Now, he confirmed what had happened to cause a lot of chaos within the Thunderbirds' lines for quite some minutes before the actual battle. The southern city's troops had attacked the Thunderbirds and gave Eden's troops vital minutes to prepare and deal with the cavalry attack.

Dave's aide joined him, as he walked a little more and looked down at his son's body. He knelt beside it and noticed a young woman's body slumped over it. He noticed that his son's shirt was wet near her face. He bent down and felt for the absence of a pulse in his son and the woman. He knelt and kissed his son goodbye.

Dave stood up, turned to his aide and said, "I don't know who this woman was but it's apparent that she was crying over his body. I might be wrong but I think she was crying for him. It might be someone he came across during his journey into enemy territory. Make sure she's buried with him."

He took the long walk to where Sam's group was attacked. He could see that there were a few fighters who were badly injured. He turned to his aide and said, "Make sure someone gets over here quickly to care for the living."

He walked to Sam's body and bent over him to confirm he was dead. He saw that Anna's body was lying half on top of him. The deep gash in her neck was enough to tell him she was dead. He tried to remain stoic as he remembered the fine times, he had had with his best friend but he knew he had to move on. They had to clear the battleground quickly. He turned to his aide and said, "Make sure you give Sam his tomb and place Anna with him. I'm sure he wouldn't mind. I hope the two of them mended their rift and became partners."

One of the wounded fighters overheard him and said, "You're right, sir, she finally won his heart."

He nodded back to the man and walked back behind the wall.

They collected the prisoners and placed them into a prepared compound within the farms. The Thunderbirds had over two thousand killed, three thousand wounded, and over three thousand taken prisoner. This excluded more than 2000 warriors from Eden's southern city. Dave lost about four hundred dead and 900 wounded, including Sam's small force.

Before they cleared the field, Dave met with his leaders. "We won that battle and I'm proud of you for your great work but the next battle won't be so easy, so there's a lot to do. I'm taking the chance that the nearest other troops will be at least a week away, so I'd like to get three thousand head of cavalry behind them."

There were many puzzled looks at him.

He continued. "The only way to do this is to use the small window of opportunity we have to get them over the bridge and hide where we were fifteen years ago. They can use the road to reduce the chance of leaving a trail. They've got to cover any trail they do leave, if necessary.

"Their mission is to shut off the three working wind generators, so the Thunderbirds' fighters will not be tempted to damage them. It means no lights here for a while but if we lose, it won't matter anyway and I don't want them to gain that technology. Another mission is to catch anyone who might want to escape to ensure nobody returns to build new armies against us. Of course, they're also our support force."

"But we're losing almost all of our cavalry here on defence," one leader said nervously.

"Yes, but we've captured almost 2000 of the enemy's horses, so can create a new cavalry here."

"And if we lose?" another officer asked.

"Let's hope that doesn't happen. We'll use our smoke signalling system to let them know when they're needed. If we're defeated here, they'll get here to turn the tide or go down with us. Nothing will matter then. We must win and having a backup outside of here will be a surprise to the enemy."

Dave paused for any additional comments then said, "Okay, when we're confident the Thunderbirds are all here, we'll send up a smoke signal that the cavalry should be able to see. They can cross the bridge, set up behind the enemy, and decide what to do from there. For example, if they want to close in on enemy forces without detection, they can. When we need help, we'll send them another smoke signal to attack from the rear. Their other armies likely won't arrive for several weeks, so there'll be some waiting involved. Are there any questions?"

There was nothing from his leaders.

"Okay, do it. I'd like them briefed and out of here early tomorrow morning."

His leaders filed out of the tent. Dave stayed behind for a few minutes to calm his nerves. He hoped that he wasn't making a mistake by splitting his forces like that. He spent the rest of his day visiting the wounded in the hospital compound.

Early the next morning, he saw the cavalry leave. Later in the morning, they had funeral services for their dead.

Dave talked to the defeated fighters over the next few days and got almost half of them to defect, leaving him with more fighters than he had before. Their hopes to have an early battle with the Thunderbirds had been a success. Soon, the 5000 seniors and young people from Eden arrived. They had about 17,000 people from Eden and 2000 defectors behind their lines ready for battle with 3000 hidden behind the enemy lines.

Over the next two weeks, they held many mock battles and practices to keep the troops fit and ready, and to integrate the defectors into their forces.

An enemy army was soon in view. They stopped out of range and made camp. Two weeks later another army arrived. In another two weeks, they saw more activities in front of them as it appeared that more enemy forces had arrived.

"Well, that's army number three," Dave said to his aide from his observation post on one of the towers, "except the last bunch looks a lot larger than the last two combined. Either that was a huge army or two of them arrived together. It's much more than I expected. That might be over 20,000 troops there and it appears they brought some siege equipment of their own. They must have brought everything here. I guess their expansion was so successful in the south that they decided to do an extra expansion this year. The first thing they're going to try to do is knock down our towers. They might not be able to spot the lookouts we have in the trees so; we'll use those from now on. Their visibility isn't the best but they'll do. Our advantage is we're defending and can keep most of our troops and equipment hidden."

They climbed down the tower and waited.

"Where's Craig?" the king demanded when his generals assembled in front of him in their camp well behind the lines.

"I thought he was with you!" one of the generals responded.

"Do you see him here?" the king shouted. "He should've been the first one to arrive. We would've noticed him if he loitered. You can't hide an army. It's rained here several times before we got here, so any blood from a battle might not be around anymore but from the trampled state of these crops, either the farmers came out here and had a party, or Craig, the idiot, came here and tried to start a war without us. If he did, he was a moron. At least I hope, even though it looks as if he did try and lose, he delivered heavy enough damage to these northerners that it'll make things easier for us, now. It also showed us that we can expect a good battle and that we were right to bring everything we have, to snuff them out. For a while, I was thinking we were overreacting.

"There's not much we can do today. We'll rest and make our plans tomorrow morning. Those farmers aren't going anywhere."

Dave sat down with his leaders over a supper of stew and said, "It looks as if the new arrivals want to rest their troops, so I don't think they're going to attack us tonight but I want everyone on high alert with a silent wake-up as we did for their first army, in case they do.

"They've got a huge force there and we can't see it all. We're outnumbered but we've got the defensive advantage, so don't get too nervous. It looks as if they've got twenty catapults which may be why they arrived a little later than we figured.

"As soon as their catapults are set up, get their sightings for our eight catapults using the rocks we've placed as markers in the field out there. I know we don't usually fire the first shot but when it looks as if they're setting up for battle, fire as many shots as you can before they start using theirs. Use our oiled fire bombs for maximum damage. Since using catapults will give away their location, move them to a new spot when you see them setting up theirs. Have the crossbowmen and women set up to take out anyone who tries to move the rocks we've put onto the field. Let's let them know we're serious. They have no idea how many fighters we've got here and that's a big advantage for us.

"Any questions?"

There was no response.

Dave continued. "Let's hope they don't start the battle tonight but, if they do, we'll have the catapults ready to fire and destroy them early if we have to."

One of the leaders asked, "What about the cavalry? Should we send them a smoke signal?"

"No, the Thunderbirds won't attack unless all their troops are here. When they engage us, we'll send it. I don't want our cavalry caught with an army of Thunderbirds behind them. I know they're several days away but I hope we can withstand an attack or two over a few days for them to get in place."

Dave heard no more comments, so closed the meeting. Everyone went to their posts.

Dave stayed up through the night but the enemy did not attack.

In the morning, the dew was on the crops. The shifts changed and the troops got fed. Dave could see that the Thunderbirds had made the final adjustments to all their equipment but most of the enemy troops were still in the background.

The catapult crews placed straw balls onto Eden's catapults, ignited them, and released the trigger. They were instantly repositioned for the next shots. By the time the bombs reached their destinations, the catapults were ready with the next shots.

Dave looked at the battlefield to see that five enemy catapults were ablaze. He was extremely satisfied with that. It was very difficult to set a catapult to hit exactly on target the first time.

He saw the teams reset the catapults and take the next eight shots getting four shots on target. They adjusted the catapults for the targets that remained and sent out a third shot. Soon those were on their way and set four more catapults ablaze.

Dave saw the Thunderbird's teams setting up to return fire, so informed their teams to move the catapults to a new location.

Dave's crews pulled the catapults into new positions and adjusted their aim at the remaining seven undamaged enemy catapults.

Within minutes the Thunderbirds were firing their catapults into Dave's compound but hit nothing.

Eden's fighters sent another round of fireballs to the enemy, knocking out four more catapults. The Thunderbirds now had only three operational catapults. Dave grinned.

Because the shots were so accurate, the leaders of the Thunderbirds quickly examined the area around them and noticed the carefully positioned rocks. Some Thunderbirds raced out to dislodge them.

Eden's crossbows began to fire now and hit many of the people who were within range of them.

The Thunderbirds kept coming though, as it seemed they wanted the rocks displaced even if it cost a few lives. Eventually, the Thunderbirds were successful and their troops withdrew.

The crossbows stopped firing.

For two hours, the Thunderbirds bombarded Dave's forces with their three remaining catapults. The Thunderbirds missed all Dave's catapults as they had moved them. Two people were killed, three were wounded, and two towers were destroyed but they finally stopped.

Dave's catapults were now ready to take another shot. They fired and hit two of the Thunderbirds' catapults. They reset and took out the last one. They rolled the catapults to new locations.

Dave felt relieved and hoped they did not have another army coming with more catapults but his troop's skills, despite not having the markers in the field, made him proud. They had practised extensively with them over the past couple of months. This was what Dave was counting on. The Thunderbirds were a disciplined, professional, and experienced army. Dave's troops were mostly none of that. Within two months, he had honed them into a fighting team of amateurs. So far, luck was with him. Over the next few days, all of them would be tested. Simple numbers meant that holding Eden would cost them dearly through this war.

For the show, the Thunderbirds massed their troops beyond the reach of the defenders. It was impressive.

Dave thought that the Thunderbirds were trying to unnerve their opponents and was sure it at least impressed most of his young fighters, hopefully not to discourage them.

Soon, the troops broke up and retreated farther into the field and forest. They also pulled back their damaged catapults.

At supper, Dave again met with his leaders and congratulated them on a good day. They argued over the Thunderbirds' numbers and upgraded them to over thirty thousand.

He said, "I'm not sure all the armies are there but I suspect they'll repair at least some of their catapults. There's a forest behind them for wood and they can cannibalise the irreparable ones.

"I have a feeling they're going to attack tonight. I'm going to take a chance that all their forces are there so, after supper, ignite the smoke signal. In a few days, our cavalry should be set up behind them.

"Make sure our fighters are alert tonight. Position our reserves oceanside to be ready to move where they're needed most. I'm heading to bed now, so I'll be more alert when I'm awakened. I'll see you all later."

He finished supper and headed off to bed.

Someone else entered his tent soon after and Dave whirled around annoyed, until he realised it was Lizzie.

"What're you doing here?" he asked, surprised.

"I missed you. You've been away a long time."

"We might be attacked tonight, so it's not a good time."

"It might be a good time; maybe I'll never see you alive again."

"That's being negative."

". . . but realistic."

He smiled at her for her thoughtfulness.

She continued. "Maybe you could practice some battle techniques with me?" She started taking off her clothes.

"Well, I was hoping to get to bed early to be refreshed for a battle we might have tonight."

"Well, you'll have to serve your wife first. It's my turn."

He smiled again, "Just don't stay here okay; I don't want to be tripping over you in the middle of the night."

"I promise."

She closed in on him and gave him a sensuous kiss . . .

Later that night, someone poked Dave and he pulled out his knife to attack but realised it was a boy who appeared to be scared.

"Sorry young man, thanks for getting me up," he said cheerily to calm the boy's nerves. He could see that it was quite dark outside. "I guess we're being attacked, huh?" he said as he got up and picked up his weapons.

"Yes, sir," the boy responded shakily.

"Okay, I'm up, so see your boss to find out what's next for you. Thanks for helping us here."

The young man ran out of the tent with Dave hot on his heels. Within minutes, Dave was near the wall.

The sentry looked at him and said, "There's been some movement on the other side of the fields."

Dave climbed up a tower, pulled out his binoculars, and soon saw hundreds of horses on their way to the wall. He looked farther behind the horses and could see archers and infantry moving up quickly.

He looked at his troops and saw two lines of archers arrayed as far as he could see. The enemy was still out of their range but he could see in the trees and at scattered spots along the wall the crossbows heavily in use as they picked out the riders on the horses.

Dave waved to several persons below him and said, "Get some wagons tipped behind the gate. I think they're going to try to take it down. We don't want to have a gap there."

The men raced off to get wagons and some help.

Everyone knew what to do. Everyone previously asleep would be up by now and in position. He was going to need every one of them.

Rocks began falling around them.

"Shit," he said, "They've got their catapults working again."

He could see the spotters already setting up the positions of Eden's catapults to fire back.

A runner called up to him, "We've spotted some boats approaching from the ocean."

Dave stood shocked for several seconds. He had to think fast. He could not spare anyone from the front line. The gate and wall had to hold the enemy back. If the Thunderbirds started flooding over the wall, Eden was in peril. He could see that the enemy's troops were now much closer as the archers were now in action and there was the odd arrow soaring over the wall; that would turn into a torrent within seconds.

He climbed down the tower and shouted to the runner, "Okay let's go." He ran toward the children and seniors. He had never planned to use them so early in the battle. They were supposed to be a last resort.

He stopped in front of them and said, "The main line is fully engaged and we spotted some boats coming up the coast. Are you ready to fight?"

"Yes," the children and seniors yelled.

"This is not a practice. This is the real thing. These are mean fighters coming. Remember don't waste your arrows. If you can't see anyone, don't shoot. I want to get as many of them as we can while they're on their boats."

One of his leaders ran up to him. "I've got forty crossbowmen for you."

"You need them on the front."

"We need them everywhere. Have you seen the number of boats coming?"

"Okay, we can use them, if you think you can spare them," Dave replied thankfully.

The leader said, "Let me know if you need infantry. I'll keep some near here along with some cavalry. If they land, we must stop them. Right now, it's an archer and catapult war near the wall. They pulled down the gate and are now trying to light the wagons on fire. Some of their cavalry had broken through but were beaten back and we're fine for now."

"Okay, thanks. I doubt we'll be able to provide any support to you for a while," Dave said apologetically.

The leader ran back to the wall.

Dave raced closer to the coast and looked through his binoculars. The boats were still out of range but it looked like about fifty to sixty large boats that he estimated could carry fifty to a hundred men. In other words, it was imperative to stop them from landing, if possible.

He looked behind him and saw the crossbowmen arrive. He asked several of them to bring the grease pots over with the straw balls. They lit several small fires near the coast, so they could light the balls.

A few minutes later, one of the crossbowmen shouted, "Let's get going, they're close enough." The crossbowmen had already placed the straw balls on their arrows, they all dipped them into the fire and shot. They reloaded and fired as fast as they could. A few minutes later the ships were in range of the older archers and they began to do the same thing.

The boats had sides that were a metre and a half high to help shield the men seated inside. Suddenly, archers stood up and shot back at them. Some of the boats were ablaze and people dove into the water, so they could swim to shore. The enemy boats still rowed closer to shore.

The older children were doing a great job with their bows and arrows. As the swimmers and boats closed in, the younger archers became active.

Suddenly, behind them, a large group of archers from the main force joined in the battle and almost all the boats were ablaze with people abandoning them. The good thing was that, while the Thunderbirds' forces were in the water, they were defenceless.

In all, only ten boats landed on the coast and a battle of archers took place. While some of the swimmers found their way to land, most of them died in the water as they swam. The ones getting to shore organised themselves and fought back, either as infantry or archers.

Dave was valiantly participating with his bow and arrows but could see out of the corner of his eyes, arrows hitting children who dropped to the ground.

As the sun began to rise, it was easier to see what was going on but the battle continued. The party of archers by the ocean had to leave to rejoin the battle along the wall but the reserve infantry had started hand-to-hand fighting to help the kids and seniors fighting along the coast.

By mid-morning, the battle by the coast ended and the last few Thunderbirds surrendered. Dave helped soothe some of the wounded children. He looked over his losses. Of the five thousand seniors and kids, there were about eight hundred dead and twelve hundred injured badly enough that they would no longer be able to fight. Another thousand had minor injuries. He had expected worse. He could see that some of the archers and crossbowmen who had come over to help had been killed, too. He wandered among them and stopped. He bent down to confirm what he saw. Lizzie was lying on the ground face up with several arrows in her. He felt for a pulse and knew she was dead.

He had wanted her to sit out the war, after all, she was old enough to warrant that but she wanted to do her share and now Lizzie lay there, dead. He knew this was no time for sentimentality and he had to keep focussed. He had taken the chance to break from the zombie mode and fallen in love with someone – now he was paying the price.

He used his fingers to close her eyes. Now, she looked at peace. His eyes teared for a few seconds. He got on one knee, bent down, and gave her one last kiss. He looked up at the continuing battle and raced to the wall.

The sentinel on the hill overlooking the bridge where Dave and Sam had had their discussions so many years ago was taking a little break. It had been boring for many days now, so when he saw the smoke, he was startled. He waited awhile to make sure it was real. It was in the right spot on the horizon to be their signal to mount up and ride.

He stood up, ran down the hill, and entered the leader's tent. The aide looked at him startled then stood up and asked, "Have you seen the smoke signal?"

"Yes, it's in the proper location for it."

The aide ran out of the tent and up the hill to verify it. He ran down toward their leader and yelled out, "The signal has been spotted."

The leader whirled around. "Has it been confirmed?"

"I saw it myself," the aide responded.

"It's rather late in the day but let's get mounted and ready to move."

The whole camp was abuzz with the news as everyone picked up their weapons and supplies and got ready to leave camp. They soon left camp and headed toward the bridge.

After they crossed it, everyone spread out and waited for further instructions.

The leader sent out several reconnaissance details that advanced first through some scrub but later through the forest that sporadically covered the area between the bridge and the farmer's enclave. They found no one and a runner ran back to inform the leader. The horses advanced quickly north as they continued this action through the night and into the next day.

When Dave got close to the wall, he climbed into one of the trees to see what was going on. Everyone on the field looked exhausted but the fighting continued. The wagons at the gate were burned through and several times the Thunderbirds' cavalry got through but Eden's cavalry was there to beat them back. It looked like a stalemate. It looked as if the other side had lost ten of their thirteen refurbished catapults and Eden had lost three of their eight. All but one of Eden's towers had collapsed to rubble. Some of their trees were burning. There were bodies strewn everywhere.

They fought on for two more hours until he heard the loud noise of horns from the Thunderbirds that signalled a retreat and a wave of tired people began their trek across the fields. Dave's fighters were too exhausted to take advantage of the situation. Most of them sat down unable to move.

Dave climbed down from his vantage point and got the children and seniors to clear their compound of their injured, and after, of their dead. He didn't ask for a briefing on the numbers. He could see their numbers had thinned appreciably. His archers were so tired they could not raise their arms. The youths began bringing out food for everyone.

Throughout the rest of the day, they repaired their damaged catapults, cleaned up the area within their compound, replenished supplies of armaments, and piled rocks in front of the damaged gate.

One of his leaders stopped by Dave. "You heard about Lizzie?"

"Yes, don't remind me."

"You don't want a report on the situation, do you?"

"That's not going to help us."

"I wonder how our southern cavalry is doing?"

"It's impossible for us to know. Maybe they've been wiped out; maybe they're intact but too far away."

"Well, the Thunderbirds didn't fare well. Their ocean attack failed."

"Yes, that was fortunate. I think they didn't consider that we'd expect they'd do something like that. It'd have finished us off right there if most of them had landed."

"Do you think they're going to go away now and leave us alone?"

"That's a dream. No, I think they'll fight. Their honour is on the line. They're invincible, right? I'm afraid they'll try again tonight. The battle won't be of arrows though. Their archers are as tired as ours are. The archers' arms are going to seize up. It's going to be a cavalry and infantry battle. Have everyone change their armband colours; they might try to confuse us."

"I doubt they will, they'll also confuse their troops. If they go heavily on the cavalry, though, they outnumber us at least two to one and they also have lots of infantry left."

"They've learned a lot about us. I think they now know we're not a little band of farmers here."

"It'll be a battle of giants."

"It'll be a battle we'll have to pull out everything to win. We're the underdog here, even hidden behind our lines."

The Thunderbirds' king was very disappointed with the results of the battle. He roared out to his officers, "What the hell was that? They're puny farmers. You let them get the best of you. Have you heard back from the Navy?"

"No one's heard from them since they set out," one of his aides replied.

"Then they disappeared like Craig! We have too many missing armies. You're not doing your jobs. A lot of heads will roll if you don't get better than this."

"It's getting near the end of the season. Winter will be here soon. We can return and finish them off in the spring," one of his officers suggested.

The king glared at him. 'We're here, now. You can't be suggesting that we go back to return next year. If you do your jobs well, we'll finish this off and get home before winter sets in. If you don't think we can do it, then there are lots of other people who can do your job. Hell, some of the guys in the cavalry have said they saw kids fighting in their front lines. They're down to using their children to fight. You think we're going to give up, now?"

Eden's cavalry south of the battle quickly continued to advance through the forest. They stopped for a few hours to rest and eat. The commander took the opportunity to talk to his leaders during their meal.

"I know we've been going day and night but we're about halfway there now, or more. When we get the next smoke signal, we've got to respond quickly, so we'll have to get as close as we can without detection. Be ready for anything."

One of his officers said, "If they were attacked, there may be nothing there when we arrive. We've already seen signs of other smoke; maybe they never got the chance to send the proper signal."

"They're using fire during the battle. I'm sure they would've had time to send the red smoke signal if they were desperate," the leader said.

There were a lot of raw nerves.

"Look guys, we have to stay positive. Keep your eyes open for the signal," he said to bolster his fighters.

Soon, they were ready to go again. They continued moving north until about two hours before sunset. In a clearing, a scout entered and said to the leader. "We've spotted a large encampment of fighters but we're still a half day from the farm."

They halted all the horses and the leaders got together. The scout repeated his message to the other leaders.

"What does this mean?" one of the officers asked.

The commander replied, "I don't know. Why would they be so far from the battlefront? Do you guess the size?"

The scout responded, "In the thousands, maybe more than us."

"I wonder if this is a reserve army, as we're our army's reserve."

"They're holding these back!" one of the officers exclaimed.

"Battling armies get tired, so fresh troops at one point can turn the tide."

". . . and they might be used to finish the battle quicker in the end," another officer suggested.

"The Thunderbirds didn't know what they were up against. Who knows what's in their minds?"

"So, what do we do?" the officer asked, "Go around them?"

The commander said, "No, we go through them."

The other leaders all smiled.

"They outnumber us," an officer said.

"We have horses and surprise on our side," said the commander. "Our skirmishers can eliminate their sentries then we all charge in from all sides and kill them before they can do much about it."

"Won't the main army hear us?"

"No, we're too far away. We're just using swords and bows. They won't hear the yells. The forest will help muffle the sounds."

"Sounds too easy."

"It won't be. Some of us are not going home tonight but we must take out this secret army they have or, even if we charge on the field later, it might not be enough. We have to do this even if we all die."

They got on their horses and got into position. The skirmishers moved in from all sides, snuck behind the sentries and killed them. The riders first moved in slowly and as quietly as they could until they reached the edge of the camp then moved in quickly, first hacking at the tents to kill the people inside. Some of them got off their horses to spread quickly through the camp to kill those exiting their tents with the increase in noise as the alarm went out.

The Thunderbirds did get a chance to muster some troops for defence but it was futile. Within 30 minutes the remaining forces had surrendered. The cavalry rounded them up into one group.

One of the leaders asked their commander what to do next.

He responded, "We hadn't expected this. We have more than two thousand Thunderbirds here and more injured. Their practice would likely be to slaughter everyone and then continue with their task. If we keep them, it'll reduce our strength by having to tie up some resources guarding them."

The commander rode over to the prisoners seated together on the ground and addressed them. "Identify your leaders and spies."

There was hesitation at first but soon the fingers started pointing.

"Will those identified please stand and come in front of me?"

Some prisoners walked out and some were pushed. More than one hundred people were standing in front of him.

When the activity stopped, the commander said, "Are all the leaders and spies out here?"

The people in the large group looked around and soon pushed out one other person.

"So, one last time, is this all of them?"

More heads were looking around then they were still.

"Okay, what do you want us to do with them?"

One voice from the prisoners said, "Kill 'em for all I care," and then others followed suit.

Eden's commander said, "Likely, if you were in our position, you would have slaughtered us but we try not to do that. If you're reasonable with us, we'll be reasonable with you. You're our prisoners and we can kill all of you but, if you let us take you as prisoners then, if we win the war, you'll be free to live with us in peace. If we lose, your army will be able to pick you up and bring you back into their army. If you try to escape from us, you're dead. Think about it. If you cooperate with us, you win both ways."

He paused to let his words sink in. "Now, leaders can create problems and are the most loyal to the Thunderbirds. We don't want that. You've said to kill them. Is that unanimous?"

There were loud shouts of assent.

He signalled his archers and arrows flew, taking down everyone standing in front of him. A few fighters on foot checked and jabbed the wounded with their sabres.

"I'm giving you a chance to take your injured with you. I want you to check your people and anyone who can move and bring them with you. If not, it might be good to end their suffering. If any are your leaders or spies then kill them yourself. So, go to it. We want this done in thirty minutes."

The prisoners ran through the camp killing some of the wounded with the armaments strewn throughout the camp and they gathered the rest of the fighters with them.

Before thirty minutes were up, they were back where they were but with another thousand fighters.

The commander said, "Everyone confirms that there are no leaders or spies among you."

The people in the group looked around them but took no action.

"Okay, I expect there's honour among you. If any of you try to escape, I want you to take matters into your own hands and kill them yourselves. If people leave your bunch, my fighters will kill them and maybe the others around them, understand?"

The prisoners were all nodding their heads.

"Okay, remember that. We're going to move you to a safe spot about an hour away from here."

He turned to one of his leaders and said more quietly, "We'll get them to the road and you can surround them with your troops and take them to that large clearing we saw back there."

"Yes, I remember. I only have three hundred fighters, is that going to be enough for about three thousand prisoners?"

"No, but I'm hoping they want to live and will cooperate. You're armed and they're not, so you've got that going for you."

"Okay, we're taking a chance here."

"I know but I can't spare more than that."

"What do I do if we lose?"

"If you want to live, surrender. We'd have lost and there's nothing more to gain. Otherwise, we'll send a detail to escort you to the farm."

"Okay, go win the battle for us."

"Good luck to you. Be tough with them. I don't think anyone will try anything. Most of them are carrying their wounded. They're not likely to drop them to break free."

"Ah, I see your plan. Eliminate their leaders then burden them with their wounded. Good plan."

The commander left a small detail at the camp to kill any messengers the Thunderbirds sent from the front and to care for their own wounded while they waited for Eden's smoke signal. The prisoners' group surrounded them and marched to the road and into the clearing.

The commander had his cavalry spread out and slowly advanced to within an hour of the battlefield.

It was the middle of a moonless but starry night when Dave again spotted activity at the other end of the field. Because there was a chill in the air there was a slight mist helping to diminish visibility. He sent the signal to his aide to get everyone out of bed.

The cavalry behind the Thunderbirds caught an enemy messenger from the front and killed him.

When the commander heard about it, he sent messengers down the line to advance closer to the front and be ready to attack. They moved within thirty minutes from Eden.

The Thunderbirds rolled up their six working catapults and began firing across the field. At the same time, their archers and infantry advanced noiselessly en mass toward the fortifications. The cavalry advanced on their flanks. When the archers got in range, they began to fire into Eden's fortifications. The infantry ran toward the gate and rock barrier while the cavalry rushed the barrier.

When the enemy catapults fired at Eden's troops, they returned fire with their four catapults. Dave's crossbows were soon firing into the attackers, then the archers. Dave signalled the man with a torch and he lit the signal fire. Soon, red smoke billowed into the sky.

Dave turned to his aide and said, "The cavalry is probably several hours away. I don't know if we can hold out that long. Get out the guns and get everybody we can armed. We have less than a thousand rounds. We'll be lucky to get 500 shots from them."

Eden's hidden cavalry stood its ground, quietly biding its time. Suddenly, the sentries could see the red smoke rising in the sky. The commander gave them the signal to wake up their resting members and advance.

Dave pulled out his gun and was firing at the infantry pouring over the barriers. They were holding them but just barely. He stopped and ran back several hundred metres to the crowd of youth and seniors and stood before them. He could hear all the shots fired then slowly the explosions dwindled then stopped.

He addressed them, "I was hoping we could hold out and not have to use you but I'm afraid there are just too many of them. We'll need you. You're all skilled in your fields. You're well trained, so remember your training and do the best you can. That's all you can do."

The king of the Thunderbirds sat on his horse and could see the battlefield and his forces overwhelming the farmers. He heard the shots ring out then eventually stop. He smiled and cried out, "We've got them. They're squirming now, even with the guns they had. Where are our reserve troops? They should be here soon. They'll ensure victory for us."

He heard a noise behind his entourage and expected his arriving forces. When he turned, instead of seeing infantry and archers, spotted horses. He yelled out, "What the hell is going on!"

Soon, the royal guards were engaged in a battle with Eden's hidden cavalry. The battle was fast and furious. The king could see that his entourage was in trouble and still expected to see his troops rushing through the bushes to save them.

Dave led the youths and seniors in the charge against the invading forces and almost immediately was hit by a spear that passed halfway through his body. The force of it pushed him back and he tumbled to the ground. The forces he was leading slowed for an instant but focussed on the job ahead and continued the charge.

The cavalry finished off the guard, killed the king and his entourage, and raced to the barrier to fight the forces that had not yet been able to enter the compound.

The remaining Eden forces, bolstered by the arriving children and seniors, fought on valiantly. At last, they were encouraged that the flow of Thunderbirds over the barrier stopped. Soon, the cavalry flowed into the compound and began to assist the remaining archers and infantry in defending the farm.

Jim arrived near the end of the battle. People had encouraged him not to go. They could not spare him but he was a fighter in his own right and got on his horse to make the journey to the farm with a few others, including his partner, Sara. She felt that, if he was going, she was also going to be there. They joined the cavalry to mop up the last of the Thunderbirds' fighters.

Within half an hour, the remaining Thunderbirds surrendered. The commander went through the same process of eliminating spies and leaders and ordered the remaining prisoners to help clean up. He sent out a party of five hundred cavalry with some wagons to fetch the prisoners who were in the clearing by the south road and to pick up Eden's injured and dead.

Jim saw what the commander had done with the Thunderbirds' spies and leaders and asked him to gather up the batch of prisoners taken weeks before and use the same process to weed them out. They found that more than a quarter of the prisoners on the field of battle were either spies or leaders of the gang. They met the same fate as the others. Immediately following the execution of the last of the Thunderbirds' leaders and spies, the other prisoners opted to join Eden. They had been afraid of their leaders.

Before everyone had cleared most of the battlefield, Jim got off his horse and wandered around it. He had never seen anything like this in his life. During the last war, he was a young boy sheltered in the hospital.

He felt like throwing up. He steadied himself. He soon was standing over Dave. He had already heard that his father had been killed. On his arrival, he found that Lizzie had been killed. All the adults that were close to him during his life were dead and he was standing over one of them. He looked at the sizes, shapes, and ages of people out there and could see the waste.

What had this battle been but a fight over a speck of dirt. It was man's greed and hate that had brought the end of civilisation and it was now preventing it from beginning again. He read a little about early history. Was it going to take hundreds of years, as during history's last dark ages after the fall of the Roman Empire for some semblance of order to return? He looked up at the sky and noticed some clouds forming. Was that an omen of more to come?

Sara walked up to him, looked at her fallen father with tear-clouded eyes and asked, "Do we have to stay here?"

"Yes, I want you to remember this sight forever. At your feet is your father. In a few minutes, we can go to one of the fields and look at your mother who died yesterday then we can go to my father's grave. They all died here for us. Somewhere in these tangles of flesh are some of our brothers and sisters."

"That's why I want to go. I don't want to see this. This is horrible."

"That's why you've got to see it. This is the price we pay for civilisation."

After visiting his father's grave and forcing Sara to see her mother and father, Jim spent the rest of the day working with the people gathering up the prisoners and getting them into the holding area. The cavalry was quite sure they got all of them. At the same time, another crew was set up to get the injured people to the hospital, whether they were friends or foes.

Jim spent the next day talking to and consoling the wounded.

Eventually, people finished clearing up the dead Thunderbirds.

Later, the cavalry south of the city arrived with its load of dead, wounded, and prisoners.

The day after that, Jim wandered to the coast. He sat quietly listening to the waves lapping the rocks and sand.

"Oh, here you are," a voice said.

"Are you looking for me, Sara?" He did not look back at her.

"Yes, this wasn't the last place I looked. I guess you're like your dad."

"Yeah," he said pensively, "even my mom used to say that. I don't go to the coast as often as he did. Near the end, he almost lived here."

"It's peaceful in a noisy kind of way."

"You know, Sara, we've known each other since we were kids because our parents were such good friends. We drifted around doing our things then got together and came to know each other in different ways and have been going together for over two years. You've been true to me, right?"

"Yes, I've told you that before. Don't you believe me?"

"Well, I admit I've had a few girlfriends before you but you had quite a reputation."

"It's been hard but I've been true to you. I don't think I could do anything anyway. You're now the top dog around here and people have a lot of respect for you. I don't think there's one man who would want to be with me even if I asked him. No one would want to mess with your woman."

"Do you like it that way?"

"Why do you ask?"

"I want to know what you think of me and if you're happy with me. I don't want to force you to be with me. You might feel you're penned in because you're stuck with me, or something. You might be bored and want to spread your wings again."

"I'm getting used to you," she said nonchalantly.

"What the heck does that mean?" he asked, surprised.

"Well, I used to be free and if I got bored with a guy, I'd dumped him."

"Well, after two years, do you want to dump me?"

She thought a while to tease him then said, "No, not yet."

"I don't think you stayed with any other guy for more than a month."

"If that; the longest might have been a week."

"Why are you staying with me?"

"I don't know. Just don't get me bored, I guess."

"I never know how to read you."

"Good, then I remain a mystery. Don't you like a mystery?"

"Not all the time. Our parents got married to their partners."

"Whatever that means; you can be together without making a big deal about it."

"Well, isn't it a big deal?"

"Is what a big deal?"

"Being together exclusively – like really committed to each other."

"We can be committed without making it into a big deal."

He glanced at her and said, "I think I want more."

"More what? Sometimes you complain I give you too much."

"It's not that . . . I'd like to marry you."

"For heaven's sake, why'd you want to do that?" she said in shock. "That'd spoil it; big parties, the whole city there and everything."

"We don't need that. We can wear what we normally wear and have a few friends and family there. It's the promise that's important."

"Weddings are for people who're insecure and I certainly don't want promises. What happens in a few years? We may not be able to stand each other. Situations change, you know," she said angrily.

"Yes, that might happen but I don't think it'd happen to us. I think what we have is special."

"That's what every guy said when he wanted to get into my pants. It's normal. It doesn't mean anything. It's all in the game."

"I don't want the games anymore. I know I'm leaving out the most important thing but you never want to talk about it."

"So, don't."

"Well, we have to deal with it . . . I love you."

"So, what's love?" she said coldly.

"I think it's when you care a lot about another person; when that person becomes the most important part of your life; when you feel that you can't be without the other person."

"That's between kids and parents."

"That's for adults, too."

"Love is for making out, that's all," she said sternly.

"What'd you do if I walked out on you tomorrow?"

"I'd say great, tough beans for you and I'd have a great time with someone else," she said curtly.

"We've been together for two years and that's all you can say?"

"Yup," she said quickly, without thought.

"If you said that to me, it'd be as if you were ending my life, my heart would be torn in two."

"Then, you're a fool. You'd get over it."

"I guess I would, in time," he sighed and said solemnly.

"If I don't say I love you, does it mean you don't want me?"

"No, I'll stick with you. It's not the end of the world. I'd rather do that than lose you. What about all the kissing, holding hands, cuddling, and talking to each other to share ideas and plan our lives?"

"Most of that is foreplay and the rest is to know what we're doing tomorrow," she shouted back abruptly.

"Ah, you're getting angry."

She cooled down. "I'm not. You're annoying me."

"You've had three children, one with me. You know I love them all. I love the other two because they're a part of you, even if you have no idea who the father is for either one."

"I do so know," she said arrogantly, "I can narrow each one down to four or five guys."

". . . and not necessarily the same four or five guys."

"So, what are you getting at now?"

"Isn't it nice to know that we had one together, at least I hope we did?"

"I have not been with anyone else," she said slowly to emphasise it, "unless you're implying that I'm lying."

"No, I trust you and you trust me, so why not formalise it?"

"There's the administrator in you – rules, regulations, everything has to be done a certain way."

"Okay, okay, I give up," he said, frustrated and threw his hands above his head. "We can live the way we are. I don't want to rock the boat. I still love you, even if you don't love me."

They sat silently for many minutes watching the waves.

"You seem to want this marriage thing," she finally said.

"Not if you don't."

". . . and you're very big on the love thing."

"Not if you aren't."

There was more silence.

She broke the quiet. "If you want to know, I do like you more than any other guy I knew."

"Well, that's a start."

". . . and when you're away, I do miss you."

"Well, to me that's love. I know you don't want to say it. It's fear. We're zombies and it's zombie fear. I can understand it." He paused. "If you don't want to say that word, then knowing that you like me and miss me when I'm gone, that's cool. You don't have to say that word nobody likes to use. All I'd like is that we both be true to the other exclusively and that we'll be together as long as we live."

"Um, how about we say that we'll be exclusively together until I can't stand you anymore? That'll keep you on your toes and make you want to do nice things to keep me."

"To be fair we should say that either one of us can't stand the other, for the same reason."

"Okay, it's a deal, if we say it in front of a few friends and family."

"It's a ridiculous promise but if it works, at least while we're together, we'll be confident that both of us remain true to the other."

He reached over to her, pulled her to him, and kissed her.

The next day, more people came from the capital city to help clean up, including some administrators. Later that day, Jim held a council meeting in one of the farmer's living rooms.

He opened the meeting. "I called this meeting to discuss many urgent things that resulted from winning this war. I looked at the coastline's map and how far our scout groups went. They likely have not seen all of the Thunderbirds' territory. In two days, we've more than doubled our size, maybe even more than that. Before we lose it, we must do something about it.

"We've lost almost a third of our population, mostly adults, and it's the same for the Thunderbirds. We must guard our expanded territory but we don't have enough fighters to do it. Our citizens are counting on our success.

"The Thunderbirds had a roving army with towns with a few women looking after all their kids. Most of the women are beyond childbearing age but there are quite a few who aren't. We can't change their system overnight, so we'll have to use it to our best advantage.

"Everything I'm saying supposes that every army the Thunderbirds had was here, as it's unlikely their king would come here without all of them. If they have another army and they attack us, then we're finished. If we're not attacked, the remaining armies will eventually retain the Thunderbird's territory. We must take the chance that we've destroyed their armies.

"I know this is only a stop-gap measure for the next ten years or so but what I'm proposing we do is, while the weather is still warm, send up to six thousand male and female volunteers south to visit every town in the Thunderbirds' territory and inform the people of our victory.

"In addition, we'll leave at least one man and woman in each town. Depending on its size, you may have to leave more than one pair behind. People in the closest boundary towns must manage the defence of our new territory.

"All the volunteers we send will have to be our people because they already know how we work and we can trust them to stay loyal to us. Prisoners will remain in our current territory.

"Why I'm saying this now, is I want this group to leave tomorrow, so we can populate every town before winter. The group will be moving south, so they may be able to complete their journey in time, as the winter will be milder as they move in that direction. I'm not sure we'll have enough people to do this. If we run out of people, men can regularly visit some of the left-over towns with fertile women. Let's make it work.

"Any questions?"

"I don't think we'll get enough volunteers," one of the women said.

"Well, we have seventeen and eighteen-year-olds that can fill the gaps. If we must, throw in some sixteen-year-olds. We've got to get our population up fast and ensure they learn our ways."

Everyone nodded in agreement.

In the morning, slightly over 6000 men and women rode out through the gate of the farmers' compound.

Later in the morning, they buried the last of their dead. An elder gave the readings for them then Jim made a speech. "It would've been nice to have all our young men and women here for this ceremony but they need to do their duty to our new combined territory. We're likely not going to see most of them again, as they incorporate themselves into new families farther south but we're the living, and life will go on for us.

"Now, we give tribute to the thousands of people who gave their lives so Josh's dream, and our dream, will carry on. The next few years, if we survive, will mark a new era of expansion and growth. Josh would've praised what we've done."

Jim continued solemnly. "Most of us are very young now and our parents are not here to lead us anymore, so we must continue what they started and remember this day as an inspiration to keep going and never give up our dream." He slapped his right fist into the palm of his other hand. "People can live in harmony and we must be the model of that.

"I'm sure all of you have suffered the loss of someone and maybe many people. We pray for them, so that, if there is an afterlife, they make it into God's arms.

"Thanks first to all the living and the dead who fought in the war. Some of you will carry its scars for the rest of your lives.

"I'd like to give tribute to all the fighters from our southern city who sacrificed themselves. They stayed true to their commitment to us and our dreams. Their early sacrifice likely helped us win the war. There are only a few of you left with us, now.

"All of you know Dave; he's been a very special person to all of us. He was a close friend of Josh and Sam and I've been pressed by many people to have him buried in his own grave and that, Lizzie, who also died, should be by his side."

There was lots of cheering.

"I had a tough time finding a volunteer from Dave's family to give this next special tribute as I don't feel right to do it myself. They're all a shy group, except for one of them. I think you'll all agree that this one is definitely not shy."

All people from Eden burst out laughing because they knew who he was going to present.

"Not everyone knows her," he said.

One person shouted from the crowd, "Yeah, the Thunderbirds."

People laughed again.

"Okay, former Thunderbirds, you live in Eden now and all of us are shy persons, except for this next woman . . ." There were some guffaws from the crowd. "Surprise, surprise, here's Sara."

Sara stepped up and swung her hip to hit him as he walked to stand at the back of the dais.

"Well, at least the babies don't know me, at least the ones who aren't mine."

The crowd laughed.

"Well, girls, these fresh new guys from the Thunderbirds are safe now that Jim has tamed me. They're yours."

There was another round of laughter, then some cheers from the women.

When the crowd quieted, she continued. "I think Josh, Sam, and Dave wouldn't mind our laughing a bit, even on a solemn day as this."

She paused then continued. "I lost both of my parents and several other members of my family in this war. I'd like to encourage all of you Thunderbirds to consider what it means to join us. The time for war is over. We must rebuild and you can be a part of it. I think you'll come to like us and the society we're trying to build.

"But we didn't come to talk about that, we're here to pay tribute to our dead and our heroes. Sam came here many years ago. He shared Josh's dream of bringing peace back to these troubled times. He was one of our best fighters, particularly in archery, and he fought in all the battles we've had since then. For you Thunderbirds, when we fought, we fought to defend our way of life. Others attacked us. We've never started a war but we ended it and all this has come at great cost of lives for us.

"Sam was a model for us. He was one of the early ones to show us how to love again. He had three women in his life and for each he showed us another way of living – a more settled way, although I guess I shouldn't be the one talking about this, right girls?"

There were some chuckles from the crowd.

"But Sam was a good and decent man and Jim has had many people tell him that he should be especially honoured by us. So, as we did for Josh and Dave, he's already buried here in his own grave with his last love, Anna. He'd have liked that."

There were cheers from the crowd.

She added, "The carpenters have also offered to put up a statue of him at his gravesite."

People cheered.

Sara said, "The few remaining people from our southern city want to rebuild. They might not live in the crumbling old city but would like to rebuild an old town north of their city closer to the windmills so they can share in the power. They also told me that they want to name their town Samstown after our hero and for all the things he did for the town over the years."

There was another round of cheers.

As she listened, she did not know what their fragile future would be but somehow, they would rebuild a new world along the coast of this ocean and perhaps spread out from there to bring civilisation back to the people of Earth.

Sara turned and gazed at Jim standing at the back of the dais. Her eyes teared. She thought of her lost parents and her new life with Jim. He was all she had left now besides her children. She walked to him, stood in front of him, looked deeply into his eyes, grabbed his hands, and yelled loudly so everyone could hear, "I love you, Jim Ferguson."

Everyone cheered, especially the women.

Sam's spirit remained near his body before and during the battle. He watched as the events took place. Soon, Anna's spirit joined Sam and they could see the battle and the field of the dead and wounded through the haze around them. They saw the burial ceremonies and the speeches delivered.

"I saw you smile. I guess you're proud of what you did," Anna said when the speeches were done.

"No, I was proud of what they'll do."

"Oh . . . When I look at all the dead people, I remember your belief in God and ask if God has abandoned them."

"No, actually we abandoned Him."

"If we're dead, is this our dying brains having a dream?"

"I don't know. Maybe this isn't real."

"What do we do now?"

He took her hand and said, "I guess we walk."

"But there's no road or path."

"I guess we can walk in any direction."

The battlefield and gravesite drifted away as they walked, or floated, as he could see no feet beneath him. Blurred images appeared ahead of them and he could make nothing out until he was close and realised that they were Beautiful and Jill. They joined together as one.

He had found life to be a journey, never knowing what he would find. This new journey would likely be much the same. He thought he would be happy but happy, sad, love, and hate did not exist here but he had something to hold onto. At first, he struggled with what it was, until he knew. He smiled; he was content.

ABOUT THE AUTHOR

Michael has had the bug to write since before he reached his teens but rarely got much time to do it. Now he is retired and trying to catch up on his life's dream. It is never too late to start. He lives with his family in Canada.